MT Burell

STRIVEN

A novel

Litavis House press

Copyright © MT Burell, 2021

All rights reserved. The right of MT Burell to be identified as the author of this work has been asserted in accordance with Section 77 of the Copyright, Designs and Patents Act 1988

This book or any portion thereof may not be reproduced or used in any manner without the express written permission of the copyright owner except for the use of brief quotations in a book review.

First paperback edition March 2021

Typeset by Afallon-glyphs

Cover design by Nick Castle
https://www.nickcastledesign.com/

ISBN 9781838387808

Published by Litavis House Press

"Nothing will send you to Hell faster than a fair face with a heart of stone."

— DAKRIS MANELL

1

I HAD EVERYTHING. Youth, good brains, some loyal friends, more passion than I could handle and looks good enough to make some nights interesting and the loneliness almost bearable. But most of all, I had potential. Heaps of it. Ok, I could only afford steak and chips once a month and I had to travel by bus, but that's small change, that's temporary. I knew it was. Well, I didn't *know* it know it, but I was convinced of it, and sometimes that's enough. Fine, let me rephrase: I had everything that mattered.

And yet I was constantly battling a tendency for self-destruction. Bewildered by my own self, my youth, by these floods of raw energy that emerged from deep inside my bones, charging forth like a herd of crazed wild horses, unbridled, unsaddled, unguided. My body and mind seemed to be constantly conspiring to produce this insistent force that had no discernible means of delivery. I was rocket fuel without a rocket, a beast without a prey, gunpowder without a gun, a gun without a bullet and a bullet without a target. What was I missing? A wise man once told me that the thing with potential is that it's everything but it's also nothing. So that may have had something to do with it.

2

THE RISING SUN had been good to me, the place of many baptisms, the place where I met Kevin.

Kevin spent the mornings working on a master's degree in video game development, the afternoons answering phones to pay for the work he did in the mornings, and the evenings dispensing wisdom with a pint in his hand. "The future is a playground," he would say to anyone who doubted his career choice, "and one day everyone will walk around with video games in their pocket." Most people laughed. Most people are average. Kevin was far from average.

We first met on a Sunday afternoon. I'd only been in London a few weeks and I was wandering around the West End looking for a job. That's how I first ended up in the Rising Sun. It was a warm summer day and there were a dozen people drinking outside. They all seemed to be in groups of three for some reason. As I stood there, I overheard this guy: "Fifty years ago it took a man three weeks of hard labour to chop enough wood to keep his family warm through the winter."

"Uh huh…" agreed some older guy, one of those who are bald but think they have long hair. He wore a sorry-looking corduroy jacket with elbow patches, and there were handfuls of dandruff scattered all over his shoulders. He rested his pint on this huge belly he had. Every time he brought the pint to his lips he overdid it with the tilting, raising his elbow up high above his ear, causing some of the beer to spill out, desperate to fall to the ground. But it couldn't. Each attempt was quashed by his mighty protrusion, catching the beer halfway on its downward journey. And there it sat, on his overstretched black pullover, next to a fainter, older stain, defeated between pint and pavement. His wasn't just a belly, it was the beer-world equivalent of no man's land.

"How long does it take now," Kevin continued, "with all modern equipment – two, three days?"

"Probably," said the belly, tilting his pint slightly and feeding the fresh stain a little.

I later found out that Hugh – that was the belly's name – was Professor of Computer Science at Imperial College. A genius when it came to coding, one of the brains behind the mobile phone revolution that began a few years later. Hopeless at personal hygiene. Hugh never got any credit for the revolution he helped to bring about, he was too absorbed with the engineering and cared too little about fame or society or even conversations to get involved with any of that. The credit went to the managers, who knew nothing about coding but a lot about talking.

"Right," Kevin said, "and what does this lucky man do – this man who is blessed with this modern equipment that gifts him free time – what does he do with the remaining eighteen days? Does he sit by the river? Does he smell the flowers?"

"Erm…" more over-tilting.

"No, he does not. He buys a bigger piece of land, grows more trees, and ends up chopping wood for three weeks anyways."

"Oh…" Splash… Splash…

"And that, that is the essence of what's wrong with modern man."

Kevin, Hugh and some older guy who was sitting at their table took a ceremonious sip from their pints, as if to mark the end of all that needed to be said on the subject.

I waited a few seconds before cutting in, not wanting to spoil their ritual. A man needs his rituals.

"I suppose," I said, "the man saw potential beyond the here and now."

"Ah, a pragmatist!" said Kevin with a knowing smile.

Kevin wasn't a tall or imposing man by any stretch, but there was an aura about him. The way he spoke made me feel a need to be succinct. Get in and get out quick, conscious that my words were thieves stealing time and space that could have belonged to his. Maybe that's why Hugh kept his replies so short. Maybe it wasn't out of a natural tendency to be concise, maybe it was awe – maybe Hugh simply knew his place. I knew instantly that I had to know *my* place, quick.

Kevin seemed excited at my suggestion. Hugh made a raspy noise that signalled agreement. I didn't know what a pragmatist was but decided to keep that quiet; I needed to get off to a good start.

"Ambition…" said Kevin.

Hugh took a sip, fed the stain – which by now had encroached on the older stain's territory – and said, "Ikaros's dilemma."

"Of course!" Kevin lit up, "Daidalos made it possible, but it was Ikaros who saw the potential."

I knew Ikaros was some naive precursor to the Wright brothers, and I suspected Daidalos was his father, but didn't ask.

"It cost him, though," I said, risking it.

"It sure did. Maybe ambition needs wisdom, maybe the root of the curse is not ambition, but ambition in the absence of wisdom."

"If ambition is the engine then wisdom is the brakes," I said, a little ashamed that I had to resort to motorbike analogies. But I was desperate to be part of that conversation, and I knew way more about motorbikes than I did about Greek mythology. Needs must, I thought, trying to reassure myself. I also wanted to let Kevin know that I knew what he had in mind. I suppose a simple "uh huh" would have been fine, but I thought an analogy, even an obviously uneducated one, might make a better impression.

"I like this guy," said Kevin, flicking his thumb at me.

My chest swelled up. I felt like I belonged. I'd done well not to ask about pragmatists.

"I'm Kevin." He stretched out his hand and we shook.

Hugh smiled, but only with his teeth. It was the best he could do.

"Dak," I said, "pleased to make your acquaintance, sir." The words flew out of my mouth before I had a chance to realize how over-the-top they sounded. Kevin was only a couple of years older than me.

The landlord came out through a door with a STAFF ONLY sign on it and called me in. A fat geezer with a huge round head and an East End accent. His name was Liam. He put both hands on the bar and leaned in as if he were about to threaten my life, then told me politely that he wasn't taking on any new staff. It was the seventh time I'd heard that today, but it wasn't followed by the usual wave of disappointment. For the first time in my life I felt that I belonged; that being inquisitive wasn't an inconvenience, that curiosity wasn't an inconvenience, that *I* wasn't an inconvenience.

Kevin and I carried on talking for a while, mostly about ambition, fulfilment, and the delicate balance in between. Hugh kept feeding the stain between interjections and occasionally showed his teeth. We discussed the attraction of achievement, wondered whether it's only a temporary sight in the eyes of ambitious men. Every word we spoke was an archaeological dig unearthing the bare bones of a deep, magical connection. A connection that ran straight through our minds and into our souls. A connection that was born of our shared struggle, a struggle to find a place in the world and *hang on* to it like our life depended on it... because, well, it kind of did.

I later found out that Kevin was from a small village on the Isle of Wight where life was simple but uninspiring. Locals resigned to having no prospects and hippies looking for a place to gloat about lack of prospects. I could not imagine him living there – and neither could he. He had moved to London a couple of years earlier, at the age of twenty-four, to make something of himself. He was already something, of course, but that's ambition for you.

3

IT ALL STARTED when I was thirteen years old. Adolescence hit me like a freight train of consciousness and hormones, and suddenly I knew. I wanted to grab the universe by the balls and rattle it so hard that my existence would become irrefutable. The trouble was, I had no idea *how,* so I spent years trying to find something that had meaning, or at least something to which I could attach meaning for a while. A song, a football, some girl, a red Yamaha.

For most of my teenage years I was told that my best course of action was to get a job, any job, and keep my head down till retirement. The implicit suggestion was that I would amount to nothing more than a humble fish in a small pond, occasionally paired with the very explicit suggestion that I would likely amount to nothing at all. Curiosity, inquisitiveness and ambition were a nuisance, something to keep in check like a sore or a persistent cough. I remember my mother in tears after one particularly harrowing parents' evening when the teacher had told her, "Dakris's classroom behaviour needs improving. He asks too many questions." Her tears eventually dried, but she never stopped wondering what was wrong with her son; why couldn't he just stop asking those darn questions?

There didn't seem to be anything remarkable about me, except perhaps that I produced a steady supply of disappointment that was worth a story or two at family gatherings, inevitably followed by sighs of resignation. Eyes rolling. More explicit suggestions of failure.

And yet, throughout this – in spite of this – I was blessed with a true north: an absolute belief in my intellectual abilities. I could out-think the lot of them! I could outdo the lot of them! …if only someone taught me how. But there's a problem at that age: you can't tell the difference between a teacher and a crook, and that can cost you. It can send you on a wild goose chase, or breed an immature recalcitrance in your heart, or both, for the rest of your life. That's where luck comes in.

Anyway, this true north, this belief in the power of my mind, wasn't really founded on anything, you could hardly call it rational, seeing as I hadn't achieved anything *yet*. And that's really what it boiled down to, that *yet* in my gut. No idea how it got there, but there it was. And a belief can be so much more powerful than knowledge. Knowledge is useful and can sometimes save your arse, like when your car is stuck in the mud in the middle of nowhere in the freezing cold but you know how to work the clutch. You'll thank your gods for knowledge then, and maybe even your dad for passing it on to you that miserable afternoon when you thought he was being pedantic about foot controls. And yet knowledge has an irredeemable flaw – it lives in your mind, and that's too high up to really poke at you. But belief, belief sits right down in the bowels of your soul. Like a ballast of the spirit, keeps you centred in all weathers. I was lucky to have that. I've known guys who gave up on themselves too easily because they lacked belief, they had nothing to hold them together when the seas got rough and their guardian angels started puking over the starboard rail.

To be fair to my parents they did teach me a great thing: work ethics. That was my other bit of luck, and you do need some luck. It didn't come for free though. Work ethics cannot be taught any more than riding a bike or using your fists. Someone can *show* you how it's done, but to learn it you still need to graze your knees and bruise your knuckles. So, while *they* taught me work ethics, I was the one who *learned* work ethics. The hard way.

4

I DROPPED OUT of school at fourteen. The perpetual stillness and that sorry combination of moralizing and pre-packaged information made me ill. Sometimes I felt sick at bedtime, when the thought of school the next morning smacked me across the head. My mother would make a pot of camomile tea for my stomach, a gesture that was both kind and cruel, forcing my insides to submit to the god of conformity. Sometimes it worked. I would lie in bed quietly, with my stomach mildly restored and my mind in knots. They didn't make camomile for the mind.

Sometimes it didn't work, and I would sit on the bed for hours, my stomach churning and my mind racing in some perverse dance of dread and futility. And sometimes it *seemed* to work, until a few hours later, when I would wake up in a sweat to discover that I had thrown up in my sleep, my body desperately trying to eject the crap that everyone was so keen to force down my throat.

Then, one day, I refused to carry on that miserable routine. I left school, amazed at how easy it was – you just dropped out, and that was that. It wasn't so much an act of leaving, more like an act of *not* doing, like discovering that there is no bogeyman under your bed after all. My parents didn't take it well, especially my mother. There were tears, there were silent treatments, screams of dejection, threats of disownment, the usual cries of "look what you're doing to your poor mother!" More tears. But I didn't really care. I felt free. I suppose I had felt free as a baby, but I had no memories of that. Now I felt *consciously* free, and it was wonderful.

A few months later I got a job as an apprentice in a mechanical factory making squirts, or "precision nozzles for high pressure fire hoses," as the designers insisted on calling them. I quickly learned that designers always used more words than necessary.

You had to be fifteen to legally work, so I forged my birth certificate and made excuses about my non-existent ID card. Eventually they stopped asking.

Work turned out to be a joyless drudgery, as meaningless and pre-packaged as school, but with more cursing and less moralizing. This new form of drudgery was handed to me by a man they called Felix. Felix was in charge of the apprentices. He must've been in his late forties but looked sixty-five. He had this massive, almost perfectly round gut, and a set of teeth that were too small for his head. He'd been grinding away at them at a fast rate. Maybe the responsibilities, maybe the dead-end job, maybe the guilt of having to steal the souls of young boys for a living. In the grind by day and grinding at night.

The outline of his body was something out of a comic book. His chest was normal, straight, almost perfectly vertical, and then – suddenly – there was this immense bulge shooting outwards, pressing away at his belt. He looked like a cross between a meerkat and a pregnancy. The belt couldn't take it. It corkscrewed on itself in a desperate attempt to keep the bulge away, but it didn't stand a chance. The mid-button of his brown smock was under constant attack, and occasionally you would hear a sudden *ping*! like a marble hitting an anvil at speed. It was Felix's mid-button shooting against the steel partition of the lathe. The delicate equilibrium between clinging thread and pressing bulge had collapsed, and physics did the rest. The fight must have been constant. Relentless.

Felix handed me a pair of protection gloves, showed me to my station and turned on the machines. They were old rusty things that smelled like burnt motor oil and made a shrieking noise that never stopped. Never. Even when I left the factory at 5 p.m., the echo of those shrieks would linger in my head. I still hear them now, every night when the lights go out and the world goes quiet, there they are – denying me the pleasure of silence.

Felix lit a cigarette, took a long drag and pointed at a forklift that was making its way towards us. I didn't know at the time, but that's how each of my days would begin from then on, with the forklift dropping a crate of a thousand freshly machined metal pieces next to my station at 8 a.m. sharp.

At one minute past eight I would pick up the first piece, hold it in a bolted metal casing under a vertical drill and proceed to cut a hole through it. The brief journey would then continue for a few seconds under the deburring wheel and finally end with a blasting of the blow gun, getting rid of any leftover shavings. Forty-five seconds later I would place the finished piece in a padded container and start all over again: one down, nine-hundred and ninety-nine to go.

Whenever the crate was nearly empty, I could spy the forklift operator getting ready to bring over the next one. A bottomless pit of crates that just kept flowing. Full. Permanent. Sisyphean. He was my torturer, and I hated him. And yet part of me envied him, how he got to lift different crates of different colours filled with different pieces of different shapes and different sizes. He got to hang on to his humanity.

And my soul wasn't the only casualty either. The metal pieces were made of stainless steel, a bastard to cut through. The vertical drill was fitted with a high-speed tungsten bit that became incandescent as it went through the steel, heating up my measly protection glove and baking the flesh of my index and thumb as they gripped tight to keep the nozzle-to-be from spinning along with the drill. One piece at a time, the stench of glove and flesh fusing together became revoltingly familiar. The skin on my thumb became so thick that it felt like I was permanently wearing a leather thimble. But at least I didn't have to sit still in a classroom for six hours a day, so that was something.

In the winter there was the added curse of the cold. The factory ceiling was falling apart, and the little heat generated by the ancient air pump would fly straight out as soon as it came in. On rainy days, the combination of the cold and the humidity made me feel like a block of wood with arthritis. The holes and cracks in the ceiling were a two-way affair: just as the cold flew out, rain snuck in. One of my duties was to place buckets around the factory floor to prevent it turning into a swamp. "The shearing machine!" was the drill. The shearing machine was this hungry animal that took in large sheets of metal and spat out little strips ready for welding. The electric cables that fed the machine were supposed to be concreted under the floor – nobody wants to drop a thirty-pound sheet of sharp steel on a bunch of high voltage cables. But the cheap concrete had eroded away, and the electric cables had become exposed like a corpse in a shallow grave – except that a corpse is mostly harmless, and it usually doesn't fry you dead when it comes in contact with water. So I made sure to keep this shallow grave dry, and always started my bucket round behind the shearing machine. I used the biggest bucket I had too, because at night some of the smaller buckets would overflow. Some mornings we would find little frozen puddles all around the factory. That's when you knew it was going to be a tough one.

I couldn't fit a coat under the compulsory overall, so I would spend three months a year feeling stiff as a board. It messed up my gut. I tried everything. I even took to wearing a pair of woollen long johns, carefully tucking my jumper in, pushing it as far as it would go, sporting octogenarian undergarments seventy years before my time. As if adolescence alone wasn't enough of an embarrassment. I was terrified that I would injure a knee or a foot and be taken to the emergency room where a cute nurse with a small nose and a soft spot for pimply teenage apprentices would give me the eye while asking me to remove my trousers; and there I'd be, revealing my grandpa's attire, disappointing her terribly and annihilating the fragile embryo of our undoubtedly beautiful love story. That's the sort of stuff I worried about, besides trying to keep warm. And I *really* worried about trying to keep warm. Whenever I needed to turn, I would shuffle around with my feet like a penguin instead of turning at the waist, for fear that the tiniest pocket of hard-earned warmth would escape my body. I looked like a wind-up toy in a forced labour camp.

During my first week of winter at the factory I couldn't wait to get home and sit next to the wood burner, hoping to restore my normal body temperature. No such luck. The cold had reached so deep into my bones that being a foot away from a red-hot stove made no difference. It was bizarre. The stove could burn my hand, I could feel it was *hot*, but I couldn't feel its warmth. So I gave up sitting next to the stove. The only thing that warmed me up was a hot bath. But even that couldn't fully restore my body to its normal functions. Every time I got out of the bath my feet would itch like mad, an unscratchable itch that came from deep in my flesh. I later found out that's how frostbites feel when they're not quite there yet. Dickens was alive and well.

5

I CARRIED ON the drudgery for over six years, churning out squirts during the day and fumbling around for meaning and adventure at night. By the time I turned twenty I became obsessed with any woman whose skirt swirled the right way and every man who seemed to know something I didn't.

I felt like an innocent man serving an unknown sentence. Is this it? Is that fifty-year-old welder with a mullet all I have to look forward to? Is that me thirty years from now? Am I the next bulge? I didn't want to be the next bulge.

It was through some shoddy efforts to address these potentially honourable questions that I stumbled across science, a magic world where bad ideas can objectively be proven wrong. Claims stand or fall on their own merit; it doesn't matter who makes them, how powerful he is or how high up in the pecking order he sits – if a claim fails to stand up to experiment, it is *wrong* – and that's all there is to it. That stuff has a lot of traction when you spent the first twenty years of your life being wrong just because your teacher or your father or whoever *decided* that you were wrong, with most discussions ending as you abandoned your line of argument under threat of a licking. That had built the illusion in my mind that being right was the sole privilege of those above me.

But then I met Ric.

6

RIC WAS A physics professor. He was from the big city but had fallen for a village girl who lived just a few houses down the road from where I grew up. Her name was Rosa. Rosa's parents were what you might call old fashioned, and they forbade her to move away from the family home. That's when Ric left a tenured position in Newtonian Mechanics some two-hundred miles away in exchange for a part-time job at our local hardware shop. It didn't seem to help at first – Rosa's parents remained uneasy at the idea of their daughter marrying a man twenty years her senior. But Ric was an intelligent man, a persuasive man. In the end I think Rosa's parents ended up loving him more than she did. By the time I met Ric he was in his mid-forties, he had been married to Rosa for five years and there were rumours that she was screwing around on him. Rosa's parents never screwed around on him.

Ric was a tall, scrawny man. He wore thick spectacles and talked physics to anyone who'd give him a chance. I instantly became his biggest fan. The hardware shop where he worked was a bit of a teenage hangout, and a few of us spent most of our Saturday afternoons there – fiddling with nuts and bolts, pontificating about the quality of different steels, lecturing customers on what parts they *really* needed. It was our neighbourhood equivalent of the motorcycle shop. We swaggered along like we were in a Brando film, minus the girls, the cycles and the cool leathers.

This one Saturday I got there around 4 p.m. The shop was quieter than usual. Ric was pretending to sweep the floor, pushing dust back and forth trying to look busy. We chatted a while about a 12mm threaded rod. I don't remember how we got on the subject, but at some point Ric started to explain how gravity attracts all objects at the same speed, regardless of weight. I laughed. I honestly didn't know, I was just an arrogant kid.

Within minutes Ric was standing on the top of a scaffold

about twenty feet high, holding a quarter inch ball bearing in one hand and a solid wood toilet seat in the other. "A bottle of scotch says the ball hits the floor first!"

I couldn't afford a bottle of scotch, but he let go of both objects before I had a chance to reply.

The toilet seat smashed to the ground a good couple of seconds after the ball bearing had bounced back into the air and rolled under a shelving unit. Gravity had pulled them down with the same acceleration, but aerodynamics favoured the slick little ball over the cumbersome slabs of wood. A customer on his way out turned around to see what all the commotion was about. Ric hurried down the scaffold to hide the wood fragments that bore witness to his illicit experiment. Dust particles floated in mid-air then slowly settled back on the concrete floors. Ric walked away and took his place behind the counter.

I stood there feeling foolish, angry at my ignorance and embarrassed at my indefensible arrogance. God, there's so much I don't know. I felt overwhelmed. And that's when it hit me: opinion was worth fuck all. You've got to stand up, step on that bloody scaffold and FIND OUT WHAT'S WHAT! I felt excited and restless, like I *had* to get going there and then and *do* something, *any*thing. Not many people can honestly say they had their life changed by a toilet seat.

7

THREE WEEKS AFTER that toilet seat gave its life to science I bought a one-way ticket to London.

That's where stuff happens, I thought. That's where I need to be to escape the ever-encroaching mullet, the obscene horror of inertia. That's where you make it! Whatever "it" is. I still had no idea, but at least I was *doing* something.

Everyone thought I was crazy. Leaving a steady job in a safe town to go to a big strange city a thousand miles away with little money and no prospects? You must be *crazy*, they'd say. I must be. I just refused to believe in slow and steady. I guess that's crazy enough.

My true north came in really handy in those moments; it's kind of hard when the facts point to either you or everyone else around you being crazy. Statistically it's likely to be you, so you're bound to buckle – unless you really *are* crazy, in which case facts don't matter, they don't even appear on your radar. So I boarded the flight to London with some trepidation.

A week later I moved into a crummy sublet above a kebab shop in Deptford, hardly fifty yards from the spot where Marlowe was stabbed in the brain. I prayed that the place would be kinder to me than it had been to him.

The shop was run by Mr Alaoui, a chubby, cheerful character with a keen aversion to work. He called himself "the landlord", but the building belonged to the council, social housing assigned to him and his family twenty years earlier. He had made some money in the 1980s when the shop was doing well and had bought his own house somewhere in the Elephant and Castle. Garage, two gardens, the works. Now he was subletting the three-bedroom council house to whoever was skint enough to keep quiet.

"If anyone asks, you don't live here, ok? Tell them you're my daughter's boyfriend. Her name is Tara, ok?"

"Ok."

"Rent is £50 a week plus bills. We split the TV licence four ways."

I moved in early on a Saturday morning. Mr Alaoui had told me that there were three other people living there. He had converted the living room into a fourth bedroom so that he could squeeze every penny out of each square foot, while homeless families were wasting away on the council's waiting list. I liked the man, but his mediocre prosperity fed on desperation, and that I never made peace with.

No one was around when I arrived. I walked up the stairs, put down my suitcase and took a look at the room. It was a disgraceful arrangement of grimy walls and musty carpet pretending to blend into each other. At the centre of the room the carpet was light brown and threadbare, getting thicker and darker as it approached the walls. It was impossible to decipher what colour the walls were supposed to have been.

I spent most of the day standing on a chair trying to turn that irredeemable mess into a living space. As I scrubbed at the walls, decades of nicotine came back to life and caked up on the scouring pad, morphing it into a useless block of sticky, waxy gunk. At around 4 p.m. I admitted defeat, walked to a hardware shop and spent a third of all my possessions on a tin of mildly disturbing peachy paint that was going for half price. I could not afford a brush, so I detached a broom from its handle, dipped it into the paint and laid it on. The first coat looked like a cat had been dragging its claws on the walls.

It was five o'clock when Mr Alaoui walked in. "Oh, you're making it nice uh?" he said with a hint of excitement. He went back downstairs and returned with a brush. I thanked him and carried on.

"I have some off-cut carpet in the garage, give me a shout when you're done painting and we'll go get it." He made it sound like he was doing me a favour.

Two hours later we got into Mr Alaoui's vintage Mercedes, drove to the Elephant, picked up the carpet roll, drove back to Deptford and laid it down. It was bright orange. Together with the peach walls it made an odd combination that was not exactly ugly but was probably capable of triggering an epileptic seizure.

That evening I sat on my bed, knackered. I turned on the TV. BBC weather was on. I wasn't interested in the forecast but didn't have the strength to get up and change the channel, so I sat there staring at the map: light rain and a gentle breeze. At least something was going to be gentle.

My only suitcase had broken during the move, I had less than twenty quid to my name and I could hear mice trying to scratch their way in between the floorboards. But I was free.

Life is anything you make of it, and here I am, making my own anything of it. A sense of happiness washed over me, and that weather forecast began to sound like the most soothing of poems.

I was going to be ok.

8

ONE TUESDAY MORNING I made my way to the job centre. Potential is all well and good, but Mr Alaoui still wanted his £50 a week.

I was walking along Tottenham Court Road and saw two homeless men sitting next to a filthy sleeping bag topped with a bunch of empty cider cans. My spine froze over. Is that going to be me? How much bad luck is there between five pints in the Rising Sun and a night under a flyover? I played it all out in my mind: the job centre clerk looked at me and told me that my National Insurance number was not valid.

"Ok," I replied, "what do I need to do to sort that out?"

"It's not that simple," he said. "In order to get a new NI number you need to provide a current one."

"Sure, I have this one," I said confidently, waving my NI card.

"This is an invalid number. It's not in the system, and if it's not in the system it does not exist," he said in a bureaucratic monotone. "It's a worthless sequence of random numbers that happens to be printed on a National Insurance card." Then he added, "In fact, it might even be fraud. NI cards should only be used for NI numbers."

"Hold on a second, I didn't print this card, this was given to me, by the NI office!"

"It doesn't matter who printed it, *you*'re in possession of an NI card that does not carry an NI number. With your name on it."

"Ok, then I'll apply for a brand new one, cut this one up," I ventured with some hesitation, confidence slowly leaking out of me.

"No can do," – he was trying to sound normal. "It says here you applied for and were subsequently issued with an NI number six weeks ago. You are therefore already in possession of an NI number; and you are not allowed to apply for a second one. One NI number per person per lifetime. That's the rule."

"I know," I replied, "the number you issued six weeks ago is this one!"

"I'm sorry, sir," – you know you're about to get shafted when they call you sir – "but as I've already explained, this is *not* a valid NI number, therefore it is *not* an NI number."

And so there I was, in a perfect catch 22 – in possession of a number when I request to apply for one, but suddenly not in possession of a number the moment he asks to see my number. I'd better find the nearest flyover before it gets dark.

When I got to the job centre things went a little better than I had imagined, except for the hangover. I kept losing focus, and the clerk's voice sounded as though it came from under water.

"Please spell your name for me."

I spelled my name.

Then he asked me something about surname and middle name or something, then he faded deep under water, and then he came back up. I heard something like "from mother?"

"What? No, no it's my surname, it's from my *father*. I got it from my father."

"So you did." His tone of voice sounded a lot like I'd imagined, straight out of some sort of Her Majesty's Institute of Bureaucracy. "I asked if it's 'm' for mother, sir. Is it 'm' for mother?"

"Oh, yeah, sorry. Yes." I bit my tongue to stop myself ending with "sir". I felt like an idiot child in the principal's office.

My NI number was fine. I picked up a gig making coffees in the City, just off Lombard Street. Serving high-fliers £1 coffees for £3.75 an hour. Our average customer earned more in the time it took them to neck an espresso than I did in a week. And yet I wasn't jealous of their life. Well, maybe a little jealous of their money, but not their life – they may have raked in the dough but it was clear to me that they left the universe positively unrattled.

Lunch hour was total war. Wave after wave of suits would descend on us with narrow eyes and a single aim: to get served food and coffee *fast*. Tons of coffee were sold in the City every day, and 80% of the takings came in between 12 noon and 1 p.m. Most suits only had half an hour to spare before they had to go back to selling landmines to their favourite dictators. That meant we only had fifteen minutes to take their orders, toast their sandwiches, brew their coffees, serve them, print the bill and try to keep the change. It was mayhem.

We started prepping at 8 a.m., sorting out every detail while Hasan, the shift manager, shuffled around old receipts pretending to be doing something important. He could hardly read, and we all knew it. Cashing up was taken care of by Dan, a branch manager who came over in the evening to do a stock check, sort out the takings and give Hasan a ticking-off for messing up every single task that involved reading – signing the wrong forms, accepting the wrong deliveries, that sort of thing. But we kept up the pretence, we needed the job.

At the start of my shift I would go to the basement to mix and grind a couple of sacks of beans, just enough for the day. Then back upstairs to purge the coffee machines and get ready for the 10 a.m. coffee break, the first battle of the day.

Ron was the guy dealing with the sandwiches. Piles of them. Slice, fill, slap, wrap, repeat – until the display fridge was full. It took him the whole morning, but at least he didn't have to be involved in the 10 a.m. rush – food wasn't on the suits' minds at 10 a.m.

As the clock approached 12 p.m., an eerie silence would descend on the café and we'd brace ourselves for the stampede. You could slice the air with Ron's sandwich knife.

Hasan would disappear into the toilet at 11.45 and emerge again ten minutes later with thick eyeliner under his eyes and so much gel in his hair that you would've thought he'd been dipped in a spittoon. I didn't particularly like the fool, but I respected his tacit admission that we too needed prepping at least as much as the coffee machines.

And then it was time.

As the first wave marched in, Hasan started shouting orders across the counter like a sergeant major in a life-or-death situation. Ron juggled three grills and two toasters, praying that the next customer would have enough bad taste or be in enough of a hurry to order a cold sandwich. One in ten of his prayers would usually get answered, but sometimes he had to go for longer – twelve, fifteen orders without a single cold sandwich. That messed up his rhythm. A couple of bread rolls and a fair few fingers would get burnt in the process, slowing down the whole operation and making things worse. Hasan, realizing that the orders weren't coming, screamed like a maniac, as if the volume of his voice was a secret spell capable of summoning more speed and accuracy in Ron's body. Hasan's face turned bright red, contrasting even more sharply with the black liner under his now bulging, blood-shot eyes. What the stupid fool didn't consider was that Ron knew what he was *expected* to be doing, he just didn't have enough hands and functioning fingers to do it with. He was cornered into doing a two-man job, but Hasan would scream the whole City of London into rubble before admitting that.

Watching Ron work was painful. Not that I had any time to stop and observe, but occasionally I would catch a quick glimpse of his personal hell, and that was enough. He was constantly on the verge of a total breakdown, launching himself from one grill to the next, desperately trying to keep up, frantically flapping his arms around like a mad hen, cursing at the Italians and their bloody rotten paninis. More prayers. More burnt fingers. More of the turnip-faced sergeant major breathing down his neck.

While all this was going on, I worked all four blocks on the espresso machine. Soggy coffee grounds flew everywhere as I hastily banged them out of the portafilters to make space for each fresh batch. In training they tell you that you're supposed to hold the portafilter handle while the coffee comes through, as the high pressure can slap the filter out of position and into your face – steamy water and all. But there was no time for that. So I'd lock the portafilter in as best I could and then – while the espresso was brewing, water shooting through the pipework like a trapped tornado – I would froth the milk, fetch clean mugs, empty the bins, top up the coffee dispenser and hope for the best, hope that the next 90p worth of boiling water wouldn't be coming to claim my face. Not a single second was wasted, not a single unnecessary or uncoordinated movement. We looked like a cross between ballet dancers and medieval warriors.

Work was so incessant that lunch hour would always fly by. As the clock approached 1 p.m. the suits would get up and leave in a hurry, like robots brought into action by a hovering mothership. Suddenly the café was empty.

The dust settled on the crumbs and the dirty dishes and the crumpled-up napkins, and we began the clean-up. The whole place looked like a crime scene. There were spent coffee grounds *everywhere*: on the walls, on the counters, in the fridges, in our shoes, down my shirt. We would scrub the splatter off the walls, take out the bins, sweep the floors and load the dishwashers in time for the afternoon coffee break at 3 p.m. Although it was a doddle in comparison to what we had just experienced, the afternoon break was the toughest part of the day because our bodies were exhausted and had no adrenaline left to help us through.

The height of our day came at 3.30 p.m., when we counted the tips. Café workers banked on tips for their survival, they're the difference between having to hide from your landlord and going out at the weekend with your head held up high. On a good day we could make over £5 each in tips, and that's a big deal when you're on £3.75 an hour. That didn't last though. A good chunk of the tips came from the 10 a.m. and 3 p.m.

espresso rush. The suits only had fifteen minutes to charge down several flights of stairs, neck a 90p espresso, pay Hasan with a £1 coin, toss the 10p change into the jar and climb back up the stairs. Management caught on quickly though and raised the price of espresso to £1. It didn't make much of a difference to the suits – most of them still paid Hasan with a £1 coin – but the jar got much less action, and so did we.

At 4 p.m. I would make the last coffee of the day – double espresso with a dash of hot milk – and place it on table three as Dan arrived to pick up the takings, now fattened up by the 10p coins that should have landed in our jar. Dan would sip at his coffee and demand to see the paperwork for the day. That's when Hasan looked much less like a sergeant major and more like a puppy who'd just peed on the rug.

9

SOME TIME LATER, on a Friday night, I found out that I could make some women hot and bothered.

I had been with a few girls, but it had always been a struggle. I always felt like a second-hand car salesman trying to convince some girl that I was worthy of her fickle attention, and would she please consider talking to me? Please? It was demeaning and I hated it. And I do mean *hate*. I hated it to the point that I would often go home alone rather than engage in the whole sorry ritual. But this, this was different.

I walked into the Rising Sun looking a little rugged after a ten-hour shift at the café, but I was wearing my brown leather boots and I felt good. I was in good shape. Kevin pushed me to keep my mind sharp, and I had started lifting weights to do the same with my body. "Life is a battleground," Kevin told me, "and London is the battlefront. You need to be fighting fit." So I made sure I was. I'd begun to train in a makeshift gym at the back of a mechanic's garage near Deptford Bridge.

The gym was run by Al, a retired boxer with an infamous

left hook and a pair of tired shoulders hunched forward under the weight of a bad divorce (are there any good divorces?). His wife had taken everything worth having, house, kids, self-respect. At the court hearing the judge reprimanded Al for referring to his wife as "that nasty piece of work." I had a feeling the judge had a retirement plan, played golf with the children and never had to sleep in a garage.

The equipment consisted of two iron bars bolted to the wall for pull-ups and such, and three wooden boards laid on top of some breeze blocks for benches. No dumbbells. There were two iron rods for barbells with weights made from concrete left to set in old oil cans. I don't think anyone had any idea how much each one weighed, you just piled them up as you went along. There was a unique smell in the air, a mixture of sweat and spent motor oil. I couldn't afford to buy 2500 calories a day, so I wasn't big or anything, but I was physically fit, like a sort of wartime athlete.

Anyway, on that Friday evening I marched into the Rising Sun feeling sharp in my brown leather boots, and despite the long shifts and constant graft I felt good about life, myself, and potential. There was a queue at the bar, so I decided to look for Kevin first and then come back for a drink. He'll probably need a refill anyway. He usually finished work earlier than me on Fridays, so I knew he would have been there for the best part of an hour. I spotted him in the far corner chatting with Gus, a guy in his fifties who managed the local post office. Gus was a sort of social outcast who enjoyed our company. He was obsessed with philosophy. I waved at them as I tried to get through the crowd – the pub was absolutely packed. And that's when it happened. A woman in a grey skirt and red shoes stared at me the way you stare at somebody who's just come back from the dead. She must have been about twenty-five years old and had a sweet-looking, almost kind face, the sort of face I didn't expect would stare at men. I was wrong. Her eyes were unambiguous, they swung in my direction and *hung on* to me.

I wasn't used to this, so at first I suspected there was something weird on my head, or a bogey sticking out of my nose. The whole thing was odd, unfamiliar. But then I caught on, and I liked it. After years of unrequited effort, laying myself on an autopsy table so that some idly ordinary girl could inflate her ego at the expense of mine – here it was. And it was high fucking time.

Up to that moment I had often felt cornered between two unpalatable choices: be alone and give up hope or be a beggar and give up dignity. I picked the first choice whenever I could and the second whenever I had to, whenever things got too much. Then I would drown my dignity in a pint, flood my brain into submission, and force my body through the motions. I had also been approached by girls on a couple of occasions, and believe me when I say I had been grateful for that, but most of the time I was caught in a dreadful balancing act that made me despise my libido, my manhood. I couldn't think of a more heartless prank; cursed to continually produce sexual energy that could only be released by giving up your dignity. What had I done to deserve this?

Girls seemed to have it easy in comparison. They mostly stood there in blue frocks or tight jeans or frilly skirts or whatever and handed out judgement, like flocks of Caesars in lipstick, crushing my fledging ego with their precious thumbs. And just like Caesar, they never seemed to earn the right to do that, it was theirs by birth. Who had decided this? I sure was never consulted. I had no choice, forced to bury my head in a game I had never agreed to join. I resented girls for it, and that cost me dearly. It nearly crippled me for life.

But the winds of power were beginning to shift now. Just as those girls were becoming women, approaching the big 30 and being overtaken by a new batch of free riders, I was starting to get noticed. Time was a great leveller, and time was here.

I walked up to grey skirt and smiled. She lowered her gaze, pretending it had all been a misunderstanding. This momentarily spoiled my mood. But I was too buoyant. I didn't let her coyness faze me. "Busy uh?" I said. Her friend smirked, confirming they'd been talking about me.

"Can I get you a drink?"

"We're ok, thanks," said the friend. Grey skirt shot her an annoyed look.

"Are you here alone?" she asked. She didn't hang about.

"Yeah, my wingman requested a day off."

"How are you going to cope without a wingman?"

I liked her.

"I probably won't," I said, "women scare me."

"That can't be right," said the friend in a tiresome voice. The friend was wearing a black top with "be your own muse" written across it in pink letters. I believed it. Her breath smelled like a dead rat, so she didn't have a choice really. Muses and halitosis don't tend to go together.

"Why not?" I asked.

"Well, you came over to talk to *us*," replied grey skirt.

"That's different, you have a kind face. I thought I might be safe with you."

She giggled.

The friend didn't. She was used to being her own muse. She had to.

One of the bar staff nodded in my direction. I ordered a pint for me and one for Kevin. He would definitely need a refill by now.

I picked up the pints, handed over a fiver, took my change and walked to Kevin's table.

Grey skirt kept sending me suggestive glances and I kept smiling back politely, thinking I might go back to the bar and ask her out. But then Gus started talking about Kant and I never did go back. We got sucked into the *Doctrine of Virtue* and we even missed last orders. But those few minutes had cast a new light on me, and I was bursting to bathe in it.

10

IT WAS A sunny afternoon and I went down to Deptford market to find some second-hand furniture for my still-bare room. That's when I met Judy.

I know what you're thinking: here we go, the whole thing is now going to be about some woman he falls for and chases after for god knows how long. It's not like that.

Judy was a seventy-two-year-old widow. She'd married into a wealthy family and had lived most of her life in Fulham but had to move to Deptford after her husband's death left her destitute. Neil, her husband, had been a consultant at University Hospital. He believed in free healthcare for all so refused to move into private consultations and missed out on the big money of the 1980s.

Judy was an odd combination of posh and progressive – for the people but not exactly of the people. She looked frail and was unsteady on her feet but had a mind like a steel trap and the mouth of a docker, a strangely aristocratic-sounding docker.

I saw her trying to carry an old floor lamp and I offered to help.

"Oh, that's awfully good of you," she said in a public-school accent. It was obvious she wasn't a Deptford local. She was the only person I ever knew who pronounced the "h" in "hot" but not in "hotel", like in Victorian times.

We got to her car, a white Mini that had seen better days. I put the lamp on the rear seat.

"Let me make you a cup of tea to say thank you," she said, looking at me with her inquisitive, luminous blue eyes.

"That's ok, don't worry about it, I'm just glad I could help."

"Nonsense. Get in the car."

Judy wasn't one for disagreement.

She lived a couple of minutes away, near New Cross Road. When we got there Judy opened the door and went straight to the kitchen, leaving me to negotiate the doorway with her unwieldy new purchase.

"Put it in the front parlour, next to the sofa," she shouted. "I won't be a minute. Milk and sugar?"

As I walked in I noticed a man, about thirty-five years old, sitting on an armchair looking out of the window into the garden.

"Hi, I'm Simon," he said.

"Dak. Nice to meet you."

"Oh yes," said Judy, as if suddenly remembering his existence, "he is Simon." Then she added, "He lives here, but we aren't fucking." Her brazenly unfiltered language startled me. I smiled nervously. Simon was unfazed, he'd clearly heard it all before.

"We're very fond of each other though!" Judy laughed.

Simon was a supply teacher, English Lit, the only one I ever met who did not wish for a permanent position. "Judy won't have it," he said when I enquired about his decision. "She needs me around. But it's nice to have a place of work to go to every now and again."

Simon told me he used to do Judy's gardening at the weekend, that's how they'd met. Then three years ago his girlfriend kicked him out during one of her nervous breakdowns and Judy offered to put him up. They became close friends and he never left. People were suspicious of their relationship, and Judy got a kick out of the fact that she could still set tongues wagging at her age. Whenever someone asked her what was going on between the two of them, she would answer, "I like being surrounded by young handsome men, don't you?" They didn't know what to reply to that.

Simon's mannerisms were a little camp. He had this way of pushing up his lank fringe with a stab of his hand, making a comb of his fingers. He wouldn't have lasted a day in a factory. But he liked to talk about his women. Overcompensation perhaps. Or maybe his upbringing – he was what you might call very middle class.

It turned out that Judy's combination of poshness and foul mouth was no coincidence. It had been nurtured since 1932, when her parents sent her to Thorpennhowe, an experimental boarding school founded during the golden era of alternative education. It was run as a democratic community and all pupils had the right to vote on all matters concerning the school's activities, including rules and regulations, deciding their own bedtime and all. They were free to do and say as they pleased, attend classes if they wished, or tinker about in the workshop or go for a swim or climb a tree. It was eventually shut down in 1984 after having been blacklisted by the government for three decades. "Freedom and government never did get along," was Judy's verdict on Thorpennhowe's fate. "It's astonishing they let it go on for as long as they did, really. We were lucky. Very, very lucky."

Simon looked at Judy with devotion in his eyes. You could tell he too felt that he had been very lucky.

I finished my cuppa, thanked Judy for the trouble and got ready to leave. As I walked to the door she looked at me with the gaze of a caring mother and said, "You're young, you need to eat some meat. Join us for lunch this Sunday, twelve noon. Don't be late, cold food is bad for the soul."

And that's how our Sunday tradition began.

11

I LEFT THE café just after 5 p.m., got on a packed bus and began the usual slog that took me back to Deptford. As I walked in I knew Terry was home. There was no mistaking the loud music and the smell of pot that came through from the kitchen.

Terry was a stocky, angry character with a thick Indian accent who insisted on telling everyone that he had been born and raised in New Zeeland. Nobody believed him, but we all played along with his fantasy, probably because none of us wanted to confront him, knowing too well that it would force him to deal with whatever messed up reasons he had for hiding behind such blatant nonsense.

He worked at the local barber shop. The thought of Terry handling a razor made my blood run cold. He once punched through the rear window of a client's car because the poor bastard had parked in front of the shop's door. Terry's fist went straight through the window, while the glass shattered in a million pieces and nearly tore his arm to shreds. He was a barely functioning lunatic, but in some strange way I envied him. I envied how his behaviour was entirely uncontaminated by thought. I wished I could've acted so instinctively, letting raw impulse drive my actions. But I could never do that, I was too much of a thinker. Thinking things through is meant to be a good thing, mature even, but what if it's a compulsion? What if someone has no choice but to always think things through? Is it still a good thing then? A rational mind could feel very limiting sometimes, though definitely kinder to the flesh on my arms.

Terry was a happy drunk but an obnoxious stoner. A knot grabbed my stomach as the heavy smell of pot hit my nostrils. I walked up the stairs, then along the corridor and through to the kitchen. Terry looked at me dead-eyed. He passed me a couple of beers that he'd nicked from the communal fridge and made a clumsy attempt at covering up the bag of peanuts he had obviously taken from my cupboard. He always nicked other people's food when he was stoned, and he was always stoned.

Sitting next to Terry was a flat-chested woman called Yona. She'd moved to London from Bulgaria a few weeks before and was clearly still struggling to make sense of it all. I'm sure Terry's presence didn't help her with that. He was shouting at the TV, waving his hands frantically. Occasionally he would stop, take a sip of beer and look around the room as if he'd just woken up in a foreign country. Then he would laugh uncontrollably, a deep, visceral laugh, before continuing to curse at the anchor-man on the screen.

Yona looked a little shell-shocked, but she seemed to have some street smarts about her. She had a pronounced underbite and a square, androgynous jaw. This boyish-like appearance put me off and turned me on at the same time, like toying with some sort of mild taboo. I had noticed her looking at me a couple of times when I came out of the shower, and I once overheard her telling Gemma, our other housemate, that she liked my hands. I think she meant my arms.

Terry was now in a full-blown argument with the TV and conversation had become impossible. I asked Yona if she wanted to go downstairs for a chat. She replied with an emotionless "yes". I grabbed a sandwich from the fridge and walked down the stairs.

Yona had no arse to speak of, and Gemma had told us that she hated her lack of curves and was saving up to get breast implants. She managed it in the end. A pair of cumbersome, rubbery things that mocked gravity, sexuality, and all that's good about either. She also ended up with no sensation in her nipples, so the whole thing was just an awkward mass of rubber, turning any hope of sexual encounters into a sad one-sided affair. What's wrong with these women? Do they really think that a man wants to have his own boob party where the woman is not invited? Are they really that clueless? Most men understand women like a squirrel understands the cockpit instruments of a fighter jet, but at least we are aware of that fact.

12

I ENJOYED ROAMING London on Sunday mornings. The quiet roads and tentative sleepiness were a wonderfully odd prelude to the relentless pace that lay in ambush. It was a dry, pleasant April morning, clear sky peppered with a few tiny white clouds and the usual Heathrow traffic. I cycled to Lewisham High Street market to get some fresh bread, then through New Cross and back towards Deptford. Two firemen were cleaning mud off their Jeep's windscreen outside New Cross fire station. I waved.

I arrived at Judy's just before noon, knocked on the door and handed her the fresh bread.

"Thank you," she said with a firm sincerity. "The world needs more men who come bearing gifts." Her words made me feel accomplished, like I belonged to some new order of man.

"Do come through." Judy held the door and moved sideways to let me in, then called out: "Simon, be a dear and pour Dak a sherry, will you?" I heard a kitchen cabinet open and close, glasses clinking.

"You like sherry, don't you?" Judy asked.

Truth be told I'd normally leave sherry alone, but this was not normality.

"Sure," I said.

Judy's house had a calming aura about it. Not in that wishy-washy hippy style of quackery and dreamcatchers. It was a perfectly ordinary house, light cream sofa, a rocking chair, reading lamp, two armchairs, a *tiny* TV set, electric heater, a blue vase, a solid wood bookcase, an old upright piano, flowery curtains. And yet I felt like I'd just entered some sort of sanctuary. The curtains turned out to be William Morris, so that may've had something to do with it.

She later told me that the front parlour – as she called it – was exactly how she and Neil had it back in Fulham. "It's what kept me from going insane," she said matter-of-factly. "After he died, I was terrified I would forget him." Judy always said "died". She hated euphemisms. "It was all irrational of course," she gave a sudden laugh, amused at her own irrationality, "so I brought our front parlour with me. This was our place. He used to sit on that armchair," she gestured towards where I was sitting. "He was so handsome, talking to me about his patients for hours. He was an old-school physician, you know, he actually *looked* at the patient. Nowadays it's all about the computers."

Judy spoke of her husband with such intensity and pride that it was almost painful to witness. I had never met the man and yet I envied him deeply. I wondered whether I would ever make such a profound mark on a woman. When I told Judy about this, her eyes welled up: "Oh darling, I feel for you. It's horrid. Today so many women are on the capitalist bandwagon that they see love as just another market exchange. The job lust has got them, and the status lust. They're infected." There was a sadness in her eyes, as if she wished she could tell me otherwise, as if she would've liked to shelter me with a lie but couldn't.

"This is happening to so many women," she continued, her mouth half open, as though shocked by her own words, "they can't see what love means. They don't seem to be interested in men in the mating years, and later... well, later it's just another acquisition. I hardly recognize them as women."

Simon arrived with my sherry.

"Simon knows all about this, don't you, Si?" said Judy. Then she turned to me: "He has suffered his disappointments."

"I have," said Simon with a cheeky grin, "that's why I'm reading *Silas Marner*. I much prefer the company of dead women."

Judy laughed. "I bet you do!" she said playfully, "they don't talk back like us live ones!"

"Yes, and I don't have to touch them. You know I'm squeamish with that sort of thing."

"Oh do shut up!" Judy could hardly speak, laughing so hard she had to gasp for breath.

But there was some truth in Simon's comedy, and he often complained about how there was not enough time in a lifetime to read all the classics, the Great Masters. Shakespeare, Hemingway, the big Russians and so forth. He talked about Virginia Woolf and Charlotte Brontë as if they were his lovers, and in a sense they were. Those women had bared themselves to the world through their words, and Simon was one of the men who paid attention – really paid attention. Not just to the lyrical language and the carefully crafted sentences, but to the intimacy that lies beneath.

Listening to Simon I felt ashamed of my ignorance. I read the newspaper occasionally and I had used books, but I didn't really *read* books. The working class are pretty unforgiving of that sort of stuff, so I left it alone. I'd been through a few physics books that Ric had given me, a few manuals on heat absorption, and I'd read a few history books, mostly war and religion (quite the happy marriage) but that was for knowledge, that was different.

I told Simon. He laughed. "But literature *is* knowledge," he said with a series of impassioned jerks of his head, his fringe flapping up and down like a panicked bird's wing.

I couldn't agree. "It's stories," I said, "I don't see the point in reading something unless it's for gathering actual information."

We could hear Judy fumbling around in the kitchen, putting plates under the grill. She loved to serve food in hot plates, do well by our souls.

"And you think information can only be gathered by lists of facts? How about the human condition?" Simon asked.

That made me think. I was out of my depth. It was uncomfortable, but I liked where I was. Things are *happening*, I thought. Was I lucky? It seemed like the right place to be and the right people to be with.

"Grub's up, boys!" Judy called.

Simon and I sat at the table while Judy laid the empty plates in front of us and then brought over a large oven dish. Cottage pie. It smelled like home.

Judy sat down as Simon spooned a large slice of pie into my plate.

"Dak thinks there's no point in reading stories," he said with a smile.

Judy laughed. "What's the point of doing *anything*?"

"Well," I said proudly, like some genius who'd just been consulted for his unique perspective, "the point of science is discovery, for example. Besides, you read the newspaper for information, don't you?"

"Oh, don't be a fool. The newspaper is just homework! If you want to discover anything about *people*, then read a novel, don't talk to a scientist." She let out a proud laugh.

I didn't like her take on science one little bit. But I had a strange feeling that this was one of those moments that mattered.

Simon poured me a glass of wine and passed the water jug. Judy pointed at the bread. "Have some bread and butter, it's good for you."

I thanked her, picked up a knife, sliced a bread roll in half and covered it in butter.

"So," said Judy, "what brought you to London?"

I explained that I had this urge to make a mark. I told her about Ric and the toilet seat, how it had made me feel that I had to *do* something.

"Yes!" Judy said enthusiastically. "So you should. Make a man of yourself. The world is desperate for good men."

I wasn't sure what she meant by that, but her enthusiasm spurred me on, so I continued, "I really want to make something of myself, I just don't know how."

"Did you hear that, Simon?" she said in a mocking tone. "He doesn't know how to make something of himself." Then she laughed a hearty laugh.

"Well, there's no need to be mocking about it," I said, annoyed by her tone.

"Well, maybe there is!" she replied in an almost ecstatic voice, as if she'd just stumbled across a great discovery. "Maybe that's exactly what you need to open your eyes," she brought her right hand to her face, making an unfolding motion in front of her eyes.

"Yes…" said Simon pensively.

Judy laughed, as if I were missing something entirely obvious. I didn't know what to say, I had no idea what it was I was supposed to be missing. I looked around in confusion.

"He really doesn't know," Judy said finally, in a sort of defeated voice. Then her tone changed, became that of a nurturing mother: "Education. It's got to be education. Any decent mark to be made begins with education."

"You need to get yourself into university," Simon added.

"Well, I would, but –"

"But what? But it's *hard*?" Judy said, mockery still lingering. "Of course it's hard. If it weren't hard the world would be full of Oscar Wildes, John Donnes and George Eliots."

I kind of knew who Oscar Wilde was. Almost one out of three wasn't too good. She was obviously right about education.

"No," I said, "what I mean is that I can't because I left school at fourteen, remember? I have no qualifications." I resented her insinuation that I was somehow intimidated by hard work. I knew I could do hard work, and I had nearly a million squirts to prove it.

Judy turned towards Simon and sighed. "He's telling me it's hard," she stated in a deflated monotone.

We finished our meal in silence.

A couple of hours later we had tea and biscuits in the front room. It was part of our ritual. And all through this ritual Judy would tell me stories of her youth – education, love, loss, poetry, music, sex, the Great Masters, life, and, of course, her Neil. Then she'd ask me about my own life and aspirations. She was the first person who had ever genuinely taken an interest in me. And she knew it.

"All these women are not interested in you!" she said abruptly, after I told her about my Friday night at the Rising Sun.

That was the Friday I had met Elly, a twenty-five-year-old Irish blonde with large wobbly breasts and slender fingers. We got drunk on cheap lager and left just before the bell. We walked to Soho to find a minicab, haggled on the price and got in. I slid my hand under her blouse as the cabby negotiated the London traffic and pretended not to look in the rear-view mirror. Elly's tongue darted around my mouth like a mad snake, and somewhere near Southwark she grabbed my crotch. That Catholic upbringing hadn't been in vain.

Judy listened to these stories with great amusement, but occasionally got cross, and often I had no idea why. Her moods were like hurricanes blasting in and out at random intervals.

"How extraordinary!" she said. "And what happens after you fuck?" She asked the question with an almost child-like wonder. I could see Thorpennhowe, how it had nourished that little girl's curiosity and enthusiasm, allowed them to be brought into adulthood almost intact. I envied her.

"Nothing much," I replied, somewhat hesitant, feeling like I was about to step into a trap.

"Well, they obviously don't care about *you*," Judy stated matter of fact. "They see your joy for life and they want a morsel. They want a *piece* of you."

Judy's words struck hard, and the mixture of sadness and nurture in her voice nearly moved me to tears. I wasn't one for reading stories, and I especially disliked vampire stories – something to do with having an over-punctilious suspension of disbelief, a blessing and a curse – but suddenly they kind of made sense. Maybe vampires aren't fictional after all, I thought. Maybe fiction isn't fictional.

"They don't even know you," Judy said. "They don't *want* to know you, let alone *love* you," she waved her hand dismissively. "My Neil and I loved fucking, but it was the love for each other and the knowledge we had of each other that made us strong. Stop thinking of excitement as something that happens to your dick!" She paused and stared at me, looking for a reaction. Then she said, "You need a woman who can excite you on the *in*side."

Judy's swearing often stirred people up and she had come to expect strong reactions. She liked that. She talked freely like that to everyone, she saw no point or sense in filtering her thoughts. To me, however, that unique combination of grace and foul-mouth was like two beautiful yet incompatible universes that had inexplicably melted into one another. It filled me with hope and a yearning for life, for Woman. I think that's one of the reasons Judy took such an interest in me, the fact that I liked what others considered an unpleasant quirk. But I didn't just like it, it was much more than that.

"Don't get me wrong," Judy went on, "fucking is good. But it's a moment, not a lifetime."

I could see her measuring her words carefully. This was important.

"When my Neil and I got married, I was free. I thought: 'this is it, perfect freedom, everything is settled and I can do what I want now.' Yes, yes, of course it was also euphoria," she added, as if addressing an imaginary rebuttal. "And of course I couldn't always do what I wanted, thank God! But the feeling was that something fundamental – my love partner – was settled for ever. I was freed from a big question. Without that freedom to live and love you're just having the prems!" She laughed.

"Premature ejaculation," came Simon's explanation.

"Yes," said Judy, "but emotional," she enunciated the word, slowly, as if talking to a child. "The *emotional* prems. Squandering your emotions.

"You need a woman who wants knowledge, a woman who wants to *know,* who wants to know *you*."

"And where do I find a woman like that?" I asked. I was being rhetorical, I think.

"Well, certainly not in a bar!" She laughed an obvious laugh.

"University?" suggested Simon timidly.

"Yes!" Judy agreed, astonished. She couldn't believe she hadn't suggested it herself. "University. And anyway, you can't carry on making coffee, you have to make something of yourself."

That I had to do.

"Yeah, but I left school at fourteen, I can't –"

"Oh stop that at once!" she hissed.

"What?"

"The self-pity. It's ugly."

"It's not self-pity, it's a fact that universities require –"

"Can you believe him?" Judy looked at Simon in astonishment. "You want to make something of yourself, don't you?"

"Yes, but –"

"Then do the fucking work! Call, ask, speak to whomever you must and make it happen!" she yelled.

I sat there speechless, like I'd just been attacked by a mob.

"Ok," I hesitated, "but I don't know where to start."

"Start where every man should start. Read the Great Masters. Don't waste any time on those books —" Judy paused, then shouted over her shoulder as if calling Simon in another room, "Si, what are they called?"

"Who?" answered Simon quietly, sitting beside her. They both chuckled at her slip.

"You know, those people, those who churn them out."

"Michael Connelly?" suggested Simon.

Judy turned back to me, "Yes, don't waste any of your time with the Michael Connellys, there simply aren't enough hours in one's lifetime. And anyway, anything anyone can possibly say has already been said by the Great Masters. Read the Great Masters. It's terribly urgent."

Well, I thought, at least I have instructions. I am capable of following instructions. For the first time since Ric, I saw a crack running through my life's deadlock. I saw the future. And it felt good.

"And don't faff around with introductions to the Great Masters. Go straight to the stories. Introductions are written by overeducated underachievers who can't write but like to talk about those who can. Don't let fools cloud your experience."

"I like introductions," said Simon.

Judy laughed. "No he doesn't."

Her face became serious again. "You don't want to wander around like a lost boy forever, do you? Good. Fortunately you don't *have* to. They all laid it out for you. It's all there." The tone of her voice lowered, as though she was stating an obvious truism. "There's no excuse really…" She paused in thought for a few seconds, then turned to Simon, "Si, do you think he should start with Forster? He should probably start with Forster."

"Yes…" Simon hesitated. He knew his role: to agree with Judy's decision — she wasn't really asking him a question. But then he added, "He has a scientific mind, though. He should probably start with the philosophers."

They continued exchanging ideas about what my course of action should be, and I listened intently, my future unfolding before my eyes. I felt excited and overwhelmed. A wave of optimism ran through me. I had no idea how I would make it happen, but suddenly it all seemed more possible, more graspable. My desire to make a mark was becoming less of a dream and more of an idea. With any luck it may even turn into a plan.

13

SO THAT'S HOW I joined Charing Cross public library. I didn't know where to start but I knew it involved books, and Charing Cross seemed like a good place to "do the fucking work!"

Truth be told, Charing Cross was a little out of the way. I had to take the 188 to Waterloo Bridge and then walk for half a mile along the Strand. But somehow I felt it was the right place. I'd heard about its history of bookshops, and I took that to be a good omen. Not that I believed in omens, but sometimes that's all you've got to go by. And seeing all those bookshops neatly lined up, knowing that some had stood through the Enlightenment, the Victorians, two world wars, a sex revolution and at least three music revolutions, from hefty leather-bound tomes all the way to nifty paperbacks – it just gave me the right gut feeling. Besides, I liked the Strand, it had an aura about it, a greatness blended with the ordinary.

I walked through the double doors, dutifully holding my utility bills as proof of address, and applied for a membership card. I leafed through a book about the Second World War. I wondered what I should read. What is my ticket to making something of myself? What does it look like? Will I *know*? How does one know? Fuck. How does one *begin*?

I remembered Judy's words. Of course it's hard. It's going to be hard. I wandered along the tall shelves, lost. Then I remembered Simon's words. I should probably start with the philosophers. I thought about the Great Masters. I thought about *it* all being laid out for me. It.

I walked to the philosophy section and picked up the *Analects of Confucius*.

14

I THINK IT was a Thursday. I got back after a double shift, knackered. I took off my clothes and ran a hot bath.

My feet were killing me.

The bathroom floor was laid with some patchy carpet that looked like a cross between old sack and a mock Persian rug. There had been a latch on the door, till Terry ripped it off in one of his drunken bouts. I don't know the whole story, but I suspect it involved some poor soul trying to escape Terry's madness by hiding in the bathroom. It clearly hadn't worked.

We now protected our privacy by leaving the door open every time we'd finished with the bathroom – that way we knew that a closed door meant someone was in it. I often fell asleep in the bath after a long shift, so I took an old newspaper to the bathroom with me. I closed the door, folded up a few pages and wedged them underneath. I lay in the bath and closed my eyes.

The first few minutes were always the best. The hot water almost burnt my skin, giving me a faint feeling of pain that quickly turned into pleasure as my muscles relaxed.

I lay there for about an hour, then got out, dried off, wrapped a towel around my waist, pulled the newspaper out from under the door and left.

As I was walking across the corridor Yona came out of her room. I almost walked straight into her. She blushed.

"You should watch where you're going, you might get hurt," I said, grinning.

She smiled shyly, her eyes darting around nervously. She finally spoke, "You should cover yourself, it's distracting."

Her boldness turned me on instantly. "Come upstairs and help me out," I said.

"I've got to go to work. Night shift." She worked in a cocktail bar just off Regent Street.

"Ok, I'll see you later."

She locked the door behind her and left. I walked upstairs, put on a t-shirt, collapsed in bed.

At 2 a.m. I was woken up by someone shouting at the telly. Terry was home. I banged on the wall a few times. Nothing. I got up, put on a pair of trousers and went downstairs.

"Come on, T, let's keep it down."

He was oddly apologetic, almost embarrassed. He put down my peanuts. "Sorry, man, I'm out of booze. Do you have any booze?" He knew I had some beers; he'd seen them in the fridge.

"Yeah, take a can from the fridge. Give me one too, I won't be able to sleep now anyways."

"Thanks, man! Sorry, man! I'll get you ice-cream tomorrow!" He meant the ice-cream he nicked from the barber shop. Ice lollies. They used them to bribe the kids, you know, so they'd stay still during the haircut.

I heard a key turning. The front door opened then closed. Footsteps. It was Yona.

"Come and join us, Yo!" said Terry. "There's beer!" It was my beer.

Yona pulled a bottle of vodka out of her handbag. She poured a glass, threw in some lemonade and sat down. Terry's face turned into a beaming child. He couldn't believe his luck. Free beer *and* vodka?

We chatted until 4 a.m., Terry shouting at reruns of *EastEnders*, munching on my peanuts, draining my beer and Yona's vodka. Yona kept pretending not to be looking at me.

"I like you," she said out of the blue, almost like she had lost a dare.

"Is that so?"

"I've liked you for a while now. You have sexy hands."

"Thanks." I couldn't find a compliment to give her in return. I didn't fancy her at all, but I was horny and a little drunk, hardly a good combination.

I stood up. "Come on then, let's go upstairs. You can make better acquaintance with my hands."

She smiled a nervous smile and stood up. That surprised me, I didn't think she would. She followed me upstairs.

We walked into my room and stood by the bed. I nudged the top-left corner, where one of the legs was missing, collapsed under the weight of the previous lodger's sexual exploits. I had put two bricks under it, one on top of the other, to keep the whole thing levelled. But the top brick would slide away from the bottom brick just a little bit every night, so I had to keep an eye on it to make sure it didn't topple. It seemed steady; it passed the nudge test.

Yona moved closer. I put my arm around her waist and went in for the kiss. She opened her mouth and presented her tongue like a corpse on a stretcher. I nearly gagged, then froze. It must be some sort of bizarre survival reflex, I thought. Seconds passed like minutes. I stood there with that lump of motionless flesh in my mouth, and a single thought occupied my mind: why do I do these things? I moved away, eager to put a stop to the sadness, but not for long. I motioned her to lie on the bed. I was getting hard despite everything, my body going through the motions like a perversely dependable companion.

I took off my shirt and unbuttoned Yona's trousers. She slid out of them a little clumsily, revealing a pair of plain, white knickers. Her androgyny had all but disappeared, she was all woman now. As she turned on her side, her buttocks looked rounder and fuller than was even imaginable just a minute ago. I was stunned. It was like a Wonderbra in reverse. I wondered how many men had been fooled into thinking that some woman had a flat arse when in fact all it takes is for her trousers to come off and bring out a perfectly acceptable level of roundness. I should know these things by now, I thought. For a second I felt like a fraud.

The bright whiteness of her knickers contrasted sharply with her olive skin, sending a throb along my already hard cock. I removed the rest of my clothes and grabbed her by the hips. She turned her body slightly, placed her hand behind my neck and tried to kiss me. I couldn't do it. All I could think about was that lifeless slab of flesh lying still in my mouth. I turned my head and began kissing her neck, pretending I had misunderstood her intention. But the lack of tongues was beginning to get to me; I could feel my cock getting soft, I didn't have long before my erection would be gone.

So I knelt up, my legs across hers, ready to enter her with an unimpressive half-mast – just enough to gain a notch on the bedpost but not enough to invite any pride. As I edged closer to her she shifted to the right. I moved left to compensate. She shifted left. At first I thought it was some lack of coordination, but then I realized it was more deliberate than that. Was it nerves? We repeated this dance of despair a few times. The blood began to drain from my cock. As I looked down to assess the loss of turgidity, a loud fart boomed out of my arse and murdered whatever shreds of mood we had left. I stood up in silence. Although I could swear Yona picked up her clothes in haste, I saw the scene unfold in some sort of slow motion. The door shut. No notch on the bedpost, not tonight. That's just as well, my bed didn't even have a headboard anyway.

15

ONCE A MONTH Mr Alaoui made a fresh batch of kebab. I always tried to make it in time for the ritual tasting.

Mr Alaoui was one of the laziest businessmen I'd ever met. He'd sit in the shop watching TV all day while Salim – his only employee – would run around in a frenzy trying to grill steaks, serve customers, count the change and answer the phone. Occasionally Mr Alaoui would be called to the grill to make a burger – that was his domain. He would solemnly take a lump of patty out of the fridge and toss it on the grill. He would then pull out a stick thermometer with the demeanour of a priest who's just about to bless the body of Christ, step closer to the grill and start fiddling with the patty. This would normally take no more than fifteen minutes, but it was enough to make Mr Alaoui sweat profusely. When he was done, he would dry his forehead with a towel, like a boxer who'd just been through a brutal round, and then sit down at the TV again. But despite his clownish manner and his aversion to work, Mr Alaoui made by far the best kebab south of the river. On the last Saturday of the month, when his wife travelled to Cardiff to visit their eldest daughter, he would order a sack of offcuts fresh from the butcher's. His wife was a short, hyperactive woman who pranced around the shop with a sense of urgency, cleaning and tidying as if possessed by a supernatural force. Her presence must've been torture for him. She did more work in an afternoon than he considered tackling in a month. I can't imagine anything worse for a man of Mr Alaoui's disposition than having a woman like that around. It was almost amusing, knowing that at some point he *proposed* to this woman, thinking that it would be a good idea to spend their lives together – and she *agreed*. Maybe that was the secret, maybe I was missing the entire point. Still, he didn't want her around when he was making kebab, he needed a religious atmosphere, something she was unable to supply.

The offcuts included everything that was left over after every last bit of sellable meat had been chiselled away. As Mrs Alaoui pulled away in a taxi, Mr Alaoui would rub his hands in expectation and waddle to the basement. His face looked almost young; you could see the boy buried inside the man. Once in the basement, he would pick up the sack of offcuts – huffing and puffing like a tired old bull – and empty the contents into an old, oversized mixer that resembled a medieval torture machine but with the added menace of an electric motor. Guts, cartilage, nerves, small bones and all.

Once I asked Mr Alaoui if testicles were part of the mix.

"Oh no!" he said. He looked excited at my question but also puzzled by my blatant ignorance. "Testicles are too good for blending. I grill them with olive oil and lemon." He brought his hand to his face and smacked his lips, "A speciality." He wasn't joking.

"You wanna try them?" he said with a hint of mischief on his face.

"Erm, sure, why not."

"They're not always easy to find, but next time I'll ask Salim to make them for us. After closing time."

"Ok."

Mr Alaoui turned off the mixer, adjusted the bowl and turned it back on. The old thing clanked into life like a bucketful of gravel in a tumble dryer.

"Look," he said, turning serious, "a girl calf has potential, you see. One day she'll give you milk."

He opened a rickety cupboard and pulled out two spice jars.

"I know, I know..." he added, as if replying to an imaginary opponent, "these animal rights types are always complaining about the suffering of cows – you know – because cows are kept pregnant for the milk... but at least they get to keep their bits!"

This really seemed to bother him, I couldn't help wondering whether this was about something else entirely. Maybe there was more to Mrs Alaoui than the prancing around and the busy-looking demeanour.

"What about boy calves, uh? If you're *lucky*, they let you grow into a bull – you know – to keep the cows going," he made a circular motion with his hand. "Thing is, they only need one bull for every twenty cows or something, so you need to be *really* lucky."

His words threw me. I hadn't expected my factual question to elicit such insight, and from a man who I'd always presumed was barren of insights. Maybe his blight wasn't laziness after all, maybe it was worse. Maybe it was disillusionment.

"So, if you're a boy calf, the best you can hope for is that your bits end up on my plate!" He gave an expectant smile. "At least your suffering won't have been in vain."

This was personal. I was convinced Mr Alaoui liked testicles more than milk.

He grabbed a handful of spices from each jar and threw it in the mixer bowl.

"Not for customers, though," he added. "Family and friends only. People don't eat testicles in this country." This fact seemed to sadden him, as if he blamed himself for having failed to instil Brits with a love of grilled testicles.

The mixer had now churned the offcuts into a fine, pinkish pulp. Mr Alaoui threw in a handful of salt and some more spices from the jars. Then he held a wooden spoon against the inside of the mixer bowl, scraping off the few bits of offcuts that had got stuck there and forcing them back into the mixer blades.

"Sometimes they put penis in the mix though!" He laughed.

I don't think he was joking.

The mixer kept rattling away.

The whole process looked more like witchcraft than cooking, and I half expected Mr Alaoui to pull out a bunch of bat wings from his apron while muttering words in Latin. That never happened, not as far as I know anyway; but you never know, none of the spice jars had labels on them. But the true bit of witchcraft was the result. Despite the process I had just witnessed and the less-than-noble ingredients behind that blended pulp, it tasted delicious. It was astonishing really, how such a delicacy could be born of such modest parentage.

When the pulp was ready, Mr Alaoui would grab a handful and roughly gather it into a ball before impaling it on a giant skewer. He would repeat this process till the giant skewer was filled to the end, then place it on a vertical grill and let it slow cook for about an hour, occasionally spraying it with lemon. Then he would take out a long steel knife and sharpen it ceremoniously. That's when Salim usually turned up. He fancied himself as a bit of an expert taster. Mr Alaoui would proceed to thinly slice the fruit of his labour and lay it on a large oval plate he kept especially for the tasting. Then he'd pause and look over his creation with a proud grin. At that very moment, and for a few quick seconds, I always felt a kinship with the man, the bond you feel with a man who takes pride in his work. And that work was definitely worth a few sins, pride included. Oozing with fat, it had a meaty – almost refined – texture, a bit like burger patty but with a much more intense taste. As the spices kicked in, I could taste the years that had gone into perfecting the delicate combinations that were so effortlessly melting in my mouth. Blended poetry. I struggled to keep my eyes open as I ate.

Most of the batch would end up in the freezer and lose much of its brilliance. That's why I always tried to make it in time for the tasting.

16

IT WAS chucking out time, and I had no idea I was about to get mixed up with the Russian mob.

Gus was trying to convince Liam to serve him one more drink.

"C'mon, mate, one for the road!"

"You travel by tube."

"You know what I mean, c'mon, show us some sympathy!"

Liam wasn't the sympathetic type. He put some dirty glasses on the bar, turned around and stared Gus down. Gus got the message, thanked the bar staff and left.

Kevin and I got out, walked to Tottenham Court Road, took a right and went down some narrow stairs into a bar with steamed up windows and a faint smell of disinfectant. The music was lousy and the beer mediocre. We walked out and wandered around Soho for a while.

We passed by a sign with GIRLS! on it repeated three times in green, blue and yellow neon lights. Once would've been enough. A skinny blonde with a fake smile called out: "Hey, fancy a bit of fun, gentlemen? It's only £5."

It wasn't our usual scene, and I never liked the idea of paying for pussy – ordinary anatomy presented as though it was some rare artefact to be witnessed at great cost. It's demeaning for a man, a failure, a con, the triumph of an irrational insecurity that he is somehow lesser than a woman whose skillset amounts to little more than a vague ability to stand around with no clothes on.

But we were bored and lonely, so we walked in.

A few middle-aged men, all seriously out of shape, sat around a small round stage; eager slaves to the Great Con. On top of the stage a peroxide blonde was swaying her hips and unclipping her bra. Strobe lights flashed about uncontrollably like a bunch of mad radioactive flowers; there was a smell of cheap vodka and body lotion in the air. I couldn't detect any disinfectant.

We found two stools near the bar and blew our last fiver on a pair of whiskies. The peroxide blonde finished her act. She came out a few minutes later dressed in a green faux-leather skirt and a low-cut top. She scouted the room for prey and decided on a balding fifty-year-old who'd somewhat managed to hang on to a vaguely youthful face.

The strobe lights stepped up their madness and the next dancer walked on stage. This time it was a small brunette with very straight hair, a wonderfully compact arse and a strangely innocent look. She started her act, swaying her hips to the music, making some eye contact with the room. She knew how to play a man's desperation.

The music picked up pace and the brunette whipped off her bra, then walked down the few steps that separated the stage from her audience. She was wearing a red thong and had a small toolbelt around her waist. She pointed at some guy in an ill-fitting suit who couldn't believe his luck, walked up to him, and straddled across his lap.

The ill-fitting suit went wild. He grabbed the brunette's hips and started throwing his head around in a frenzy, his tongue sticking out, flapping left and right while his head darted around as if mounted on a crazy rubber neck. Small brunette took a can of whipped cream from the toolbelt and placed a squirt of it on her belly button. The suit's head came to a sudden halt. He stared at the white stuff for a few seconds, then licked it off. The audience cheered and the brunette walked away, looking for her next fool. The suit looked ecstatic. I wondered how his life might have worked out if he'd put all this energy and excitement into making something of himself. We have to get out of here, I thought. This is where a man's soul goes to die.

As I turned to Kevin to call it a night, I saw him looking at me with a goofy smile. Small brunette was walking straight towards me, pointing and winking and swaying her hips. The strobe lights swung around and slapped me in the face with green and blue and yellow. I turned my head slightly and gestured to her that I wasn't interested. Then I pointed towards another customer and gave her my best fake smile; no need to be a prick about it, she was at work after all. Small brunette ignored my attempt at politeness, took out the whipped cream and squirted a dollop on each of her nipples. She stood straight, her breasts sticking out, offering me her misuse of dairy and sugar. Her right arm was stretched up in the air, her index finger pointing toward the ceiling in a sort of Freddie Mercury-esque pose. The audience looked on in expectation. I suppose that's what they call being put on the spot.

I smiled, dipped my finger in the cream and smeared it on her nose. She chuckled. Then she wiped off the cream and gave me a mock-menacing look. For a moment I saw the girl behind the stripper. The audience let out all sorts of disapproving noises.

Small brunette carried on swaying her hips for a couple more minutes, then stepped back on the stage, waved at the audience and disappeared through a black curtain.

Kevin and I were about to call it a night for the second time when small brunette came out through a side door and walked straight up to us. Behind her was a tall, boring-looking blonde in knee-high boots that she probably wore to conceal a pair of bowlegs.

"Hi, I'm Tatiana," said the small brunette.

Tatiana had a gentle oval face and a sincere-looking smile. Her teeth were slightly spaced apart and she had intense brown eyes. She spoke in a thick Spanish accent.

Her friend started chatting with Kevin. The music was really loud now, and I couldn't quite make out what they were saying. Kevin was nodding and smiling. The blonde looked a little less boring as she perked up with the conversation. Her boots were still knee-high and her legs still probably bowlegs.

Tatiana stepped sideways and lowered her wonderfully compact arse onto the stool next to mine.

Within seconds a waiter appeared and started hovering nearby, clearly expecting something from us. It turned out that's how the girls made their living, by getting customers to buy them overpriced drinks. The waiter would serve the girls a drop of some non-alcoholic drink, usually orange juice or apple juice, and charge the self-appointed fool a fiver for it. A pint in the Rising Sun was under £1.50. The drink would barely last five minutes of inane conversation, after which the waiter would reappear, hovering. This ritual would carry on indefinitely, until the customer could no longer afford the juice, at which point the girl would move on to the next mouldering soul, and the circle would begin again: hovering, overpriced juice from concentrate, fake smiles, more hovering.

"Thanks, mate, but we're leaving," Kevin told the waiter.

"If you sit with the girl you need to get her a drink."

Tatiana looked at me pleadingly. I had the impression she wasn't just doing this for money; she looked like she *had* to do this.

Kevin stood up and put his coat on, prompting the waiter to turn around and take his hovering elsewhere. Tatiana leaned toward me and whispered in my ear, "I'll get the drinks, just stay a while." Then she slipped a tenner into my front pocket.

We sat back down. The waiter reappeared.

"What are you girls drinking?" he asked smugly. He was beginning to annoy me.

"Orange juice. Twice." said Tatiana.

The waiter got a tiny notepad out of his breast pocket and pretended to scribble down the order.

"And for the gentlemen?" What a phoney prick.

"We're ok, thanks."

He looked at us in contempt, then turned around and walked off. I really couldn't stand the fucker.

"I've never seen you here before," said Tatiana.

"Nah, we usually go to the Out Bar."

"The Out Bar? I don't know it. Is it a strip club?"

"No, it's a bar. In Holborn."

The waiter arrived with the drinks. "That'll be £10."

I handed him Tatiana's tenner. He put it in a black waist bag and left.

"So, why did you come here tonight?"

"You didn't just spend £10 on orange juice to ask about our drinking habits, did you?"

"No…" She smiled, showing me another glimpse of the girl. It was a quick smile though, and she suddenly turned serious, as if she'd caught herself out. Squirting whipped cream on yourself for a living must harden you up more than most.

"I just wanted to be away from *him*." She nodded to her left where there was a middle-aged man in a tattered black leather jacket, sitting alone, sucking at some blue cocktail. He looked depressed and had tufts of grey hairs pouring out of his nose and ears.

"Oh, I see. Pardon me if I don't feel flattered," I said.

A few minutes passed and Tatiana hadn't touched her drink. The waiter came back, hovering and giving her looks, reminding her she was on the clock.

"Turn to your right for a second," she whispered, "look towards the emergency door."

I did as she asked. She tossed her drink in a nearby flowerpot. Judging by the yellow leaves it probably wasn't the first time.

The waiter zeroed in. "Drinks for the ladies?" His intonation rose excessively at the end of each question. I imagined what it would feel like to smash the empty glass across his face. The sound of his cheekbone cracking, blood splattering *everywhere*. The image was so vivid in my head that I felt a sense of liberation mixed with panic; there he was, the annoying prick lying on the floor, customers leaving in a hurry, horrified but too afraid to do anything about it. That's what it must feel like to be Terry, I thought. I probably could've taken him on too, he was a skinny little fucker. But I couldn't go through with it, I just wasn't that sort of bloke.

"Same again?" He pulled out his phoney notebook and scribbled down the pretend order.

Tatiana leaned in, took my hand and slipped me another tenner. She seemed to be taking a shine to me for some reasons. Maybe she saw the vulnerability buried in my shallow grave of swagger.

"This can't be good for business," I told her.

"It's ok, I get £3 for every drink. I made enough for today anyway. I'd rather sit in peace for a while."

"What brought you to Soho then?" I asked.

"We're not really allowed to talk about our private lives."

"I can't stand small talk, even if you're buying your own drinks."

"It's complicated."

It was.

Tatiana asked me to go back the following Friday. We got there much later, around 2 a.m., and had to pay the full admission price. Kevin fancied this woman who did some shifts pulling pints at the Out Bar. She happened to be working that Friday, so I hung around in the wings while Kevin sat at the bar and talked to her between pints.

We walked in. Same dispirited audience and deranged strobe lights. Same scent of cheap vodka and body lotion.

Tatiana was sitting at a table, talking to a short, chubby man who was laughing mechanically throughout the conversation. As soon as she saw me she downed her drink, and stood up before the waiter had a chance to launch. She walked up to me, took my hand and led me to a small table in the corner. It was Kevin's turn to hang in the wings now, and peroxide blonde's turn to keep him company. Knee-high boots was having a night off.

Tatiana went all out that night. She told me that she was from Colombia. She had been sent to London with two other girls to work for a Russian gang, something to do with settling a cocaine dispute. She told me that she liked me; I made her feel normal and safe and optimistic. She usually had a few hours to herself on Sunday afternoon. Would I like to meet for coffee on Sunday? We arranged to meet for coffee on Sunday.

17

THAT SUNDAY I learned that Marisol lived in a five-bedroom house in Brixton with seven other girls. Tatiana was a stage name. Marisol was her real name. The Russians kept their girls under close surveillance, except for Sunday afternoons when they could be out for a few hours. The Russians had her passport too.

We sat a while, then finished our coffees and walked to Marble Arch and through Hyde Park.

"I need to get back in half an hour." Her voice was sad, but with a hint of expectation.

I put my arm around her waist and leaned in for a kiss. Marisol closed her eyes and let herself go so fully that she almost fell over. I had to bring my other arm around to hold her up. She had a little, energetic tongue and she kissed with the intensity of a woman who'd never been kissed but the know-how of one who had.

I took her by the hand. We walked along a narrow path and up to a small group of buildings near Brook gate. We kissed again, her little tongue dancing around mine with great passion. My dick got hard, but we were in the middle of Hyde Park and I knew we didn't have time to go back to mine. I broke off, the pain of what couldn't be outweighing the pleasure of what could. Marisol looked at me for a second, put a hand on my cock and dropped to her knees. I couldn't believe my eyes.

She unzipped me and took me in her mouth, gently circling the head with her tongue. Then she gradually picked up the pace, working at it with the same great passion that she had shown in her kissing. I always suspected that great kissers were also great cocksuckers. It's the most focused form of passion.

Cocksuckers. Why does it sound like I'm trying to insult her? How did cocksucker ever become an offensive term? Some insecure, fake macho probably thought it up and the rest of the flock just went along with it. A closet poof too busy overcompensating to know that the last thing you want to do is give cocksuckers a bad rep. Cocks need sucking, ergo the world needs cocksuckers. Good ones. Ones who know what they're doing. And if you know what to do with a cock there's nothing contemptible about you, so how the hell did we end up calling contemptible people "cocksuckers"? That's such a bad move. Cock-wasters – now there's an insult! Those who waste perfectly good cocks, *those* are contemptible. But cocksuckers, cocksuckers are a great addition to the universe. We've got to change things around; we've got to shift to cock-waster. It's just logical. And sensible.

Marisol was a great cocksucker. She kept working at it, occasionally looking up at me with that strangely innocent face. That face, combined with the devilish act she was performing, rattled my brain. Two intense yet irreconcilable facts happening simultaneously, like that moment when you're sitting on a train as it leaves the station, it's pulling away, you're travelling on, rolling along; until the train on the next platform is gone and you realize you're sitting in a motionless carriage, staring at an unmoving and unmovable train station. For that split second your brain is living two realities, both simultaneously true and false at the same time, making your stomach surge. Marisol sucked and stared. My stomach surged and my brain rattled. She was an angel and a whore, a fire-eater and a nurse. Afterwards I felt shaken, like I'd just been through an earthquake. And I was the only survivor.

Five days later Kevin and I were back in Soho. The ill-fitted suit looked particularly dispirited; motionless and sunk in his seat as if under the weight of an invisible boulder carefully balanced on his head. The strobe lights were at it with their usual madness and the cheap vodka and body lotion kept fighting for supremacy.

Marisol and I sat down at our usual corner table. Kevin and Peroxide joined us a couple of minutes later.

I looked at Marisol as we talked. She was beautiful. She was becoming more beautiful with every story she told.

"I have a friend who lives in Amsterdam," she told me. "She says that there's demand for couples, you know, to do sex shows. We should go together, we can make good money."

"I'm a Londoner now, I can't leave."

"Londoner? You're not even from this country, yes?"

"Doesn't matter."

"How?"

"Doesn't matter where my mother's vagina happened to be located the moment I pushed out. I'm a Londoner, it's a state of mind."

"So you don't wanna come with me?"

"Look, even if I did, what about your passport?"

"I'm nearly there. A couple more months and the whole thing will be over."

"You mean, you can go wherever you like?"

"No, they expect me to go back to Colombia, but fuck that. I'm not leaving one prison for another. I want to do my own thing."

"In Amsterdam?"

"In Amsterdam. Come with me."

I thought about the sex shows and about Marisol's magnificent arse. I could be the envy of every man in Amsterdam. I could make people dream! Dream of making love to a magnificent piece of arse!

The waiter broke my trance, "Drinks for the ladies?"

We went through the motions. The yellow leaves turned a little yellower, almost brown in fact.

Then, out of the blue, tattered leather came over and sat at our table.

"Hey, what time is your act?"

"Listen, mate, we're having a chat here, why don't you find yourself another girl?"

"Erm... I'm sorry, I just wanted to see Tatiana's act. She's so talented!" He had an annoying, squeaky voice and his breath stank of gin and pickled onions.

"A quarter past one," said Marisol.

"Thank you, thank you," he said. He had a wimpy voice, too.

"Ok, see you later, pal."

"Erm... can I ask one more favour?"

"What?"

"How are you guys getting home after the show?"

"We're taking the night bus from Trafalgar. Why?"

"Well... I need to take the night bus as well, but I'm afraid to walk through London at night. Can I walk with you?"

"You were fine last week," I said.

"And the week before that," added Kevin.

"Erm... yeah, I usually take a minicab, but I haven't got enough cash tonight."

"Fine, you can walk with us. We'll be leaving after Ma – Tatiana's act."

"Thank you, thank you," he replied in an almost subservient manner. Then he stood up and went back to his table.

Marisol finished her act at half past one. We chatted a little longer, tossed another tenner to the waiter and got ready to leave. Kevin walked over to Tattered Leather to let him know we'd be going soon.

Marisol walked me to the toilet door. "There are no cameras here," she said with a cheeky smile, then gave me a quick kiss. "Ok, go! I'll see you Sunday."

I went back to the main foyer to meet Kevin. Tattered Leather was waiting by the door, fidgeting. We walked out, took a right on Charing Cross Road and made it to Trafalgar. We stood at the bus stop. Suddenly Tattered Leather looked really nervous.

"What's the matter, mate?" asked Kevin.

"Erm... nothing, nothing, bus stops make me nervous." Kevin and I looked at each other but said nothing, both wondering what sort of weirdo we ended up dragging around with us.

Then I noticed Tattered Leather waiving vigorously, like he was trying to attract someone's attention. Just as I was about to ask him what on earth he was doing, he scarpered. Seconds later there were three large, thuggish individuals walking towards us, all wearing shiny leather jackets. Untattered. Two of them were absolutely huge. Jackets the size of pop-up gazebos. They moved clumsily but somehow quickly at the same time, like agile gorillas. A thought flew through my head: they had probably been built in a factory. I just couldn't imagine them having been babies or having a mother or a childhood. The one in the middle was nearer normal human size – only just – and kept moving around on the spot, like he was shadowboxing or something, compulsively flicking his nose with his thumb every few seconds. He had a sleazy ponytail to complement his receding hairline. He spoke in a thick Russian accent: "I see you've been making friends with Tatiana."

"I guess I have," I said, surprised that my mouth could move enough to produce entire words. My limbs had stiffened up and my gut was thrashing about inside me like a mad snake. I was bricking it.

"Tatiana can't have any friends," said the ponytail.

"Can't she?"

"No."

"Why not?"

"Because we say so."

"Yeah, because we say!" half-echoed the other two. Their voices were like sandpaper mixed with thunder. They looked even bigger now.

"If you know what's good for you, you'll get on your bus and never go anywhere near Tatiana or set foot in our club again."

"Yeah, again!" came the echo. They moved like a pair of Frankenstein's monsters and sounded like the Terminator.

They stepped closer. One of the Frankenstein brothers had his belly right up against my chest. It pressed hard against my ribcage, like an overinflated lead balloon.

"I hope we don't have to repeat this message to you again," said the ponytail. "We may not be so, what you call... *understanding* next time." Then he turned around and walked off. The Frankenstein brothers looked at each other for a second then scrambled after him.

I never made it to Amsterdam and I never saw Marisol again.

18

I WAS in the library three or four evenings a week. I sat at the reading table with a persistent will to learn *something*, anything. The old classroom-style chairs were terribly uncomfortable, and the table had all sorts of crap scribbled on it. TOM WAS HERE! carved in biro next to the drawing of a cock and balls made me chuckle. I moved from side to side against the backrest trying to scratch my back, it itched like mad from all the coffee grounds stuck down my shirt.

It was during one of these evening sessions that I picked up Karl Marx. The man was a borderline sociopath, but he did say some things that needed to be said. I was flicking through one of his books when I saw it: find a job you love, and you will never have to work a day in your life. Well, he didn't quite write that. It was more along the lines of how work for the sole purpose of earning a wage alienates man from himself, and how man's gratification comes from the work he does as a spontaneous activity, as something that satisfies his need to create, his need to express himself, to make his own self *visible* – something I later found out had also been said by Khalil Gibran, confirming what Judy had been telling me for months: the Great Masters already knew, it's all there laid out for us. There really was no time to be wasted, nor much point in reading anything else. So anyway, Marx didn't quite tell people to find a job they loved, and neither did Confucius for that matter, but Marx did get close enough, or at least that's what I got out of his writings anyway. And that really pissed me off. The world had known this for more than a century! And here I was having to discover it all by myself. What if I had never picked up that book? I would've just been left to deal with my feelings of inadequacy as if I was some kind of whacky wimp who couldn't just bow his head and carry on with the job. I was *really* pissed off. I should've felt inspired, I know. Enlightened even. And don't get me wrong, I did feel grateful at finding this piece of wisdom, I felt liberated to know that I hadn't been the only one or even the first one to feel inadequate in this profiteering mess. Someone had even written a book about it, more than a century ago! But I was also *seriously* pissed off. I had spent ten years in school, all that moralizing and pre-packaged drivel, all those nights of camomile and knots and puke and nobody had ever breathed a word about this... this guy who'd put it all in black and white. And the doctors? The fucking doctors told my mother I had caught some sort of stomach bug. Yeah, a stomach bug that lasted for the best part of two years... Don't doctors read this stuff? They bloody should! Making a kid feel like it's normal to take his soul to the morgue every morning. The fucking nerve on those whitecoats. I had been shafted and I hated everyone.

But most of all, I was pissed off at the men in my life. Too busy to help young boys make sense of this whole scam. Who knows, god forbid, those boys might grow up to be better men than *they* were. No, they just sniggered at our cluelessness and took pleasure in our confusion, in how we were going to suffer the same pain as *they* did, stumbling through the same unfulfilling lives like concussed hitchhikers stranded in Hell.

Nobody on the factory floors ever said a word about this. *Nobody*. The foremen and the bosses, ok, that's understandable, they need misery, that's how factories survive, that's how bosses stay bosses. But *schools*? The educators? Wasn't education supposed to set you free? Fucking phoneys. It was a scam, and I'd been dropped right in the middle of it.

19

IT WAS 6 P.M. on a Thursday and the place stank of piss. I moved further down, near the gardening section. No luck. The piss seemed to follow me around. Never mind. I didn't care much for gardening anyway. I saw a homeless guy sitting at one of the reading tables, muttering to himself. On cold days there were a few of the homeless sitting around, trying to keep warm. Some pretended to read a book, others would snooze with their head on the table or lean back on the chair and snore with their mouth open. I wished they had a place to go, somewhere they could keep warm without interfering with my reading. I felt bad at having had that thought, but piss is piss and my nose didn't give me much of a choice.

I tried again, this time moving as far away as I could from the reading tables. I found a corner at the back. There was a chair behind a pillar. I sat down. It was the cognitive science section. I went on reading about the art of war for a while, then took a break, used the loo, came back and started browsing the cog sci books, *The Cognitive Revolution*, *Modularity of Mind*, and *The Man Who Mistook His Wife for a Hat*. And that's how it all began, that's how piss led me to cognitive science. I didn't know it at the time, but that section, tucked away where the stench of piss didn't quite make it, was going to change my life.

I could've got into anything really. I was hungry for passion, for something to grab me by the skull and claim all my energy and devotion. It just happened to be cognitive science – it could have been anything else. Except for gardening perhaps, I didn't care much for gardening.

20

ANOTHER YEAR had begun, and the universe remained thoroughly unrattled. I carried on making overpriced coffees for overpaid suits, and occasionally took Elly out for a drink and a fumble. When I could afford it, that is. The war on loneliness is an expensive business.

That Friday we got some good tips at the café, Japanese brokers visiting the London offices. The Japanese were among the best tippers, second only to the Americans. So I went home, washed the coffee grounds out of my hair and underwear, put on my best jacket and took a bus to the West End.

We had a bit of a routine, Elly and me. We'd go to a pub for a couple of beers, then pop to the offie, get a bottle of wine and take a minicab back to hers. She was staying in a loft conversion near Kensington Gardens – family friends with new money. Lots of it. Elly herself didn't have any money, but the family friends had converted their loft to put her up for the duration of her studies. Beautiful views. You could see Kensington Palace from the dormer.

Elly was training to become a teacher. Imagine those giant breasts wobbling about in the classroom as she moved her arm up and down across the whiteboard. *Slowly* at first, as she wrote across the board... and then vigorously, *woosh*, as she rubbed it all out and began again. I felt sorry for the boys in that class. Their head would be thumping so hard... they didn't stand a chance of learning a thing. Poor bastards. It was quite unfair really.

Anyway, Elly and I would get to the loft around half past

eleven and pull out a chair. Elly liked to have sex on a chair, something about it that reminded her of dry humping, alleviated the guilt. She would sit astride my lap, unzip me and guide me in with those long fingers. That turned me on immediately. Though truth be told I had mixed feelings about the long fingers, sometimes they made my dick look small. But never mind that now. As I was saying, she'd guide me in with those long fingers, and then she'd move slowly from side to side while we passed the bottle of wine back and forth. Sometimes her big breasts got in the way, so she'd cradle them in her forearm, gathering them up close and creating a long, supple cleavage – freeing up just enough space for her body to keep moving. Then she'd take the bottle from my hand and gulp down some more of the wine, gently rocking her hips. The drunker she got the hornier she was and the hornier she was the faster she moved. Bordeaux did it best.

This particular Friday we met in the Rising Sun, ready for the usual routine. But after a few drinks Elly got flirty with Jim, one of the staff working the bar. He was a short guy with a boxer's nose and big teeth. I liked Jim. I didn't know much about him but he seemed like a nice guy. But it bothered me that Elly had opted for the short guy with the boxer's nose and the big teeth. It felt like a personal attack, though I didn't care enough to make a fuss. I went to the bar and ordered another pint, found a stool and sat down. The place was heaving.

Liam walked over, placed one hand on the draught pump and nodded towards Elly. "You need a leash for that one," he said. Liam was Irish, he knew all about Catholic upbringings wreaking havoc. He was a Londoner, too. An East Ender born and bred who wore Arsenal shirts five days a week. He used to wear them at weekends too but got tired of getting into brawls with boozed-up Spurs supporters. Weekdays were safer. But he was Irish, and nobody dared argue otherwise. Nobody except Gus.

"C'mon, mate, you're a Londonah, innit!"

"Leave it, Gus…"

"You support Arsenal!"

"I ain't got a choice, Chelsea fans are twats."

"You were born in Bethnal Green!"

"Jesus was born in a stable but 'e weren't a donkey."

"Oh…"

That would usually put an end to it, till the next Friday at least. So many words have been written about identity and nationality by so many phoneys, and Liam nailed it in a single sentence on an average Friday while pulling pints and staring down the drunk and disorderly. A master of multitasking.

I didn't care about Elly flirting with another guy, chances were that it would still be me ending up on that chair tonight. But somehow it bothered me that people might think I was a mug. Nobody likes to be made a mug of. Well, *I* didn't. I picked up my pint and walked over. I nudged Elly in the arm with my elbow. She turned to face me. "Look, if you needed a wingman for the night you should've asked. Don't pull this crap on me, on my home turf of all places."

Elly gave a drunken smile and then made a clumsy attempt to lean in and kiss me. I took a step back. She stumbled forward and fell on me with her chin on my shoulder. Her hair smelled of coconut and fags. She straightened herself up, trying to regain what was left of her balance. "Oh, you've a REPUTATION to uphold now, d'ya? What, I'm not good 'nuf for ya? IS THAT IT?" Words flew out of her mouth in a messy slur.

"You're pissed." I told her.

"Yeah, and you LIKE it when I'm PISSED, I'm HORNY when I'm PISSED, and you LIKE ME HORNY DON'T YOU!" Her lips were all twisted, like pieces of crazy rubber. She spoke with her eyes half-closed and her voice was hoarse from the shouting. Everyone was looking at her now, even the people who were pretending not to look.

"I suppose I do. But I don't like *this*," I said.

"What!? WHAT?" she shouted.

"The circus act."

"FUCK YOU!"

"I'm going home."

I waved goodbye to Liam. He gave me a forced smile.

As I walked towards the door, Elly ran up to me and grabbed me by the shoulders. I turned around.

"Do you love me a little?" she asked pleadingly.

I sighed. I'd been ambushed and I had no answer. Well, no answer that would please her anyway. And I honestly didn't care.

21

THE NEXT EVENING I had dinner at Judy's.

"We were going to invite the neighbours," Judy said, "but the wife's not right at the moment. And anyway, you're the only person we like." She was in great form.

Simon arrived a little late. He walked in and went straight to the bathroom. Judy turned her head and shouted in his direction: "Will you be needing a bidet, dear?" Then she laughed her deep and sincere laughter.

"He's just joined the Teachers' Union, you see," she said quietly. "I think they're mostly about drinking, reading Shelley to each other and sharing women." Then she turned and shouted towards the bathroom again: "Isn't that right, Si?"

Simon came out of the bathroom with a big smile on his face, "I don't know dear, I haven't had my first meeting yet."

Judy slapped him gently on the thigh, laughing. Simon poured three sherries and we sat down in the front room. I told them about my exchange with Elly. "Isn't that odd?" I asked.

Judy frowned, staring me straight in the eye. Then in a sharp, almost screechy tone, she said, "Odd? The woman *loves* you, you fool! Is fanny all you're interested in?"

Maybe it is. Would that be so bad? She made it sound bad.

"What if I am," I said, "how's that worse than what she's doing?"

"And what is she doing?"

I knew Judy was being rhetorical, but I carried on against my better judgement. "She's not content with having my outer body once in a while, she wants my spirit, my viscera! That seems much more unreasonable to me."

Judy said nothing for a while, then spoke in a low voice, "You're broken, aren't you..." She turned to face the wall, like all hope had been lost. I felt abandoned.

"Once bitten, twice an arsehole, I guess."

"Do you want to be an arsehole? Because it doesn't have to be that way."

Doesn't it? What would she know, she was sent to Thorpennhowe for god's sake! She never had to drill through a thousand squirts or fish coffee grounds out of her groin. It's easy to be understanding when you've had your ego massaged from the age of nine.

"Look," I said, "the first girl I declared my love to grabbed my arm with both hands and said, 'I'm a fly!' "

"A fly?" Judy laughed in bewilderment.

"Yes, exactly. And when I asked her what she meant, she said that flies grab onto shit. Get it? So don't come and spin that yarn about women's feelings..."

"So women can be ghastly, of course. Especially the pretty ones. They develop this contempt for the world, for men, quite early in life. Sexual power can be tough to handle, particularly if one discovers it at a young age. You've been on the receiving end of that and you've been hurt – that's unfortunate. But you shouldn't go around hurting women because women hurt you."

"It's not like that," I said, "it's not like I have a plan. It's just how things, you know, develop."

"Oh, stop being so fucking feeble!" she shouted.

Judy was an old-school feminist. She took no crap from men but demanded a lot from women. This often made her come across as being kinder to men, but she could be vicious if she sensed foul play.

"How am I feeble?" I'd lost all faith in the conversation, but still carried on.

"You're letting it *happen*, you're letting the hurt happen! You're letting your own hurt turn you into a bully."

"You're making it sound like revenge. It's not revenge."

"Never mind that," she said dismissively. "You know what? I don't care what it is, whatever it is, you need to reverse it. I told you that you ought to read Forster: *connect — connect without bitterness*. But you won't listen, will you…"

"That's unfair, I always take your words seriously."

"Oh I know that, but I also see how quick you are to run away from the tricky parts!"

"Just because I don't follow your every word doesn't mean I'm running away."

"Doesn't it?"

"What, you expect me to follow your every word like some retarded robot?" I was beginning to get angry.

"Well, you're getting angry, so I *must* have touched on some truth!"

"Yeah, right, because you only get angry when others tell the truth about you…" I said smugly, regretting it immediately.

"Oh don't you be rude to me, young man, I remind you that you are in *my* house! I'm sure your parents taught you manners, didn't they teach you manners?"

She wanted it to be revenge. She really wanted it to be revenge. It wasn't. I guess if it had been revenge she could've waved it off like some annoying insect. But it was no insect. It was an elephant.

I didn't have the strength to carry on arguing after that. It was no use. Judy would either win the argument or accuse me of being disrespectful to my host, or to the elderly, to a woman, or whatever she could think up to shame me into backing down. That's the worst thing about being prepared to change your mind, the constant reminder that others are not, and the resentment that goes with it.

After dinner Simon poured me a brandy. Good brandy, not that students' stuff.

"Why did you do it, then?" he asked.

"Do what?"

"Fuck her. Why did you fuck Elly if you didn't care?"

"It was something to do."

"You ought to be careful with that. You could be gambling away your emotions."

"Oh I've got plenty of those."

"I'm serious. Your emotional self. You can't just turn emotions off and on as you please, you know. What if a good woman comes along and you find that they're switched off, extinguished for the purpose of fucking women you don't care about. That's a high price."

Then he told me his story. I always knew there was a story, and here it was. He had spent several years squatting in a disused office block near London Bridge; drinking, fucking, scavenging for food behind the stalls in Borough market. He told me about Katy Barnes, who volunteered for a charity that brought basic necessities to the London squats — soap, toothbrushes, sterile syringes, that sort of thing. His eyes were moist, those places were here with him. Katy Barnes was cute, clean and kind, a sort of forbidden, unattainable fruit. Simon told me how he idolized her, how he dreamed that she would be his saviour. He knew it was just a fantasy, but he liked it, and sometimes fantasy is all you have to keep you going when things get dark. And things do get dark, especially in a disused office block.

Then one day the police raided the squat near London Bridge and threw everyone out on the streets, and Katy Barnes invited Simon to stay with her at her brother's. One evening, when her brother was out, Katy Barnes asked Simon to help her pack lunchboxes for the homeless, and he did, and they ended up in bed together.

"This was it. This was no dream, no fantasy," Simon told me, his voice trembling, his eyes watering up.

I felt happy for him, happy that he got to experience that. You don't often get to be with your dream girl.

"And that's when you made sweet love to her?" I suggested.

"No, that's when I *fucked* her."

"Uh?"

"I couldn't do it. I couldn't make love to her. There was no love in me to make. So I stuck it into her, and as I did I looked into her eyes and I heard myself say: gotcha!" He paused, trying to hold back the tears. He looked shaken, as if Katy Barnes's ghost was lying right there in front of him, naked.

"I hated myself for it," he said finally.

"But he didn't just carry on, did he?" Judy said.

"I didn't. I couldn't." said Simon. He looked pale, this was *real*. "I knew I had to strip myself down to my core, uncover my authentic self."

"And how do you do that?"

"I don't know." Now his eyes looked vacant, like he'd seen a second ghost, one he couldn't ignore. Probably his own. "But I lay on the floor for two days straight. Then got up and joined AA."

Pride shimmered in Judy's eyes. "Many would have carried on," she said, "just carry on! Not Simon. Simon took stock. And he read *Sons and Lovers*, of course. Have you read *Sons and Lovers*? Well, you bloody well should. It's time to take stock, Dak, time to take stock." Judy had calmed down by now, which made me more willing to pay attention. But her eyes were solid, unwavering lakes of steel; "You need to be careful with the fucking. We all do. *Explore* yourself with women, so that when a good woman comes along you can be ready, capable of handling life in a profound, loving partnership."

Her words moved me, which annoyed me somewhat. Now I *had* to concede the argument.

The she announced, "Look, I'm going to tell you something, just ideas that come into my mind about women."

My ears perked up; no one had ever taught me anything about women.

"I told you you've been hurt, probably many times. I think you've borne your pain nobly, but of course it's only bearable with some denial of how it hurts."

"Maybe he's right, maybe it's not revenge," said Simon.

"Yes..." Judy replied with a hint of incredulity in her voice, as though she knew that it was perfectly plausible and yet she was convinced she couldn't possibly have been wrong.

Her eyes widened, "Yes, of course," she said to Simon, "but he needs to allow himself to recover." Then she turned to me and repeated it again, but at a slower pace, like she was giving me important instructions, instructions that were a matter of life and death, "You need to allow yourself time to recover, time to try and bear the truth about women, how beastly they often are. Don't be fooled, there are some dark souls behind those bright smiles!" And then she laughed, and I couldn't help thinking that she was laughing at my naivety.

"You're free now. You've left that horrible factory and you've freed yourself from your parents' demands for mediocrity. You're free." Judy knew how to win me over, even though she wasn't trying. I knew she wasn't trying. She was a remarkable person and sometimes I really liked her. Loved her, even.

"But freedom is not chaos, my darling. That's what *children* do, they yell and stomp and think that's freedom," she turned briefly to Simon, shrugging in disbelief that such obvious truths needed to be stated. "Only children confuse freedom with chaos. And it's chaotic to be so perverse, to toy with a woman, to toy with her *love*! And to think that you can switch your emotions, your *humanity*, on and off at will." She sighed and shook her head.

"You make it sound like I'm lost," I said.

"Oh no, of course you're not lost, you just don't like being where you are. It's a dull place to be."

Judy's words darted around my brain for the rest of the day. I never imagined freedom could have a double edge, but here it was, long and sharp, and it glistened under Deptford's streetlights. I had a vision. I saw Marlowe's brains splattered across a filthy tavern's wall. Maybe it had been the same double edge, the same cursed blade killing men and their potential all through the ages. I felt fear; raw, aggressive, insistent fear, the fear that jumps at you from behind a dark street corner, throws you down and kneels on your chest. I couldn't sleep. Even the mice gnawing at the floorboards sounded louder than usual. I got up, went downstairs, borrowed some steel scourers off Mr Alaoui, took a pair of pliers from Terry's toolbox, cut the scourers into one-inch pieces of rough steel and pushed them into the crescent-shaped gaps that had appeared between the floorboards and under the skirting. You could see where the mice had been doing their shifts. The patient little bastards were nearly through. But the steel kept them quiet for a night or two, they needed time to regroup, get around this sudden metal problem – they didn't like the harsh edges, you see. Even scavenging rodents have a sensitive side.

22

IT WAS A cold Sunday morning and I was sitting in a caff near the Embankment trying to keep warm. My monthly bus pass had expired the day before and I didn't really need a new one until the work commute on Monday, so I walked the six miles from Deptford to Westminster to save a few quid. I got to Charing Cross just after 10 a.m. and the stiff wind had made its way into my bones. The skin on my face felt like it was going to crack and fall off at any moment. I went into this caff, the Bean or the Pea or something, and ordered a pot of tea.

A tall blonde marched in. I was sure I knew her from somewhere but couldn't quite place her. She was one of those blondes who look straight ahead when they walk, avoiding all eye contact like it's some sort of radioactivity that would melt her head into sludge. I didn't like her, but she had a beautiful face, which annoyed me somewhat. It made the not liking more difficult, it kind of ruined it – made it laborious. I told myself to get over it, it's only symmetry after all.

We were all slaves to symmetry really. And what a daft thing to be enslaved by. Then I remembered. She was that half-minx who shook her arse at the Out Bar, draining life from the boys and turning it into self-importance. Cheap alchemy. Now she marched in trying to look sophisticated, reading glasses an' all. That's why I hadn't recognized her, she had glasses on, and her hair was all fluffy and loose. She looked like a phoney porn gig, dirty secretary style. You just knew that she never had to do any work to get her ways, never had to win anyone over. All she had to do was turn up. No charisma necessary, no work – another great Caesar appointed by birth right. You could tell she never had to suck cock to hang on to a man.

I felt angry at the whole thing – at the injustice – at what a man had to endure just to be considered worthy of the Caesars. And yet we couldn't help it, the injustice. The whole thing made me ache inside. Time would surely humble her eventually, but that didn't make me feel any better, two wrongs don't make a right an' all that. Injustices can't be fixed by maths, take a little misery from young men and pass it on to middle-aged women. That fixes nothing, except maybe a sense of revenge. I wondered if revenge was the same as justice. It probably all adds up to suffering. And you knew her suffering was coming, you knew that in the end she'd get what she was putting in; lofty, overpriced chickenfeed. Life is relentless like that. Some call it poetic justice, but I found very little poetry in this whole mess...

As I walked to the till I stopped by her table. She looked up and smiled an effortful smile, the smile you get from someone who never had to do any work to win anyone over. I certainly did not see any poetry in that.

A few seconds later she recognized me, "Oh, hi, you're Kevin's friend, right?" The smile became a little less effortful. She stood up and we talked for a while.

I made a couple of wisecracks about the Out Bar crowd and

she laughed. I could see her nipples hardening under the blouse. Turgid, proud, moulding the fabric into a sweet hazelnut shape. I was getting hard. Well, sort of. It was more an experience of hardness rather than hardness as such. My penis was actually flaccid, but I had an odd sensation of holistic erection darting through my loins. That's when her voice began to fade, my mind turning blank with instincts. I stood reminded of Homo sapiens's self-delusion, that we somehow convinced ourselves we are above nature, above animals. "Don't be an animal!" they say. "You're not an *animal*, are you?!" "Only an animal would do that!" "Pfft, animals!"

Why don't we go and tell that to the bonobos? Probably because, deep down, where our animal instincts still lie – and god knows they're still there – we know that the bonobos couldn't care less, they'd just laugh it off, or whatever the bonobo equivalent of laughing it off happens to be. They might even throw in some shit slinging in the process, just before they pull the flesh off your skull. That's how bonobos settle more serious matters. We Homo sapiens could certainly do with a bit of shit slinging coming our way, but we're so caught up with not being "animals" that we would even frown on *that*, even in cases where it's thoroughly deserved – and we're not short of those. Not the bonobos though. Bonobos don't frown. Bonobos are the apex of nature. Bonobos are free.

As she stood there yapping away and thrusting those hard nipples in my face, I couldn't help imagining what would have happened next if *we* were bonobos. If *we* were free. I imagined myself turning her around, forcefully, and entering her from behind. Feeling her pelvic muscles twitch as I thrusted forward, hard, growing harder still as I caught a glimpse of a smile appearing on her lips.

But we were Homo sapiens, the pinnacle of evolution. We wore *shoes* and *hats* and used lavatories. So I had to stand there like a fool, pretending that her nipples were outside my peripheral vision and their silhouette through the blouse was just a piece of heartless geometry. That's the sort of behaviour you need to have if you want to stay alive in this shoe-wearing lavatory-using farce. Humans are so hopelessly fucked. Except the Barbarians. The Barbarians were alright.

23

I'M NOT SURE how it happened. Between her yapping and my misanthropic musings she ended up in her underwear.

This could be fun, I thought. Not bonobo-level fun, but fun.

She was about to sit on the top left corner of my bed when I grabbed her by the waist and gently led her toward the middle. Getting on that bed from top left would've displaced the brick that kept the whole thing from tilting over and throwing its occupants on the floor. I had a feeling she wasn't the type who would see the funny side of that. My mind wandered. I wished I were with a woman who *would* see the funny side of that. A woman who would laugh at the whole surreal situation, the thud, the brick lying on its side, the bed tilting, the rolling off, the tumbling onto each other like sacks of potatoes in underwear – laugh at the whole lot and still mount me afterwards, and mean it.

Something told me that Tall Blonde wasn't that kind of woman. So we got onto the middle of the bed and started fondling each other. But my heart wasn't in it, and that meant that neither was my cock.

I knew it wasn't going to rise. I felt the pang of adolescence flooding back to my body and mind. Suddenly I was transported to that eerie New Year's Eve, barely fifteen years old, when I was lying on the floor with my dick in Sara's mouth, petrified, cold sweat slowly forming on my brow, giving sex a bad name while desperately disappointing Bartol.

Bartol was my best friend at the time (though I probably wasn't *his* best friend) and the guy who had arranged the whole thing. He was two years older than me and had been with Sara a few times. He decided that it was now my turn. "Having sex with a girl is like a thousand wanks all at once," he said as we sat in his father's workshop, trying to make sense of carburettors, expansion chambers and adolescence.

Bartol had lost his virginity only a few months before, but he talked as if he had been with a hundred women. He was obsessed with sex and would hardly talk about anything else, except two-stroke engines. Naturally I was curious about girls' bodies, and I often wondered what it would be like to be naked with a girl, touch her, feel her skin on me, share our bare selves with each other. I knew what a woman's body looked like from a couple of magazines I had stashed under a bucket of Lego bricks – the unmistakable sign that I had outgrown some interests in favour of others. But the thought of actually *being* with a real girl terrified me. The unbearable pressure of being a man, or even having to act like one in front of a girl in flesh and blood, was too much for my immature brain. But I was curious and impressionable, and Bartol was older than me, which gave him this aura of unwarranted wisdom. So I went along with his promise of a thousand wanks. "Don't worry," he said, worrying me even more, "she's experienced." That I believed, she definitely looked like a woman to me. To this day I'm baffled by how a sixteen-year-old girl can appear like a grown woman to a fifteen-year-old boy.

Bartol grinned. "It's all arranged; the New Year's Eve party."

A two-month sentence, handed down to me by a benevolent judge. He made sure to remind me periodically of my upcoming doomsday, "Three weeks to go! How do you feel?" I felt terrified, but I never voluntarily gave him a glimpse of that.

Any vague curiosity or excitement that I might've felt was hopelessly vanquished by an army of what-ifs. I spent the week before New Year's Eve in a constant daze.

"My aunt Mirna is going to a party," Bartol told me. "She said we can use her house."

Having a physical location made the whole thing feel more real. Inescapable. An additional lump joined my already overcrowded throat.

"But aunt Mirna won't allow us into the bedrooms."

A sudden sense of relief washed over me. Was this my pardon? But then he added, "You and Sara will have to use the bathroom floor." Permission to stand down denied.

And then it was time. I showered and dressed almost ceremonially, like a field marshal preparing for his own state funeral. I set off early to help Bartol with the preparations. We put out crisps, crackers and cheese boards, then set the stereo on a bookshelf and used aluminium foil and a spool of reclaimed copper wire to extend the speakers' cables so that music could be heard from all around the room. We had organized a mixed-tape competition, and I diligently prepared mine with a couple of brand-new tracks I was sure nobody would've had the time to add to theirs. People began to arrive at around 8 p.m., complimenting Bartol and me on the whole set up. A hint of pride emerged in my ocean of anxiety.

The party got underway. Everyone was drinking sweet wine and dancing to the mixed-tapes, and everyone knew how lucky I was going to get. Everyone but me.

At 10.30 p.m. the bell rang. Bartol patted me on the shoulder. "She's here."

Sara had short brown hair and wore a long fur coat. Bartol handed her a drink and nodded in my direction with a smirk. She smiled at me but then proceeded to avoid me for the next twenty minutes, joining the rest of the party. When she finally spoke to me it was with a hint of wickedness, "I hear you're the chosen one."

"We don't have to, you know, if you don't wanna," I replied, looking for an honourable way out.

She chuckled, letting out a grunt. "C'mon, let's see if we fit on that bathroom floor then."

She took my hand in an almost kind gesture and started walking towards the bathroom. I followed her like a child on his first day of school.

Sara locked the bathroom door and began to remove her blouse, then she unclipped her bra and flicked it on top of a cabinet. She had tired-looking, droopy breasts, not the sort of breasts you would expect on a sixteen-year-old. Maybe that's what happens to girls who have too much sex, I thought. I didn't know much about sex.

"C'mon, take your clothes off!"

I was trembling. "This floor is freezing!" I said in an effort to pre-empt any suspicion of more embarrassing causes.

My mind was momentarily distracted by a knock on the bathroom door. "Come on guys, I need to *pee*," said a female voice. I could hear giggling in the background and realized that a crowd had formed outside the door. My virginity was attracting more interest than the mixed-tape competition.

"Leave us alone!" I shouted half-heartedly, hoping Sara would suggest we could not possibly continue under these adverse circumstances. No such luck. She cracked a faint smile and started running her fingers down my chest. A loud voice in my head screamed, "She's going to touch it!" followed by a menacing voice, "You'd better be ready." Panic set in.

There was a second knock on the door. This time it was Bartol. "How is it going in there, S? Is he doing well?"

"It's soft," she replied matter-of-factly.

"Take it in your mouth then!"

The crowd gasped. The moment of truth was finally here.

Sara did her best to suck on what all visual cues suggested was *my* flaccid penis, and yet my sense of touch refused to believe and my blood flow refused to get involved. Nothing. Like she was sucking on somebody else's cock.

And now here I was, nearly ten years later, going through all that again, like a lame curse that visited me at random intervals. But even curses are less powerful when you have experience on your side. I knew I needed to buy some time. So I went down on her.

24

THE FOLLOWING MORNING I felt like a junkie. What is it with bedding new women that is so bloody addictive? At least with cocaine or tobacco or whatever you get some sort of high before the inevitable mess of withdrawal – but this? This is just relentless work. Deluded attempts at some sort of oxymoronic intimacy that inevitably escalate into a toxic mixture of indecency and despair. No high, no hit, just hard work – and dejection. How can something so tiresome and underwhelming be so addictive? And it's definitely not for the sex. Sex doesn't even matter. Last time I picked up a woman in a bar the thought of sex went right out of my mind the moment we got into a cab – I had her, it was practically done, what would be the point of actually going through with it? I genuinely hoped she'd pass out or fall asleep or something, that way I would be able to hand out some guilt-free rejection.

Judy told me that promiscuity was a proxy for love. No surprise there, Judy thought that everything was about love. "Stop revealing your dick instead of your heart!" she told me. Maybe she was right on this one. Maybe some things were about love after all.

Don't get me wrong, it wasn't always like this, it wasn't always about the notches. It was worse. I was caught in a spiral, a delirious loop of failed intimacy and rampant sexuality, a kind of emotional self-torture device, teetering on a double-edged precipice between the Madonna and the Whore. I was Dakris Manell: utterly preventable Freudian cliché. And I was trapped; wrapped in that antithetical madness, strapped to a diabolical see-saw of desire, drunk with the beautifully toxic vacuity, wallowing in the Whore's crevices while yearning for a touch of the Madonna, for that connection that would make everything ok.

Judy knew it, she sensed it the first time we had tea at her house. "You have such an appetite for life, Dak. And since one can't really separate living from loving, then you want to love –

naturally. Love is a beautiful thing, surpassed only by the *will* to love. And you have that, which is wonderful."

"It's painful, that's what it is."

"Yes, that too."

I could tell that Judy felt for me, genuinely, but she also knew the danger such a craving can bring. "You're embracing life in the most meaningful way," she said, "expanding yourself in so many ways. Be careful though, don't make it an obsession; your time will come, you are on the right road. But you do have to accept that a lot of women simply are not. It's bad luck courting at such a time."

And that's what my dreams of the Madonna were: an obsession. A recurring insult of sexless devotion, an insult to my own intelligence, my own humanity, and to womanhood itself. It appears that Freud got this one right; it's almost a shame he was such a fraud.

Judy told me I should stop for a while, step back. I wish I'd listened to her. "Remember Forster," she said, "*Live in fragments no longer.*" Her eyes glistened with urgency. "Pause, Dak. Pause and reflect before embarking on love affairs again." But I couldn't. Judy called it "being in the grip": you don't, you won't, which basically means you can't. That's the grip, and I was in it.

To make matters worse, my obsession with the Madonna was mired in the most ancient of delusions, a Darwinian curse carefully concealed by the feigned warmth of fairy-tales: the delusion of "fair of face, fair of heart" – a delusion that has destroyed many a man and crushed the spirit of many more.

I needed something to help me break the infernal circle. I desperately did.

25

I HADN'T SEEN Lauren in years.

We'd met on a coach trip to Paris that I had boarded to forget about a bodged engagement a week before my twenty-second birthday. We didn't say much on the coach, but we both got caught looking at each other a couple of times. She grinned at me, casually flashing those irresistible dimples, like a cat on a mission. I grinned back.

I'd won the weekend trip at a raffle and dragged my friend Marvin along. He had been to Paris once before and spoke a little French, which helped us get sandwiches at a petrol station somewhere near Arras.

Marvin and I avoided some of the guided tours but still did the usual walk along the Seine and sampled the local wine, or at least what we were served in place of the local wine. Most of the time we ended up drinking a mildly sour red liquid that tasted like an attempt to drag vinegar back in time.

We were taken in by the atmosphere, our friendship, the sense of adventure. We didn't need much more than a couple of petrol station sandwiches, and we didn't think much beyond that. Life was simple and frugal, despite the wine. And so I smiled at the belles and Marvin practised his French by sweet-talking the waitresses.

On the first day we got back to the hotel around midnight. We were standing by the lift when Lauren strutted in.

"Mind if we share the elevator?" she said in a sweet New York accent. Her long dark hair was pulled back in a ponytail and she wore no make-up, which made her look even younger than her nineteen years. She had deep, shamanic brown eyes.

"Sure," I replied. Marvin lowered his gaze, staring at his feet. "Which floor?"

"Third, please," she said with a smile.

I had never seen anything like it. It put everyone else's smiles to shame, made them look like puny attempts at half-hearted smirks.

The next morning we went on a visit to the Louvre. Lauren and I kept losing touch with the group, doing our own thing, talking and laughing like old lovers who had reunited after years of solitude. Her love of life was infectious, as was her laughter. She made me want to show off my sense of humour, something that only ever happened with friends. And I mean blokes. She adored wordplay and double meanings. That was a stroke of luck, words were my strong suit. And so I played to my strengths. Every time my words made her laugh I felt like a sculptor who'd just chiselled away a little piece of marble to reveal the hidden beauty beneath.

We walked out of the museum and wandered around town for a while. We talked for hours: cooking, happiness, headaches, singing, misery, sea otters, cheap wine, heartbreak, sweat, getting a bargain at Greenwich market. Our connection was exhilarating, nobody else seemed to exist. Our laughter echoed through the streets of Paris, and with every echo we grew a little fonder of each other. More wordplay, more wandering along the Seine, more chiselling away at the marble.

Marvin never forgave me for spending so much time with Lauren. A few days after we got back to London he invited me to lunch. We went to our usual place off Russell Square, sat down, placed our order, thanked the waitress. He crossed his arms and stared at me with a mixture of regret and belligerence, then screamed from across the table: "I WAS LOOKING FORWARD TO SPENDING TWO DAYS CATCHING UP WITH YOU, YOU AND ME, BUT YOU HAD TO GO CHASING FANNY!"

What could I say? He was right, so I said nothing. I took it on the chin and hoped it would pass, but things were never the same between us. From then on, he became more distant and less keen on spending time together.

But I liked fanny, and I most definitely liked Lauren.

And now here I was, holding Lauren's letter in my hand.

> Dear Dak,
>
> Why did we lose touch? It's been ages! But guess what, I'm going to be in London for a few days next week. It's for work this time tho'. I wish I was back in College, it was a simpler time.
> Anyway, would be nice to catch up. Will be landing at Heathrow Tuesday 11.05 a.m. See you there?
>
> Love always,
> LAUREN

We did lose touch. We wrote to each other for a while after Paris but it kind of fizzled out. Life got in the way, and truth be told I wasn't interested in a pen pal. You don't become pen pals with a woman you want to go down on. It's not like I deliberately stopped contacting her, I just welcomed the cold turkey when it drifted in. It was easier that way. But love? Always? We had never even kissed. What kind of love did she have in mind? What kind of love could she possibly be *feeling*? From what I remembered she wasn't one of those who throw the word around willy-nilly. Had I missed something? The letter did say "Dear Dak", so it was definitely intended for me. Maybe the seed we'd planted in Paris had taken root over the years. Or maybe I'd got her all wrong and she was just full of shit.

I decided to go to Heathrow and find out.

26

LAUREN HAD LEFT London three days after returning from Paris. She had moved back to New York and taken up a job as a fashion designer, soaring to the top in half the time it takes your average Jane to get a whiff at the ladder – all that raw energy had to be channelled somewhere. Now they were sending her to London to inspect their new Soho branch. She might stay here for good, I thought. This might change things. This might change everything.

I got to Heathrow just before 11 a.m. and walked into the waiting area. I sat down next to a tatty sign that said "meeting point" in faint red letters. Every time the automatic doors hissed open I looked up expecting to see Lauren walk through. No luck.

At around 11.35 a.m. I was getting impatient. I stood up to go looking for Lauren outside passport control. That's when she walked in. Though "walk" doesn't quite do her justice. She didn't walk, she glided. Glamour flowed effortlessly with her every move. She was only 5'1" but stood tall against the odds; her back straight, her head up high, her posture impeccable. She flowed through the room. Her green silk dress hugged her figure firmly, dancing along with her like a passionate lover and shadowing every flutter of her hips. She was a film star from a bygone era – but in full colour. I bet those silkworms had been proud to serve in such creation.

At that moment I realized that I'd never seen Lauren's figure in the Parisian winter. I knew there may have been a fine body swaying under the long brown coat and the baggy jumpers, but I had no idea how utterly generous Nature had been. The way her narrow waist swivelled gently along and then suddenly burst into a pair of perfectly proportioned hips, made my head spin. That dress had no choice but to hang on to every curve.

Lauren walked right past me as if she had no business being there. I waved at her. She turned her head slightly and smiled that smile of a thousand muscles – her eyes doing more work than any lips ever could. It felt like Paris.

A couple of hours later we were sitting across from each other in a hotel bar, talking and laughing as if time had stood still. It all felt very surreal, but exciting.

Lauren told me about her work, her dreams, surviving Manhattan. I spoke about my evenings in the library, my struggles with the rent, my encounters with the Great Masters. I always thought of fashion as something shallow and inconsequential, but Lauren talked about it with such passion that you couldn't ignore it.

"Imagine you have a picture in your head," she said, gesticulating enthusiastically, "and then you get some pencils and BANG! that picture is now on a piece of paper, a piece of your mind is there, staring back at you." She smiled, dancing on her seat with excitement. She exuded passion. I could sense the vine of danger growing around me.

"Now imagine that's a picture of a dress, and you get out your sewing machine and BANG! now it's not just a picture, now it's there, you can touch it, feel it, wear it to the senior prom."

It didn't seem that different from motorbikes. I wondered whether she knew how to enter my mind.

Lauren took a sip of her drink. "I enjoyed my time with you in Paris," she said, "I wish there had been more time together."

Her admission emboldened me, "Yes, it would've been nice to get more time together, I might even have plucked up the courage to ask you out."

But then I retreated, "You probably weren't interested anyway. You always kept your distance."

"I couldn't resist you," she said with a faint smile, "but I was *determined* to resist you. That's why I stayed away."

I don't know how, but I knew this sort of intentional avoidance was a sign of trouble. I felt a churn in my gut, as though a warning shot had just been fired in my direction.

"Oh darling, why did you want to resist me?" I said, badly faking enthusiasm.

"My soul, it's damaged. I've been playing tricks for too long." She looked away for a moment, then said, "I wouldn't be able to forgive myself if I wasn't honest with you, and I just couldn't trust myself to be honest. My act is too well rehearsed."

I knew exactly what she meant. I felt guilty that my act had been through its own rehearsals, but the guilt was not enough to erase the hurt from her words. She could still be mine, I thought. She would be mine as much as she could be, but would that be enough? I didn't just want her to be mine, I wanted her to give herself up to me, like a hatchling under its mama's wings. Unlimited, defenceless, *whole*.

I finished my drink, and my heart sank a little further under the weight of that distant Parisian winter.

27

TWO DAYS LATER Lauren and I met in Covent Garden for a drink.

I arrived a few minutes early, stood at the bar, ordered a double whisky and pulled up a stool. The barmaid had a kind face. She took my money and handed me the change with a smile. It looked sincere. Then Lauren walked in. She stopped at the door, took a quick look around, saw me and began to walk in my direction. I could feel the air wavering around her hips as they swayed, elegantly moving toward me. Her killer smile slowly unfolded on that strangely familiar face, summoning those bewitching dimples. She could give me a hard-on just by looking me in the eye.

Lauren sat on the stool next to me and we talked. I didn't know it at the time, but she was becoming my incurable disorder, and I was the luckiest man alive.

After a few minutes of small talk her eyes started darting around the room, as if looking for something.

"Is everything ok?" I asked.

"This place looks dull."

"Not from where I'm standing!" I said with a smirk. "Maybe I'm having better luck with my company."

"You're a dick," she said matter-of-factly. She always did that when my words edged in.

I ordered another round. I turned to face the till and noticed a small container, about the size of an ashtray, filled with bits of sponge shaped into little cubes. I started fiddling with it, picking at the little spongy cubes. "What's this?" I asked the barmaid.

"We use it to remove lipstick from the rims of glasses before we put them in the washer."

"Oh crap..." I'd just collected a thousand cold sores on my fingers.

"You shouldn't touch something if you don't know what it's for," said the barmaid.

"Words to live by," said Lauren.

"If I did that my sex life would be dead."

The barmaid smiled. I felt charming, proud. I could probably have her.

Lauren's face hardened. "Let's get out of here," she said.

She's jealous, I thought. That's promising.

"We could get a bottle of whisky from the offie and go to Hyde Park," I said. "It's supposed to be a full moon tonight."

"I'd like that."

A brief, no-nonsense reply. I liked it.

We stood up and walked towards the door. I couldn't help thinking about the barmaid. How long before I would've charmed her into my bed?

Lauren walked in front of me and through the door. She had the stride of a panther. Her shoes must've had at least a 3-inch heel. She should have looked like a clown on stilts in those things. Instead she walked with a single, harmonic flow. It was a spellbinding cocktail of skill and grace. A cross between a ballerina and a military parade. You never realize how grotesque most women look in high heels until you've seen a truly graceful one. After that, every other woman looks like the unwitting star of a gag reel. You can't help it, you can't un-see it. In a way Lauren ruined high heels for me, forever. Except, of course, she didn't.

We walked by Speaker's Corner and found a bench. Lauren sat next to me yet far enough that our bodies weren't touching. She often did that, giving and taking away in the same breath. I had a bad feeling about it. It stank of sexual withdrawal. It was bad enough when some clumsy, inept woman did it, but seeing it in a brazen vixen like Lauren was unbearable. My jaw clenched.

"I have company," she said.

"Company?"

"Shadows, I suppose you'd call them." She looked sad but spoke in a playful tone.

"Yeah, life does that to you. Just make sure you don't drive me crazy," I said.

"Oh I'm pretty sure I would *enjoy* driving you crazy." She sniggered. "Perhaps I'll spark some inspiration in you." Her words were both alluring and hurtful. I knew I was fucked but I still couldn't let go.

We kept talking for a while. It was astonishing how we could jump from one topic to the next so instinctively, so seamlessly, like two streams of consciousness embracing.

"We could get together some time, you know, properly," she said. The look of sadness had turned into mischief now.

"You mean like in a relationship?"

"Oh *damn* you! Why do you have to use words like that!"

"Sorry, I didn't think words were the problem here," I said.

"I haven't done relationships in a while. I just ride practicalities." Her mischievous look intensified, like it was feeding on something. There was pride in there, too, but I couldn't work out why.

"Practicalities?"

"Yeah, practical arrangements," she said coyly. It wasn't shyness or anything, she just liked being ambiguous. She had a big smile on her face.

"What sort of arrangements?"

"Hook ups. For convenience – like, we finish work at the same time, uh? Ok, let's get it on then!" She threw her head back in laughter. More pride snuck in.

I couldn't work it out. She was telling me of her emotional disconnect, the stuff on which tragedies are built, and yet she seemed amused. And proud. Definitely proud. I mustn't forget about the pride. It was there, leading.

"Do I really need to know that?" I said jokingly, trying to hide my discomfort. I knew she'd been with men, but I didn't like hearing about them. Bad luck. Lauren liked to tell of how much she had enjoyed other men. But then I realized, what she liked to talk about was how much she had enjoyed sexual encounters; she hardly mentioned the men themselves, they didn't seem to matter much at all.

"You must know I'm a slut!" she said, laughter creeping in.

My face betrayed me. I instantly knew she'd found me out.

"What, you thought I was a good girl? I'm definitely not a good girl. Well, I'm good at some things, so I guess I'm some kind of *good* girl, just not a good girl."

I looked at the corners of her mouth, curling. Looking was all I could do. So that's what I did.

"But don't worry," she added, pretending to be reassuring me but actually teasing me further, "I'm a careful slut." My face muscles relaxed for a second, but then she said, "Still a slut though! Can you handle that?"

Lauren knew how to disarm me. This doesn't look good, I thought.

"Well, who knows, maybe *you* could be my new practicality."

"I'm not for hire," I said.

"What, you're only interested in a *relationship*?" She made a mocking gesture as she said the word.

"I didn't say that. I just don't care much for senseless rubbing and small talk."

"Hey! I'm not shallow if that's what you're implying!" her tone was kind of serious now, but then she sniggered. "Well, maybe I am a little bit!"

"I like depth, that's all. Fucking is good, don't get me wrong, but it gets old quick." I could hear Judy's words in mine. I thought of Simon's story, of Katy Barnes, of the switch that isn't there, and I saw the pillows we hold down over our emotions' noses and mouths in the name of a shag. I felt the weight of loss and desolation, emotions squandered and gambled away. Was Lauren a gambler? She certainly sounded like a gambler. But, and this chilled me to the core, what was she gambling *on*? I looked at her, my heart heavy with sincerity, "I want a woman to do more than just keep my dick wet."

"You said dick!" she replied mockingly, in a sort of girly voice. Then she chuckled to herself, biting her lower lip. Even in these mundane moments Lauren exuded sex.

"You find dick amusing?"

"No, not at all, I take dick *very* seriously."

"You just said you take dick." I sniggered. Suddenly we were two twelve-year-olds, discovering lame innuendos for the first time. It was surreal.

"Maybe things can be different with you. We can definitely talk!"

That was true. We had been talking for nearly three hours. It was Paris all over again.

"Maybe I can open up a little," she said tentatively. "You need to be patient, though. I need time. Time to overthink, freak out, try and bail and then get it together. I told you there are shadows. I don't know... Maybe I'll open up maybe I won't... What do you want from me anyway? I've got nothing else to give you right now."

Every single word that left her mouth was a nail through my chest, and for a split second the thought of leaving that bench and cutting all ties with her crossed my mind. But I knew that my limbs wouldn't comply. I knew it instantly. I had no say on the matter, my attraction for Lauren was inexorable.

Truth is, I had some shadows of my own. I'd been with women I liked and women I fancied, but they were rarely the same women. That lack of alignment weighed heavily on me, warped my judgement, wrapped it in an oily rag of malaise. It's a tragedy, really. And you can't force yourself to fancy someone you like, and you certainly can't make her fanciable when she just isn't, not to you anyway – that's a lost cause. But I had tried, with disastrous consequences for my soul, and sometimes my manhood. So you labour under the illusion that you can like someone you fancy, maybe even make her likeable, surely she can be likeable! Look at that face, that smile, those eyes, she *must* be likeable. And so the road to Hell begins, sloping merrily in a gentle breeze before taking a cold, slippery turn into a bog of dead souls.

Our conversations did get a little deeper as the night went on, and Lauren did open up a little. She had something more to give after all. She told me about the shambles she'd left behind, about the crockery flying, doors and hearts ripped off their hinges; she told me about the shattered dreams and a busted eardrum – his. Her eyes were fiery and she spoke with a raw energy. For a few fleeting moments the gate to her soul came ajar. Well, it wasn't quite a gate, more like a double reinforced concrete wall. And yet, for the first time, I had got something real out of Lauren. Something beyond laughter, something I could hang on to.

28

THAT NIGHT I dreamed that I drank scotch straight from an oak barrel, a cute blonde gave me the eye and Lauren was kind to me, looking after me, guiding me as I staggered. I laughed in my dreams.

I woke up the next morning to find that there was no oak barrel and that the bus drivers were on strike. No sign of the cute blonde either. I got up, got dressed, walked four miles to Elephant and Castle, went down the escalator, handed my tips from the day before to a listless-looking woman at the ticket office and travelled to Bank by tube. I arrived at the café an hour and fifteen minutes late and Hasan docked me two hours.

At 5 p.m. I went to the toilet, took off my shirt and washed my armpits in the sink. Then I sprayed myself in deodorant, put on a clean shirt and went to see Lauren.

We met at her hotel, on Marylebone Road, a bloody long

walk from Lombard Street. By the time I got there I was ready for another dose of deodorant. I was feeling tired and sweaty from all the walking and I didn't really want to be there, even though I'd been looking forward to seeing Lauren all day. I was irritable and I didn't like it. Hasan and the bus drivers had been crapping all over my beautiful plans for a romantic encounter, turning my Juliet's balcony into a latrine. Lauren must've picked up on it because she asked me if I wanted to use the shower. I took her up on the offer.

It felt good to be in a fully furnished room with a shower, a tiled bathroom and the subtle scent of clean bedding. In Deptford I'd go to sleep with the smell of fried onions in my nostrils and wake up to the fumes of floor cleaner. The staircase between the kebab shop and our living quarters was like a chimney, shepherding every manner of malodour up and under my door without fail. Not to mention the kitchen; the kitchen always looked like a warzone. I was the only tenant who ever took out the rubbish: Gemma wouldn't touch it because it's a man's job, Yona wouldn't go anywhere near it because it clashed with her false nails, and Terry was just a lazy cunt. One summer I went to see my parents for a couple of weeks, and when I got back there was ten days' worth of rubbish piled in the corner, flies the size of walnuts circling in excitement. So it was nice to be in a classy hotel room for a change.

I came out of the shower feeling grateful. Maybe Lauren was kind to me after all; maybe it wasn't all a dream, maybe she *was* looking after me. I wondered whether I'd get the oak barrel too, and became hopeful about the cute blonde. Who knows, the night's still young.

Lauren was standing near the window, staring at the traffic below. I walked towards her. "What am I going to do now?"

"About what?" she said.

"My clothes are all sweaty, I've got nothing to wear."

She smiled. I put my hand on her arm and leaned in to kiss her – she turned away. Suddenly I was very aware of every noise around me: cars honking in the streets below, police sirens wailing, the bathroom fan humming, a couple arguing in the next room, the minibar buzzing away, buzz, buzz, buzz... I froze, then took a slow, deliberate breath to make sure I was awake. It couldn't be. It simply could not be. Then my heart took a ten-foot drop; this was déjà vu, and not a good one.

Lauren and I had met for a drink the day after we came back from Paris. We talked and laughed almost as we had done along the Seine, but something was off. She seemed distracted, absent, and she would go from warm to cold and back in an instant. That threw me to the point that I never tried to kiss her. She didn't try either – it seems she wasn't one for doing the work. And so we never went beyond the talk and the laughter; we finished our drinks and walked out into the streets. When we reached Charing Cross station I asked her to come back to my place, thinking that if we got to spend some more time together she might thaw a little. But she refused. And that was that. I turned around, walked to Trafalgar and got on the N1. And that was that, until tonight. Tonight was meant to be different. She seemed eager to spend time with me, to be in my presence. And yet here I was, standing like a fool, as warmth follows cold follows warmth – my head spinning, her head turned away, my pride dented. She was the fire-breathing dragon and the damsel in distress all wrapped into one.

"Why didn't you kiss me that night, after Paris?" she said.

"I'm trying to kiss you now."

"I need to know. Why didn't you?"

"I asked you to come back with me. You didn't."

"I hardly knew you!"

"That goes both ways."

"You should have chased me."

"Chasing is for dogs."

"What?"

"I'm not a dog."

"Well, men who really want me chase me."

"Maybe you never met a man who knows his worth."

"That's harsh!"

Maybe it was. I didn't reply.

"Just know this," she said in a suddenly soft tone, "if circumstances hadn't been what they were, things may have gone differently. There are reasons... reasons why I only had the one drink that night and didn't go home with you. I still remember your smile in the street as you wished me goodnight."

I didn't know what she meant, and I had no energy or will left to find out. I lay down on her sofa and went to sleep.

The next morning I woke up to the sound of water running. The thought of Lauren's body naked in the shower rattled my brain. Then I remembered the night before and sobered up – quick. The flirting, her sass, the innuendos, my growing obsession; it all seemed so pointless, so futile. I felt drunk. Buzz, buzz, buzz...

Lauren came out of the shower wrapped in a white towel, her wet hair gathered up in a loose coil. She looked sweet, inviting, sweet as anything you're ever likely to see. I suddenly felt a surge of energy. That was the thing with Lauren, she could knock me down hard and then pick me up even harder. It was exhilarating, uplifting, nauseating, exhausting.

I got up and walked over to her. She plugged in the hairdrier and turned to face me. I put my hand on her hip and stared her straight in the eye. Her eyes smiled, and a glint appeared. A coy but determined glint. I immediately knew that she wanted me, craved me. Then, in an instant, she lowered her gaze, turned around, switched on the drier and began doing her hair.

I walked to the minibar, took out a can of pop and drank it down. The buzzing intensified. I just couldn't get my head round how quickly Lauren retreated, how easily she could tame her desire. Come and gone in a flash. It can't be much of a fire if she can extinguish it at will, I thought. Or maybe it *is* a fire and she's just able to wipe it out – just like that. I didn't know which discovery would be worse: a measly flame flickering timidly in her bosom or an uncanny power to turn a blaze into dust. My stomach fell out of my stomach and into my bowels.

Later that day I decided I was going to put an end to this. I would hand my ego over to Lauren one more time, but only if she gave me another glimpse of that fire I saw when she had wrapped herself in the white towel, that determined glint.

Lauren's dance of giving and taking had become too much, perverse even, and I needed time to regroup. I swore I wasn't going to leave myself exposed unless I caught another glimpse of that desire in her eyes. One more time, just one more time before I throw another piece of my soul into this.

It was around 10 p.m. when Lauren walked me to the bus stop on Baker Street. The bus drivers' union had called off the strike after just one day – too many opinions, too many mouths to feed and not enough solutions.

I saw the 191 in the distance. I stuck my arm out.

"Goodnight," I told Lauren.

"Oh I'm not sleepy," she said. She had a strange look of excitement on her face. "I'm going to check out that shower head at the hotel. It's got loads of different settings!"

Here she was, standing next to a man in the flesh, and all she could do was get excited about flicking herself off in the shower, alone. What if I had got her all wrong? What if the fire wasn't there at all, or worse, it was just some lame little glimmer good only for toying around? I thought about Kevin and what he would say if I'd asked him these questions. I boarded the bus and played the imaginary conversation in my head: "I suspect she may be frigid," he said. You could always rely on Kevin for an objective view.

Frigidity would explain the deep well of sexiness Lauren carried with her: it was a hope, a daydream, an illusion, a way of making herself drunk on sex so that she might forget that she could not actually *experience* sex. My mind wandered. Was there hope? Maybe there was hope. Maybe there were glowing embers buried deep in the icebergs of her loins.

The sign said "Tooley Street". The bus slowed, rocked sluggishly from side to side and came to a stop. A woman got on and climbed the stairs to the top deck. I turned my head and looked out of the window. Tower Bridge looked majestic as always, splendour erupting through the night lights. London, my only true love…

29

I WOKE UP to a loud shrill. I staggered out of the sofa, stepped into the corridor, eyes still half-closed, and caught a glance of Lauren's buttocks waving through her silky night dress. A delightful symphony of curves. I was suddenly hurled into a wakeful state, as if a wrecking ball had swung past me and punched through a wall two feet away. A wrecking ball in silk.

We had been out together again, trying to make the most of her short stay in London, my doubts still clobbering me over the head, Lauren's give-and-take still burrowing through my heart's resolve. That's how I ended up on her sofa, yanked out of sleep by a 7 a.m. wake-up call.

Lauren's buttocks danced through the doorway and disappeared into the kitchenette. The silky walk lasted no more than five seconds, but its gentle waves rippled through the ground like an earthquake. Something had shifted, and there was no doubt in my mind that things were never going to be the same. Lauren never turned around to look at me, but I couldn't help feeling that she knew I was there, that she knew of the earthquake she had so effortlessly caused in those simple seconds. I wanted her more than anything in the world. Grab her, firmly by the hips, kiss her, wrestle that nightie off her body, gently bite her thigh as she lets out a half-suppressed cry of surprise mixed with pleasure. Lie naked together, drenched in sweat, covered in that scent that only feral instincts can draw out of you.

And yet, we hadn't even so much as kissed. Worse. Our bodies hadn't even touched, except for the ephemeral contact that comes with teasing each other's personal space, and that one time a hundred moons ago when she took my arm as we walked along the Seine.

I would like to be able to tell you that my catching a glance of Lauren that morning was serendipitous; the very moment I decided Lauren and I were going to be together. But I can't in good conscience do that. I have a feeling she was the master puppeteer in all this, and she had just decided that the story needed a turn. And that's what she did. I imagined her soft velvety hands, ever-so-gently tugging at the strings. Shifting, turning – changing everything.

A sudden thought broke my reverie; was I becoming too soft for my own good? I tried to push it out of my mind, but it lingered.

Meat Loaf burst through the radio next door. What if she is the only thing that's good and right?

The self-delusion was strong, and the music industry wasn't helping.

30

LAUREN AND I had dinner at my place. We talked, teased, laughed. I made strawberries and cream with honey and hazelnuts on top. When you are on £3.75 an hour you learn to indulge in simplicity. Or you don't, in which case you can truly go mad.

I cracked open a beer. Lauren worked at the white wine. I kept seeing the image of her body waving underneath the silky night dress, like a tattoo carved into my mind. Something seemed different about Lauren too, something about her demeanour, as if her reticence had tired a little. Something had shifted; she had let go of something. Maybe the earthquake had worked its way inside her too.

She was giggling, which was quite unusual. Smiles and laughter were her thing, giggling not so much. But that night, as she sat opposite me and listened to my stories, that night she cocked her head, touched her hair, lowered her gaze – and giggled. She looked delicious.

I got out of my chair, took a sip of beer and told Lauren to stand up. She gave another giggle but did as I asked. I glided my hand around her waist, pulling her closer. Her face looked perplexed, but there was fire in her eyes. She both knew and didn't know what was about to happen. She blinked. Then I pulled her body to mine and kissed her. A long, intense kiss. It was like the beginning of spring, the origin of all Sunday mornings, it was cookies and cream, it was where the fresh smell of rain comes from.

I felt intoxicated by the sheer intensity of the moment, but also relieved that she could kiss. There's no greater tragedy than a sexy woman who is a bad kisser. The frantic slobber, the lazy lump, the jittery slug, the corpse on a stretcher. Absolute tragedy. But not tonight. Tonight I was lucky. We were lucky. And so I felt grateful, happy, and spectacularly horny. I put my right hand on Lauren's thigh and slowly slid it up under her dress, feeling every texture of her skin as I moved. Her dress felt light on the back of my hand, her flesh felt like home.

My brain was a few seconds ahead of my body, picturing the moment my fingers would brush against her knickers, sliding my thumb over the side and across the hem, resting my hand there; firm, gentle, aroused. Expectant. My hand tried to catch up with the fantasy; I felt the smooth curves where thigh gives way to hip and hip to waist. My brain missed a beat. Not a stitch in the way. Just the silk and velvet of her skin, tiny goose bumps prickling up under my palm.

We parted for a second. Lauren bit my lip, then smiled her most mischievous smile, looking at me straight in the eye. I felt primal. I picked her up, threw her over my shoulder and carried her to the bedroom.

I walked up next to the bed, put Lauren down and kissed her again. We parted briefly and I took off my top. She stood looking at me with a hint of curiosity on her face. We smiled at each other. Incredulous smiles. Lauren lifted her arms up in the air as I pulled her dress over her head, revealing her perfectly naked body. She looked beautiful. She was. I cupped her neck with one hand and her arse with the other. She bit her lower lip and stared at me with a mix of yearning and mischief. Floods of desire burst through her eyes.

A beam of light came in through the open bedroom door and splashed across Lauren's side, bringing out every succulent detail of her womanhood. I wanted every inch of her, every curve. And every inch and every curve was made for this moment – yielding to my hands. As she stood, perfect in my arms, a gentle scent of cinnamon and rose wafted from her neck. I kissed her on the shoulder. Lauren savoured my kisses with a raw passivity, reacting in a sort of slow motion, both helpless and provocative, paralysed and powerful, Yearning and Mischief – a meeting of goddesses. Then she turned slightly, tilting her head to the side and stretching her neck across my face, beckoning my lips. My lips responded.

My brain was on fire, but my dick lagged behind. "I'm nervous," I told her.

That surprised me. I'd been nervous before with women, every first time in fact – more or less. I always found it nerve-wracking, baring myself for a stranger. And I don't mean physically, I knew I had an attractive body – Al's concrete cans made sure of that. No, the whole emotional nudity is what got to me. That's a tough one to shake off, all the expectations of performance and all that. More demands, more hard-earned dignity to be thrown under the feet of the latest Caesar. And it wasn't just nerves, either. There was an intuitive repugnance for the gratuity of such demands, demands that I was too strong to avoid and too alone to vanquish. I ended up feeling like a caged animal, despising my captors by instinct and accepting them by necessity. So it should come as no surprise that I'd sometimes feel uneasy with women. But it never crossed my mind to actually *say* it. That did surprise me, those words leaving my mouth. But that was the thing with Lauren, my inner self just fell out. Unadulterated.

"Why are you nervous?" she said, her voice still trembling. My lips had done good work.

"Well, you know..."

"I don't."

"I've thought about this moment for years..."

"Have you?" She smiled playfully, but her question sounded insincere, almost like she liked the idea but didn't quite believe it or wish to admit that she did. Lauren often asked empty questions like that when she needed to buy herself time to think, hold on to the upper hand.

"There's no need to be nervous," Lauren smirked, yet spoke in a gentle, almost caring tone. Then she put her arms around me and kissed me again. She began softly at first but quickly became impassioned, biting my lip a second time. This time she overdid it and it hurt, but it was honest, instinctual – so I sort of liked it anyway. She had me.

I pulled her towards me, pressing her body tight against mine so I could feel every bit of her skin. I *had* to. I felt her pubic hair bristling against my manhood. I lowered my hand between her legs and felt her lower lips. She closed her eyes as if ambushed by a trance and let out a little moan. She was wet, her juices flowing in expectation. My cock twinged. Her nipples hardened and pushed firmly against my abdomen; smug, regal, bound by pleasure. For a moment, *I* was the puppeteer. I picked her up and laid her on the bed.

"You're such an animal!" she said in flirty voice.

I liked that. I felt a connection with the bonobos. Maybe Lauren did too. I knelt on the carpet and went down on her with a compulsion I hadn't felt in years.

I had been going for about fifteen minutes and my dick was getting harder. I stood up and lay on the bed.

"C'mon, get on board," I said with a grin.

"What?!" she seemed disoriented, as if she'd just awakened from a long sleep, "I was planning to be *laid*, and now you tell me I have to do *work?*"

Even in this raw moment she couldn't let go of the exterior, the upper hand.

Lauren moved towards me, grabbed my head and forced it back down between her legs. I complied, disenchanted by her apathy but lured in by the possibility that she might bare her vulnerability for me, right there, with her thighs in my hands.

After another ten minutes my jaw was beginning to tire, but I knew she was close, I could feel her skin quiver. Her voice began to tremble. I kept going.

And then I was home. Lauren's orgasm tore through the room like wildfire. Her body gave a violent spasm as her thighs clenched around my head. She arched her back in a beautiful curve of indulgence, and let her pleasure run free, rippling across the brickwork and morphing into mild entertainment as it rose through the windows and hit the eardrums of my next-door neighbours.

They were quite gracious about it, the neighbours. A few weeks later I was in Mr Alaoui's shop when Ian and Deirdre, the couple living next door, walked in. They waved at me and ordered cheesy chips to take away. I waved back. "Has your friend gone back to New York?" said Ian. It appears that word had got around fast. Deptford doesn't get many New Yorkers visiting. I was about to answer when Deidre butted in, "She enjoyed London, uh?" she said, then stood there with a grin. I did indeed think that Lauren had enjoyed herself in London, but there's nothing like having it confirmed by another woman.

Lauren collapsed onto the bed. I lay down, feeling grateful and proud at the same time.

"You're a miracle worker," she punted.

"Don't say that."

"Why not?"

"It makes orgasms seem unrealistic."

"Sometimes they are." Her chest was heaving, her eyes half closed, "But not with you, apparently. You know your way around a woman's body, don't you...?" Her face had an air of suspicion, but it still felt good to hear those words. Egos care more about words than facial expressions.

"Ok," I replied with a grin.

Lauren turned her head and looked at me in the eye, "But remember this: we're talking about orgasms, ok? Not *love*." her face wrinkled as she spoke the word, as if it came attached with acid reflux.

"Ok." I said, a strange feeling of daze shooting through my core. "Anyway, it's you, you draw it out of me."

"I bet that's a line you use with all your women."

"*All* my women?"

"Oh don't play dumb, you've been around the block a few times," she said with a half-smile. Then she lay her head on the pillow, stretched out her arm and patted me on the head, "Good job," she whispered, wedging some distance between us.

The latent flattery softened the blow a little, but not for long. I knew not to be fooled by the seemingly generous comments; less than fifteen minutes later Lauren looked at me in disappointment and denounced me for hesitating the moment before I kissed her: "I saw your head move back an inch. You hesitated. You totally did."

Her tone was almost pitiful, like she was relaying a most miserable story, a story of great defeat, a story of emperors with no clothes and no balls – a story which in an instant overshadowed the timid shred of enthusiasm that had appeared on her face a few minutes earlier, when she so coolly and factually talked of miracles. She couldn't help it. She had to make sure her eager taking arm kept ahead of the small giving stump. Always.

I took Lauren's hand and put it between my legs, trying to direct her attention away from her selfishness and back to my own. My persistent hard-on reminded both of us that I too could do with an orgasm.

Lauren began to run her fingers along my shaft, gently. It felt good, but there was no fire. It looked like she was toying around. I had expected Lauren to charge into my body like a wild beast, like she was dying of thirst and my body was the last mountain spring. Instead she approached it more like a teenage girl amusing herself with a curiosity. I was stunned. How could a woman wrapped in such elegant eroticism turn out to be so less than ordinary? It was a painful thing to witness. She moved like a fox and talked like a slut but fucked like she'd just come out of a 1950s good housewife guide. I felt a sharp sense of sorrow, transcended only by the realization that I was a fool. The great promise was a hoax, a sexual and emotional miser in a vixen's clothes. I wasn't just a fool; I was a fool chasing a mirage.

I sat up for a while and looked out of the window, staring at the clouds. It was a tough comedown to handle.

After that Lauren and I napped for a few hours. Occasionally my eyes would open and I would take a quick look around, as if trying to work out where I was. Then I would catch a glimpse of Lauren's naked body lying next to mine, take a conscious breath for a second and close my eyes, falling asleep again with a dopey smile on my face. I was the most relaxed I had been in years.

We woke up some time around 6 a.m. and briefly looked at each other through half-closed eyes. I could smell Lauren's sweat, subtle hints of salt and rose. It turned me on instantly, but only in my brain. My body was utterly spent, ripped apart by all the adrenaline rushes and the ruthless withdrawals. Lauren stood up and staggered through the doorway. She nearly fell over but held on to the door frame just in time.

"I know I've had an effect on you," I said, "but I didn't expect it to be so profoundly disorienting."

"Nah, it's probably the lack of sleep."

Serves me right, I thought, that's how you fish a boot.

Lauren came back from the kitchen holding a glass of water and stood next to the bed looking around, sipping from the glass; naked, glowing. She was so sexy it was painful.

"Do you fancy some breakfast?" I was trying to shift my focus away from her tantalizing figure – my body just couldn't keep up with my brain.

"Breakfast?" she said, her eyebrow distinctly and unambiguously arched.

"Yes, I think there's some bacon in the fridge. I'll make us a couple of eggs. Fried or scrambled? I could get fresh bread from the market. It'll be lovely."

"You're not too kind, are you?"

"Erm, no... I don't think so." Shit, why do I take her cheap baits?

"Good. Kindness is weak."

She was a sniper, and my enthusiasm had dared to raise its head above the parapet. It never stood a chance.

Then Lauren came back to bed and we sat chatting for a while; hopes, dreams, let downs, hard work, orgasms, the soft feeling of fresh linen. I just wanted to spend the rest of my life in that bed, lying motionless while she cradled my head in her hands and whispered gentle sweet nothings in my ears. The weather was vicious, gale-force winds and persistent rain. The Met Office had issued an amber warning and a bunch of bus routes had been suspended. And yet, as I write these words, I can't help remembering blue skies and a vividly orange sunset.

31

THERE WAS a series of loud, thumping noises coming up from the kitchen. The old floorboards were rattling, sending shockwaves through the whole building. I hurried downstairs.

It was just gone ten o'clock. I walked into the kitchen to find Terry standing in a corner, panic-stricken, as the washing machine leapt a foot into the air, swaying side to side like an insane automaton. Before I had a chance to register what was going on, Mr Alaoui came marching in, his usual waddle replaced by a cloddish run. He stood still for a split second, facing the machine as if trying to threaten it into submission, then he flared out his arms and leapt forward face first, his belly making a flabby noise as he landed on top of the machine. I had never seen the man move so quick. But the white beast kept going, tossing him around like a bag of potatoes loosely strapped to a mechanical bull. A very angular and loud bull. No one dared approach the off switch. A trench of sweat appeared along Mr Alaoui's spine, and I could swear I heard his teeth rattle. Finally, Terry grabbed the cable and yanked at it, pulling it out of the socket. The machine slowed down and came to a clunky stop. The room was suddenly rid of chaos. Mr Alaoui looked pale.

We stood there for a moment, looking at each other in disbelief. Nobody said a word, but it was clear we were all thinking the same thing: what on earth possessed this thing? We didn't know whether to call an engineer or an exorcist.

Then I noticed that the machine door looked different; shiny, and unusually clean. I saw a bundle of paper on the sink and picked it up. It was an instruction manual. Attached to it was a piece of adhesive tape with which the delivery guy had stuck it to the side of the machine. It said in big red letters:

> WARNING: DO NOT operate washing machine
> before removing transit bolts.

I showed it to Terry. He walked off sheepishly, mumbling something about a toolbox.

32

THAT FRIDAY was Lauren's last day in London. My head was a circus of doubt and excitement. She was the songs of Calypso and I was an improvised Ulysses. There was a reason Kevin called him "that daft Greek hothead."

We left the Out Bar at 1 a.m. and walked towards Trafalgar Square to catch the N18 to Marylebone Road. The cocktails had worked their magic and we were staggering through Soho, laughing at each other's jokes and failing at coordination. Somewhere near Old Compton Street we turned into a narrow passage and a few steps in I realized that Lauren was gone. I stopped, turned around and saw her adjusting her skirt, grinning like a Cheshire cat.

"What's funny now?" I turned back around and kept on walking.

She didn't answer but quickened her step, caught up with me and grabbed me by the waist.

"Oh, coming up from behind uh…"

Lauren dipped her hand in my front pocket for an instant then pulled it out, slapped me on the back and fell into step beside me. She looked at her feet, then turned to me, still smiling from ear to ear, though the Cheshire cat had now transformed into a mischievous siren. I reached into my pocket and her smile turned into roaring laughter as I pulled out a pair of white lace knickers. That was the thing with Lauren, she knew how to give me a hard on deep in my lizard brain. My penis was just along for the ride.

"You appear to have misplaced something," I said.

"What, a girl can't express her desire?"

I grabbed her by the waist, pulled her to me and gave her a long, sloppy kiss. I had a quick look around. The passage was deserted. I could see the cars' headlights at the other end, going back and forth along the main road. I picked Lauren up and put her down against the wall, holding her left leg up with my hand. She whimpered. We went at each other's lips like birds of prey.

Someone coughed, and we noticed a homeless man sitting in a dark doorway a few yards away. We sniggered. Lauren adjusted her skirt and we walked on. She was temptation on legs. Great legs.

"I love the way your thigh fits perfectly in my hand," I told her.

"You're just a sucker for small candy."

"I don't like candy, but I'm making an exception for you."

Lauren smiled her beautiful smile. I chuckled, looked up, took a deep breath and revelled in her lavish presence.

* * *

A while later we arrived at the hotel. Lauren unlocked the door and we walked in. I took off my shoes, then went to the bathroom and splashed some water on my face. I came out and searched the minibar for some gin and a can of tonic.

Lauren walked over to me, grabbed my hand and shoved it under her skirt, "C'mon!" she said, "Feel me up a little, throw this girl a bone!"

"Oh, ok," I said, pretending to have been startled, "I may have to go on a recon mission first, see if I can find a happy button."

"If at your age you're not sure where to find the happy button, then you shouldn't be allowed to play with one." Lauren's wit always turned me on, made me want to feel her – all of her. But it was impossible. No matter how much I felt her flesh, entered her, breathed her in, no matter how deep I thrusted inside her, we were still separate individuals, and that seemed like a dreadful limitation.

I turned slightly and put my arms around Lauren, gently kissing her neck. One of her dangly earrings rested on my nose. "You're not wearing your studs today?"

"Studs? What studs?" she asked.

"Your studs, you know, earrings."

"Oh, my stud earrings! Sorry, I got confused,"

"Yeah, the word 'stud' confuses you, uh?"

"Yes! It has so many meanings! Like it's got to cover so much territory on its own!"

"Yeah, when are other words going to come out and help?"

We laughed. She laughed. She looked resplendent.

Then we got into bed and started kissing. As I caressed her body Lauren trembled in expectation. I put my hand on her inner thigh and moved upwards until I reached her groin. I stopped for a second then spread my hand. I felt Lauren's wetness flowing, her body more eager with every touch. I was aroused beyond sanity. I threw my trousers on the floor and entered her, slowly, pushing gently at first, then thrusted forward all the way. She moaned. Her moans had this low, primeval tone – deeply erotic yet oddly soothing. Like an ocean wave. They wrapped me up and sucked me in. I kept moving back and forth in long, deliberate strokes, my hands firmly on Lauren's hips. Her moans intensified, punctuated by short, high-pitched cries that broke through like strikes of lightning between bursts of thunder. A Morse code of lust and delight. I liked it. I mean *really* liked it. It did more than turn me on, it possessed my brain.

Then Lauren opened her eyes wide, buried her head in my chest and whispered, "I'm going to come." She thrusted her hips forward, lifting her back from the bed; her body gave out and she burst into orgasm. Pure joy.

Her flesh quivered as I slowly withdrew from inside her. I turned over and lay on my back.

Lauren lay there with her eyes closed and a tiny smile on her face. She put her hand between my legs, then opened her eyes, sobering up in an instant. "You didn't *come*?"

"Not this time. But I enjoyed watching you!" I smiled. I felt truly happy.

"Why the *fuck* didn't you come?"

"What do you mean? I just didn't."

"Then why. The. Fuck. Didn't. You. Carry on?" She flipped from ecstasy to discontent in a heartbeat. My heartbeat.

I willed myself to stay with that feeling I'd experienced just a few seconds ago, but I couldn't hold on. A sudden deflation grabbed me and threw me down. I resented Lauren for blasting the joy out of such a hard-earned moment so easily, so carelessly.

We woke up an hour later in each other's arms. Lauren's flight was leaving in five hours. We made love once again. Lauren dug her nails in my back and we climaxed together. We struggled to catch our breath, then laughed in amazement and ran out of breath again. A thrilling cycle of pure happiness. Or perhaps we were just high on adrenaline. It felt like happiness. Lauren called me a miracle worker once again and this time I soaked it up and it felt good. I figured that was her way of telling me she liked my company.

We showered, gathered our clothes off the floor, got dressed and took a bus to Paddington Station. We walked over to the platforms and stood near the gates. Lauren looked up at me and smiled. I gave her a long, passionate kiss. She responded.

"Take care of yourself," I told her. I meant it.

"I'll be good. Well, sort of..." She laughed. I felt a pang, born of the knowledge that I wasn't going to hear that laugh tomorrow, and the day after that, and the one after that. That's when Knowledge is a bitch.

Lauren joined the queue at the gate, took out her ticket, showed it to the woman in uniform and went through. I looked at Lauren walking towards the train; I stood there waiting for that moment, that Hollywood moment when she turns around one more time and gives me a knowing smile. I waited. She put the ticket back in her handbag, got on the train and disappeared.

33

I HAD A tough shift at the café. Ron was off sick, so I had to take care of the sandwiches while Hasan took over the coffee machine. Ron had perfected the sandwich routine over the years and he ran a fine-tuned production line. I couldn't hope to get anywhere near his rhythm. Not that it would have mattered, as no humanly achievable rhythm would appease Hasan's appetite for screaming like a maniac. But I reckon that day I got more than the usual share.

As lunchtime approached, I threw myself at the grills, trying to catch up with an ever-growing list of orders while Hasan shouted at me to move faster, grill faster, scrape faster, bag faster. He spent a lot more time and effort berating me than he did looking after the coffees. And so the coffee kept flowing, reaching the half-cup mark, turning beige and watery, then flowing some more, till the cup was filled to the brim. Then, suddenly, Hasan would turn around and look at the full cups in horror, shocked that the machine had betrayed him, that it had dared to take on a life of its own and mock him so brazenly in front of all the customers. That's when he'd grab the cup and throw half of the liquid into the sink, presenting the customer with a sort of pale slurry. Coffee tends to cool when the filter overruns, so it was lukewarm slurry.

Sometimes the shouting rally went on a little longer. When Hasan eventually turned to the machine, the coffee had overflowed, and little bits of grounds had stuck to the side of the cup to create a dismal, sandy-looking installation. When this happened, Hasan would wipe the cup with his sleeve, thinking that customers wouldn't notice. But they noticed. That was the thing with Hasan, he wasn't just an idiot, he was an arrogant idiot. One of those who think they are ahead of everyone else, smirking away as they enact their idiocy, thinking they are *outwitting* us, when in fact they couldn't outwit a tin of beans.

Word got around and the café was quieter when Hasan worked the machines. Though we were still busy enough to earn me a few finger burns.

I was too exhausted to make it to the library that evening, so I went straight home. I sat on the bed, thinking of Lauren, reliving what had happened only a few days earlier. We'd had tears and laughter, an approximately safe amount of sentimentality, just the right amount of mutual humiliation, a hint of dirty talk, some inspirational reminiscing, glorious foreplay and a couple of incontestable orgasms. It had been a good week, despite the angry-looking blisters bubbling over my fingers and thumbs.

I closed my eyes, trying to remember Lauren's smell and those few moments of bare emotions she'd reluctantly given me. I felt a dull ache in my gut. I opened my eyes. The ache lingered. A mild shadow of terror. My instinct was trying to warn me about something that my mind refused to accept. Lauren was trouble, and not always in a good way. Talking to her was a constant battle, exhilarating but ultimately wounding.

Her wit was undeniable, and that's what dragged me back to her; my mind becoming aroused before my cock had a chance to get involved. But even that wit was wrapped in a blanket of tricks. It was the wit of defence, lining the walls of her soul and hanging on for dear life. Sometimes it felt amorous, sometimes rehearsed, but it always left a bitter aftertaste. And yet I still wanted her, *craved* her, longed for her to open herself up to me, to weave herself into my soul – but she couldn't. She just couldn't. To Lauren, opening up was a heavy burden, a strain, an unwanted price to be paid for some honest strokes and a few moments of ecstasy; it was lifeblood she sacrificed sparingly and unwillingly, cringing as though attacked by leeches sent by Satan himself to claim her soul one, single, painful drop at a time. Because to Lauren, baring her emotions was like ripping apart her own self, tossing away her existence, abandoning her soul in a dilapidated car park.

I lay down and went to sleep, feeling almost as dismal as Hasan's coffees.

34

WHAT I REALLY needed was a way out. I couldn't quite see one, so I settled for a change. Anything, *anything* but stillness.

I saw this advert in the paper, a restaurant in Holborn looking for a waiter, no experience necessary. Perfect. From Holborn I can get to the library on foot, arrive a little earlier, put in a few extra hours a week. I was getting tired of the 11 bus. In a couple of days I would finish *The Marvel of Language*, and I felt excited about my next pick. Whitman perhaps.

It was a French restaurant with red tablecloths and wicker chairs. The manager kept me waiting a good fifteen minutes before the interview, some sort of tactic no doubt, unnerve the employee even before day one.

Finally, Ms Gina Reynolds walked out of the kitchen, came over and sat opposite me. She wore a polka-dot blouse and a tight pair of grey trousers that left little to the imagination. Her hair was entwined in thick curls, shooting off in all directions like mad ropes. She had a flat chest and a thriving belly roll that filled out the top of her trousers starting just above the Venus mound. It was almost cute but not quite. White wine probably.

"Why do you want to work here?" Gina Reynolds didn't waste any time.

"I want to build a career in hospitality, and everyone knows that French restaurants are the best. I want to learn from the best." (I couldn't tell her the truth, could I...)

She didn't look impressed. She must've dealt with smart arses before. "Why this particular French restaurant?"

"It's one of the busiest in London." I had no idea whether that was true, but it wasn't unlikely – we were in central London, and I had noticed two large dining areas in the next room; I figured it was worth a shot. "I want to learn the ropes in a place where I'm under pressure." My words almost scared me; the stuff was just pouring out of my mouth as if I'd spent weeks building a back story. I had no idea where it was coming from. I felt smug but unsettled, like a new King Midas for bullshit.

"Ok," she said, "I'll give you a week's trial. Barbra will show you to the changing rooms."

I followed Barbra up the stairs. Barbra slowed halfway up and spoke over her shoulder, "I know I'm fat. But I don't move like I'm fat."

She didn't move like she was slim either, but somehow that wasn't important enough for her to report. I suppose beliefs are less work than dieting – though maybe not in the long run.

There was only one changing room. Male employees had to sit on the stairs while the waitresses got changed. Then the waitresses would call us in when they were done and we'd get changed. There were clothes hooks all along the main wall and a narrow bench running from side to side. There was a large, heavy-looking table in the middle. One of the waitresses always hung her bra in full view, on a single lone hook next to the rest of her clothes. All the waitresses changed into a plain, white t-shirt bra before their shift, so that the lace or the embroidery or nipples wouldn't show through the white uniform shirt – and hung their regular bras, underwire and all, on a hook. But most of the waitresses put their other garments on the same hook, usually on top of the bra. Not Silvia though. Silvia liked her bra on full display every time. And every time, Paco, a sixty-year-old illiterate dishwasher, pointed at it and giggled like a pre-pubescent imbecile.

I'd never waited tables, so I needed a bit of practice if I was to get through the one-week trial. I asked Yona to show me the basics. We got some dishes out of the kitchen cupboard and she taught me how to carry three plates in one hand, using my forearm to balance two of the plates on each other. After a few attempts it seemed straightforward enough.

"Of course," Yona said, "it's a lot less pleasant when they are piping hot."

Ah, not so straightforward. I should've known there was going to be a catch.

My first shift was on a Saturday morning. As it turned out, hot plates were not among my worries. I arrived at the restaurant at 8.15 a.m., walked through the kitchen and sat on the stairs. A few minutes later Silvia called me in. I entered the changing room and put my bag on the bench. Silvia turned slightly and moved away from her clothes hook, making sure her dangling creation wouldn't go unnoticed. She looked at me, searching my face for a sign of recognition. I didn't oblige. I was neither sixty nor an imbecile.

I was buttoning up my shirt when Ms Reynolds walked in.

"You don't need a uniform. Put these on."

She handed me a pair of overalls.

And that's how it started. Every shift there was a reason why I wouldn't need a uniform. Chairs needed stacking, wine crates needed shifting, lorries needed unloading and – more often than not – the crapper needed unclogging. Three times a day.

And so the girls put on their white uniforms and I kept being handed the blue overalls. Sometimes the green ones. Equality is a great thing, until there's a clogged crapper to deal with.

But the worse of them all was the cooker. Ms Reynolds was a health and safety fanatic (not *my* health and safety, mind) and she demanded that the whole kitchen be scrubbed after every shift: appliances, floors, walls, the lot. Apparently they'd had a mouse infestation the year before. The restaurant came really close to being shut down and Ms Reynolds nearly lost her job, so now she was absolutely obsessed with drowning every corner in bleach. Which meant shifting the cooker – a big, heavy stainless-steel bastard – four times a day: twice to pull it away from the wall and twice to put it back on top of the bleach.

Day by day the overalls became my uniform. Hasan didn't seem such a bad prospect after all, but it was too late, I was Gina Reynolds's errand boy now. At dinner time the waitresses shook their arses and raked in the tips. I had nothing to shake, so I took my £3.75 an hour and stressed about the rent.

35

I CARRIED ON seeing Elly on and off, until it became clear that the poor girl could only fuck when she was pissed. A minor tragedy really. Those long fingers, the wobbly breasts, all that goodness gone to waste. The Catholic upbringing had struck deep, blown a frosty wind on her budding sexuality.

This one time I invited her over for dinner, thinking we could spend an evening without all the acting and the gaming. I occasionally had romantic spurts like that. If only women knew how to fuel them. They seemed to spend a lot of time *talking* and *fantasizing* about romance, but very little time fostering it.

I began prepping at 5 p.m., chopping and slicing and sucking at a can of lager. BB King flooded the waves with his poetry.

The phone rang, it was Elly. "What time do you want me over?"

"At this rate I'll be out of lager by eight."

"Ok, I'll make sure to be there by 7.30 then."

I hung up and went back to chopping, then took a bag of mince out of the fridge and prepared the burger patty. This kind of cooking was good for the soul, like yoga but with lager and the blues. Some things could be improved by lager, and almost anything could be improved by the blues.

Elly knocked just before 7.30. I went to the door with my apron on.

"Oh, look at you!" she said with a cheeky smile.

She was wearing a short leather skirt, showing her firm, solid thighs wrapped in black stockings. I handed her a can.

"Thanks, love," she smiled. "What's on the menu, then?"

"I made burgers. From scratch."

"Delicious!"

"Well, wait till you try them..."

"I'm sure they'll be lovely, but you should've waited before you told me, at least if they are awful you could say you bought them ready made."

"Don't worry, if it all goes tits up, I have a can of Spam."

I put the burgers on a plate and sliced some cheese. We sat down and tucked in. Elly made all the right noises. No need for Spam this time. I imagined her making those noises later in the bedroom, but the kitchen was a good start. One room at a time.

I started clearing the table the moment we finished eating. I wanted to get out of the kitchen before Terry came back. His presence was one loud cockblocker.

Elly stood up and picked up two empty cans.

I put some dishes in the sink, turned around and kissed her. A long, intense kiss. She knew what she was doing. Her tongue moved around expertly, not too fast, not like those rattle-snake tongues that work away as if they're competing with you, trying to outrun you. But not too slow either. A steady motion. My dick rose. I took her hand and led her towards the bedroom.

"It's a little early for bed, don't you think?"

"I thought we'd be more comfortable there."

"Doing what?" she said with a fake smile.

"I dunno, chatting." I was playing along but didn't like that she seemed half serious. It's never a good sign when a woman makes you feel like sex is for your own benefit, like she is doing you some kind of *favour*. I'd heard the moans and seen the eyes roll back. I knew what sex could do to a woman.

Of course, there was always a chance that she was being sincere. Maybe she was frigid. In which case it was always going to be too early for bed. I decided to find out sooner rather than later.

"Come on," I said, "it might be fun."

"Just one more drink, please?"

"Ok, but I'm out of lager. Tequila ok?" I had a fresh bottle of Cuervo that I was supposed to take to work for those hard-to-handle moments. I didn't like the idea of opening it. And for what? I felt pretty feeble minded, but I went against my gut and took the tequila out of the cupboard. I held the bottle by the neck and turned the stopper, clockwise. The seal cracked, and so did my self-esteem.

I poured two glasses and we sat around a while longer. Elly told me about her job, some sad gig at a call centre. She kept looking at the wall as she talked. It felt as if there were three of us and she was more interested in talking to the other bloke. I didn't know what it meant but I suspected it wasn't good.

Half an hour later we were in bed. At least she's a woman of her word, I thought. The sex was uneventful. We dry humped for a bit, I got hard, she removed my trousers, I pulled down her skirt, she lay on her back, I did my missionary work, she made some noises. The noises were nowhere near as inspired as those I'd heard in the kitchen. She kept asking me if I was ok, which put me off – I was trying to mount her for god's sake, not have her do me a root canal. I nearly bailed out a few times. Then I willed myself to come, did, rolled off. Elly was asleep within twenty seconds. I lay there with my right arm under her head, my balls relieved and my manhood dented.

A few minutes later she started snoring. Not one of those cute, girly snores that sound like a kitten who's not quite got the hang of purring. It was a roaring, guttural snore that made the whole bed rattle. I nudged her a little, trying to move her onto her side. Nothing. Those solid thighs were attached to a solid core. She wasn't a big woman, 5'7" maybe, and must've weighed around ten stone, but boy, she was solid. It was like trying to shift a concrete bollard. Even her flesh didn't budge. Unyielding. Maybe that's why she is so aloof about sex, I thought. Sexual action, participation, all that stuff needs *some* yielding.

She woke up suddenly, as if startled. "You ok?" she asked, confused.

"Yes, are you?"

"Erm, I think so. Did I fall asleep, you know... during *it*?"

"You mean while we were fucking?" I couldn't believe what I was hearing.

"Yeah... did I?"

"No. Soon after."

"Oh, ok, good," she said furtively. "But we did, you know...?"

"Did we have sex? Yes."

"Oh, ok. That's weird, it doesn't feel like it."

She had hardly drunk. I'd seen her in the Rising Sun downing three pints, washing them down with vodka shots and still walk in an approximately straight line on her way to the off-licence. Nah. This must've all been part of her aloofness act, in case someone thought she might've had sex for reasons other than an accidental indulgence or as a duty to man. A sad pretence. I didn't know how to feel – pity? dejection? Dejection won me over. Pretence didn't do women any favours. It was one of those things that made me less likely to sympathize with their plight.

I thought about Lauren, how she spat it out like it was – no filter. And yet, when it came down to it, when sex came into the picture, Lauren was just as aloof as any other woman. The dejection grew. I thought about the first time Lauren told me she wanted to sleep with me. Of course she didn't actually *say* it, that's the whole point, she wouldn't; she couldn't. What she said was "I wonder what your bed feels like." That's what she said. It was as though all women were caught in this compulsory conspiracy of pretence, so compelling, so very nearly pathological that it cut through all individual differences – tall women and short women, blondes and brunettes, the stiff ice buckets and the hot stoves, the lambs and the lionesses, the firebombs and the peacemakers, the bourgeois housewives and the flapper girls. They just couldn't help it, something to do with pride or honour or whatnot. The dejection grew some more, then lingered – insistent.

Elly moved closer and put her hand on my flaccid penis. Was she deliberately trying to confuse me?

"Give me a kiss," she said pleadingly.

I mustered a little peck on the lips. Just about.

"Come on, a proper kiss!"

"I've got nothing left, I'm sorry."

"Oh, ok, let's get some sleep then."

I thought about willing myself to get hard, to go through with it. But the pretence of the night before was still heavy on my mind. Fuck her, I thought. But not literally, of course.

She turned around and grinned nervously, "I was horny for a moment then."

"Sorry, not feeling up to it." I felt anxiety rising as I spoke those words, like I was doing something illegal, immoral even. I wondered if women felt the same way when they turned down a man. Maybe they did and we're more alike than we dare to believe. Or maybe it's just us. Maybe we really are at their mercy.

I couldn't sleep after that. I lay there for over an hour. Then my back started hurting so I got up, went to the kitchen and washed some dishes. I could hear her thunderous, relentless snore through the closed bedroom door. I shut the kitchen door and turned on the radio. Some bird was screaming "My body is too bootylicious for you." The poor deluded cow. If fools stopped paying gratuitous attention to her, then we'd see. We'd see how the value of that body tumbles at the rate of Turkish currency.

I wasn't in a good place. This too shall pass.

36

HEALTH AND SAFETY turned out to be bad news for my education. Most evenings I was too exhausted to make it to the library, and when I did make it, my back would hurt after a few minutes of sitting on the old spartan chairs. I tried standing for a while, but my knees and leg muscles ached from Gina Reynolds' errands – the wine crates, the potato sacks, the stainless-steel bastard, all demanded their toll. On days when I had an afternoon shift I'd try to go to the library in the mornings, but that wasn't very good either. Even when the two bricks held through the night, my backache had to contend with Terry's screaming matches and a mattress that was absolutely knackered. It was like sleeping on a giant beanbag above a mad dog's kennel. Turning the mattress over had become as useless as trying to reason with Terry, so I took to sleeping on the floor, which helped a little with the pain. But most mornings I would wake up stiff as a board and it would take me a good hour before I regained enough flexibility in my core to sit down or get on the bus. I was back in that bloody squirt factory. Full circle. Infernal Circle. I really hoped it was just Limbo. I rummaged around for some consolation. At least I was putting some hours in at the library.

And then, just like that, Lady Luck gave me the eye from behind her blindfold.

37

MY WAY OUT came in the form of an Angolan freedom fighter.

His name was Upendo, and he worked the photocopiers in Charing Cross Library. Post Room Manager was his title, but he mostly worked the photocopiers. It seems there were a lot of managers in the public services at that time.

It was a Tuesday morning and I was halfway through *The Structure of Scientific Revolutions*. Upendo was scattering leaflets on the reading tables, something to do with a guest lecture on humanity. He waved a leaflet at me. "You doing mornings now?"

"Yeah, evening shifts at work."

"You like it?"

"Yes, I prefer mornings, it's quieter. And the reading rooms are less stuffy."

"No, I mean your job, you like it?"

"Ah, no. It's fucking up my back. Not too kind to my intellect either."

"Let's go over there for a chat," he whispered, pointing to the photocopier room. There was nobody in the library, but I guess rules are rules. Or maybe force of habit.

"I'm leaving in three weeks," Upendo said. "Going back to Angola. Things are bad. Flags have changed colours, but people are still trapped. They need all the help they can get."

The colonial powers had left via the front door and came back in through the rear windows. Crumbling, bomb-stricken windows.

"You mean you're joining the –"

"Don't ask. The less you know the better."

I didn't ask.

"They'll need a new post room manager. They'll be advertising the post soon, probably Friday. Do you want the job?"

I wanted the job. I *really* wanted the job. I wished there didn't need to be a war. I felt guilty at my excitement, but only a little.

"I'll tell the Head Librarian today. Can you come in tomorrow lunchtime?"

"Yes."

"Good, you can speak to the Head Librarian then. Tell him I told you about the job, tell him you believe in free education for all."

"I kind of do."

"Fine, tell him." I think Upendo was a pragmatist, though I wasn't sure. Kevin wasn't around to confirm. Kevin would have known.

"Make sure it's tomorrow," he said, "before they advertise. If he thinks he can save a few quid by employing someone without paying for an ad, he'll be tempted."

"I'll do that, thank you."

"No worries. I'd rather the job went to someone who actually likes libraries." Maybe Upendo was a romantic too.

He picked up another pack of leaflets and we walked out of the photocopier room.

"So, you coming to the guest lecture tomorrow night?"

"I can't, evening shift. Being human, though, uh. Sounds interesting. Biologist?"

"Nah, anthropologist."

"Ah…"

"I have to pick him up from Euston, take him for a coffee and *talk* to him."

"That's bad luck. No one should have to talk to an anthropologist."

"True dat."

The next day I turned up at lunchtime and asked to speak to the Head Librarian. I did and said exactly what Upendo had told me to do and say, and I got the job. I was ecstatic. Dakris Manell: Post Room Manager.

They started me off on evening shifts, 4 p.m. to 8 p.m., when it was quiet and Upendo had time to show me the ropes. He handed me a thick file; it said "Post Room Manual" in big bold letters. "Everything you need to know is in there. Study it."

The post room manual had an index page: stock check, stationery cupboard, making booklets, clearing jams, staff reports. Every month you had to run reports, telling staff how many photocopies they'd made and reprimanding anyone who went over the limit. Library members paid for photocopies, they paid in advance, and they had no upper limit. They could pay for a million photocopies if they wished, and they'd get them. There was a whole section in the manual called "Setting up a member account".

Then Upendo talked me through the opening routine. "On a morning shift you need to start the photocopiers at 7.45 a.m. They need time to warm up and you have to get them up and running by 8 a.m."

"Ok."

There were lots of English "schools" set up in people's spare bedrooms at the time. Some of them eventually made it big, leased buildings on Tottenham Court Road and had cappuccino machines in the front office. But most of them were struggling supply teachers, casual labourers in Oxfam suits who needed the extra cash and used the library to prepare their classes, hoping that one day they would be able to afford a front office. Or at least a cappuccino machine. They never knew until 8.55 a.m. whether they were going to be needed for their supply teaching, so they'd queue outside the library before opening time, come in at eight o'clock, prepare their classes and wait. They couldn't spare the additional fifteen minutes it took the photocopiers to warm up, and Upendo knew what it was like to be out of a job, so he'd convinced the Head Librarian to let him set things up at 7.45 a.m. The Head Librarian agreed, on condition that Upendo worked the extra fifteen minutes for free.

A couple of weeks later, as Upendo got ready to fight the militias, I turned up for my first morning shift. I woke up at 6.30 a.m., shined my shoes, put on a blue chequered shirt and took the 188 to Waterloo Station. I got off the bus and walked across Waterloo Bridge, always my favourite bridge. The air was thinner, the sky was nearer, and I was floating. For the first time in my life I was going to work with a shirt on. Not a uniform, not an overall – a shirt. My own blue chequered shirt.

I arrived at the library at 7.35 a.m. The one-man English schools were already queuing outside. I knocked on the door. Someone called me a tosser and shouted something about jumping the queue. The Head Librarian peeked through the narrow glass, opened the door and let me in. I was the king of Charing Cross.

I walked through the main reading room and towards the rear of the library. I took out the key to the post room door and held it for a few seconds in my hand. I was a man with a key. There was a queue of people outside waiting to get in and use my machines, in my post room that I opened with this very key. I put the key in and unlocked the door. I might as well have been unlocking the gates of Alexandria.

At 7.45 sharp I flipped the switches and carried on Upendo's legacy. I fed the machines with a few reams of paper and sat down at the tiny desk in the corner. I was Dakris Manell: office worker. It seemed surreal and yet it seemed the greatest accomplishment ever recorded. No squirts, no smell of lubricant, no metal shavings down my shirt, no drills screaming in my ears, no sergeant majors, no coffee grounds down my pants. Just me, a desk and a chequered shirt. This is what having a career must feel like.

That afternoon some guy asked me if I knew how to unscrew one of the little side doors on the machine, where the birth certificate he was trying to photocopy had got caught. The thing was stuck deep inside and the door didn't open enough for his hand to get through. There was a 5mm bolt holding the door hinge on the other side and he couldn't figure out why it wouldn't give. It was a locknut; you need two spanners to get those out. I told him no, I have no idea, I'm not good with mechanical things.

I was an office worker now.

38

I phoned Judy to tell her about the job and she invited me to supper. Liver and onions. Simon opened a bottle of Cabernet, Judy made bread and butter pudding and I told them the story.

"This Upendo character must've had his eye on you," Judy said. "What were you doing that attracted his attention?"

"I guess it's because I was there early mornings, you know, when no one else was around."

"Hmm…" she curled her mouth in doubt.

"He must've seen how hard Dak was working," suggested Simon.

Judy agreed, "Yes – yes, he did… He saw how serious you are about bettering yourself."

"Maybe I was just lucky."

Judy looked vaguely annoyed at what she so clearly saw as an obvious banality. "Of course you are *lucky*," she said, "you're lucky to have a friend like Simon. You're lucky, you're so lucky to have my constant and vigilant love, and you're lucky that Upendo could *see* you. You're not a fool, you don't believe you're self-made, do you?" Her eyes were glistening with laughter. "You're not like – what's his name, Si? That chap on the telly?"

"Richard Branson?"

"Yes, Richard Branson! Prancing around on TV telling everyone how he's a self-made man. What a fool! Can you imagine, Si, how foolish one must be?" Judy's face was a chaos of amusement and seriousness. Her eyes streaming with tears of laughter.

"I suppose success got to his head," said Simon.

"Yes, and he forgot he has a mother!" Judy took out a tiny white handkerchief and dried her eyes.

Simon turned to me and spoke under his breath, "Sometimes I wish *I* forgot I have a mother…" We grinned. He'd had his share of imposed mediocrity.

Then Judy turned her eyes upwards, as if a thought had been

suggested to her by some higher power; "Libraries are fascinating places, aren't they... So, what have you been reading?"

"I've kind of been flirting with all sorts," I replied.

"Uh-uh, flirting with knowledge. I like that. Don't you, Si?"

"Yes, it's the greatest privilege."

"So it is," Judy said, then turned to me: "It's also very true of you, you as you are just now; it's what you are and what you are doing. Excellent. Absolutely excellent. That's exactly what you need. And don't bother trying to make it serious, that will come naturally."

Finally. I had the universe by its dusty balls. That's what the encouragement of a good woman will do when delivered at the right moment. And Judy always knew the right moment. She made me feel I was part of something. Something important, something *intellectual*, and unique. I was going to achieve great things.

The whole thing felt normal and surreal at the same time. Especially books. I'd only ever owned two books in my life, some comic book on space aliens and *The Wizard of Oz* – birthday presents when I was a kid. I remember being utterly bewildered on both occasions. A book? Why would anyone do that? The only answer I could fathom was that books must've been cheaper than toys. There was no other logical explanation. I never read either.

"Have you read Forster yet?" Judy said. "You *need* to read Forster. It's impossible to understand life without understanding love, and it's impossible to understand love without having read Forster. Life, love, all different sorts of love – and loss of love. It could well serve for training counsellors."

"I've mostly tended towards philosophy. Mostly." I said.

"Ah," she said, with a look of inevitability on her face, like she'd been expecting this moment all along, like I was a twelve-year-old boy informing her that my voice had broken. "Simon likes a bit of philosophy. I think he's reading Sartre."

Simon nodded.

"You're not reading Sartre too, are you?" Judy asked.

"No, a bit of Marx, some Lao Tzu, Plato." I thought she wouldn't be interested in the sciencey stuff, but then I felt I was betraying her, so I added, "But I've really got fascinated by cognitive science. I'm reading a lot of that at the moment."

She turned to Simon with wide eyes, "Science! Like Feynman!"

"Judy loves Feynman," said Simon.

"Oh, it's much more than love, Si. He saved my life!"

"Yes," said Simon, "isn't that love too?"

She ignored his question and turned to me. This clearly could not wait. "It was a few months after my Neil died. I was in a bad way. I had been sitting in bed for days, drinking gin from a bottle and watching TV. I wasn't a well woman; I'd given up, really." She shrugged. "The TV was on constantly. We didn't have remotes in those days and I never got out of bed, so the TV stayed on all the time." She turned her head and pointed at the old telly on the floor, next to the electric heater. "Then one evening I saw this man. He was talking about light bouncing around and swooshing back and forth, *waves* getting shorter and longer. It was Feynman, of course. He was sitting in this big armchair and he just talked and talked and shifted in that armchair like a little boy and laughed. It was his dad, you see. His dad had taken an interest in him from an early age, nourishing the little boy, so Feynman never had to lose that curiosity little boys have, you know, that 'why, why, why!' " Judy laughed for a second, then turned immediately serious again: "Most boys have it beaten out of them," she closed her eyes, as if feeling the pain of those beatings. "Feynman had been lucky; he could talk so freely. And I just listened to his voice, I let it envelop me," she made a gesture with her hands as if she was splashing water on her chest and face. "And the depression just lifted – gone." She sunk back into her chair. I think she was reliving those moments.

I had read great things about Dick Feynman, how he mesmerized his students, how he perfected the balance between lecturing and theatre – a modern Renaissance man (minus the cataclysmic paintings), and I wasn't the least bit surprised at the suggestion that he might've had some telepathic healing superpower. I didn't know what Feynman himself might have made of cognitive science, though I suspect he would have been sceptical of it. Nevertheless, Judy's suggestion that what I was doing was even remotely close to what the great Richard Feynman had done gave me a great sense of worth.

The bread and butter pudding tasted especially sweet that night.

39

EVENING SHIFTS were quiet, so I got a lot of reading done. Judy's words echoed in my mind, and I felt safe on what I now considered Feynman's path – arrogantly of course, but arrogance too has its place – and in the company of the Great Masters. As I alternated between Orwell and *Learnability Theory*, Cervantes and *The Great Cognitive Debate*, I felt my mind expand and contract like a beating heart and, like a heart, it sometimes had palpitations that made me anxious, contaminating my other heart. I was haunted by the realization that I could never get through all the books in the world. I had been having this recurring dream where I would get lost in an infinite library, running around a labyrinth of towering bookshelves, breaking into a cold sweat. I often wished I'd been born before Gutenberg, when the task might've seemed more manageable, more finite. Then I'd remember the inescapable grip of family history – life before Gutenberg was a serf chained to the land, rotten teeth, illiterate, forlorn. My destiny sealed all through the ages, slave to the plough, pissing on wool to keep myself warm, frying lice on the Somme. The world was full of real nightmares, worse nightmares than labyrinthine libraries. I was lucky. Lady Fortune had offered me a sniff at her horn, I had paperbacks and Everyman editions. I just wanted a chance to picture success, that's all. I envied mountain climbers – at least mighty Everest has a peak, and you could stand right on top of it.

Sometimes I would pick up some book on prisons or hurricanes or The Beatles or whatnot and flick through it – usually out of boredom or enticed by good cover design – and I would immediately get this feeling of urgency that I couldn't shake off, this feeling that I was wasting time with mediocrity. There's nothing more crippling than being immersed in mediocrity. It terrified me.

Simon came to see me at the library one afternoon. I was tidying up the notice board, pinning up posters that announced new publications. He handed a couple of hardbacks to a clerk, then tapped me on the shoulder, gave me a big grin and pointed at one of the posters. On it was a picture of a woman with a rolling pin. It said, "An Evening with Maureen, OUT NOW!"

"Why would anyone borrow *that* when they could be reading *Anna Karenina*?" Simon asked.

"I guess Judy would suspect escapism." I hadn't read *Anna Karenina*. I couldn't cope with the knowledge that it would've taken me the same time as three books, maybe more. I couldn't face forfeiting two books, maybe even four if I counted *The Old Man and the Sea*. I just couldn't, even if the reward was a grasp of the meaning of life. But I didn't say.

"The unbearable burden of freedom," Simon added.

"Chasing freedom To, forgetting to grapple with freedom From."

"And no one wants the freedom to enter a dark house without a hand to hold and a light to guide them." Simon smiled, a full, loving smile. We could feel Judy's presence. We could always feel Judy's presence.

"The only way out," Simon said, "is to avoid reading stuff by anyone who's still alive."

"That's quite radical," I said.

"Perhaps. But I seem to be in good company only when I'm in the company of the dead. Present company excluded, of course."

"Of course." Well, I thought, at least he doesn't think I'm dead.

As we spoke, I saw the spirit of superiority behind Simon's eyes. I knew I had it too, and I liked it. We were special, which meant *I* was special. The whole world was living by spurious celebrities and starchy Blairites, false idols and cardboard Messiahs – but not us, not me. I was going to live by profound poetry and Great Masters, by insight, by the visionary wisdom of the dead. I had got it. Fuck the living! Fuck the lot of them with their squirts, their cappuccinos, their health and safety and their toasted paninis. Fuck their French onion soup, their sergeant majors, their counterfeit Apollos. Blow all that to high heavens! And damn them all into Hell. I've got it. *I* have got it.

Of course I didn't know about hubris. I hadn't read about hubris. The working classes are not taught about hubris. We probably don't need to know – unless one of us finds a way out, then he'd better make sure he's up to speed on Ancient Greece.

Later that day Simon went to pick up Judy and we attended a reading at the British Library, something on literary criticism by a tubby guy called Adam Norther. Literary criticism. What a pompous name. Some elite club whose members fancy themselves as intellectually able to criticize Shakespeare or T.S. Eliot when they couldn't write in a lifetime what either of those two jotted down while taking a piss in the woods. The depths of their arrogance baffled me. And the way they dressed matched their phoniness. The men usually had a neck beard and always made a point of wearing corduroy – like working men, though they'd never done an hour of manual labour in their lives – while the women wore loose, lifeless clothes, hippy scarves and naff hairdos, as if their intellectual mediocrity was all they needed to attract interest. So, no, I didn't go for the reading, nor for the fashion sense. I went for the good company and the free cheese and wine. Ok, if I'm entirely honest I also went because Simon and Judy's invitation made me feel like a true intellectual, so I guess I too was a bit of a phoney and so I almost – almost – deserved to pay the free-entry price: two hours of literary egomania.

Adam Norther claimed the full price, he made sure of it. He blathered on and on about his book, how it revealed all about *The Little Prince*. He had the balls to call his work "a literary theory." You know you're dealing with smoke and mirrors when you see those two words next to each other. Guessing games can be fun, of course, but when you start calling them "theories" you know you've become an insufferable pretence. But most baffling of all were those people who *bought* Adam Norther's book. I mean, you can write a book about any old tosh, all you need is a typewriter and some time to waste, but people actually *buying* it? Why would anyone want to read about someone talking about *The Little Prince* when you could actually just *read The Little Prince*? I'd rather buy a book on coffins or stray cats or a limping donkey. At least you might learn something about coffins or stray cats… There was no risk of learning anything from Adam Norther's self-delusion. Well, except the depths of Adam Norther's self-delusion, I imagine you could learn quite a bit about that if you were interested in that sort of thing. You could learn, for example, that he spent years writing about *The Little Prince*. Why would anyone do that? A mediocre intellect, sure, but why do *that* with it? If you must produce mediocrity, then produce mediocrity that you can call your own, write a book of toilet humour or the first Great British Guide to Concrete Mixing or whatnot; don't vomit all over other people's toil.

I was furious, and the more Adam Norther's jaw kept moving the more worked up I got, which made me even more furious, because it proved that Adam Norther's jaw was actually having some sort of effect and wasn't therefore entirely insignificant.

Judy pointed out that Germaine Greer spent a lot of time writing about writing, so maybe I was missing something. I don't think Judy had any idea what that something might be, but she gave Greer the benefit of the doubt. I didn't. I was sure if someone was missing something on this one, then *she* was. Just like when she called me a rapist – Greer that is. She didn't even know me and she called me a fucking rapist, just like that. I couldn't believe it. I didn't want to believe it. But there it was, in black and white. All men are rapists, that's what she wrote, and I'm a man, so… you do the maths. The gall of some people. And I'd even *bought* that rancorous manual of hers – I wanted to know women's plight, to understand. A word of advice folks: if someone is trying to understand you, don't begin by throwing criminal accusations at them, it tends to cripple their good will.

And what of men who may feel an urge to rape but fight it with all their will because they believe it's wrong? They needn't bother, apparently, they're rapists anyways. Judy defended Greer, of course. Something to do with it being "time to get angry". Greer was angry apparently, so that makes it ok to accuse people of being criminals based on their sexual attributes alone. I wondered whether Judy or Greer would smile knowingly if I were to call all women whores when I'm angry. And being a whore isn't even a crime, mind… – so I expect they should put a hand on my shoulder, give it a little squeeze and encourage me to be bolder in my indiscriminate accusations. Maybe a pat on the back even, a little show of camaraderie in the anger-makes-it-all-ok enterprise. I didn't say that. Greer was one of Judy's heroes, and you didn't mock Judy's heroes, not if you valued your sanity – or your testicles.

All the while Adam Norther went on and on about the red rose, how it *clearly* symbolized love and *obviously* signified pain – it appeared Adam Norther believed that the presence of adverbs made statements magically true – and how the fox *manifestly* symbolized de Saint-Exupéry's conscience, as well as apparently symbolizing anything else that Adam Norther cared to think up. Just like that. No need for evidence or experimentation. No double-blind trials. Any old thing that whizzed across Adam Norther's vacant skull was good to go.

What the fuck did Adam Norther know about what was

going on in de Saint-Exupéry's mind anyway? Nothing, that's what. He knew nothing just like the rest of us. Except that the rest of us were not standing on a podium in the British Library pretending to be experts in telepathic communication with deceased French aviators. Most people didn't do that, most people had either too much decency or not enough presumption. But not Adam. Adam stood up, raised his head, stuck his chest out and masturbated in public – for two long hours. He threw around phoney words like "tropes" and "constructs" and all that fashionable nonsense. He talked about literary formulae as if he knew something we didn't, and he did it with pride, as if soiling literature with his ego was some sort of service to humanity.

Then, just before 9 p.m., Adam Norther stepped down from the podium. Simon and Judy applauded. I picked up a glass of free wine, drank it, said my goodbyes, and decided that I would go to the Rising Sun for a pint – and to see if I could get myself a woman. I bet Adam Norther never seriously entertained that possibility.

40

WEDNESDAY NIGHT was gay night at the Out Bar. Kevin and I couldn't face going home so we went over for a drink after Liam chucked us out of the Sun.

Gus decided not to join us. "You're not going home?" he said as we took a left on Goodge Street.

"Home?" I said. "What home?"

"Oh, you don't have a home to go to?"

"I have a room, in a house. Well, I say 'have' but I don't, do I… So, there is a room in a house. Nobody to go home to. No home. Just a house with a room in it."

Gus smiled knowingly, but there was guilt in his eyes. I think he felt guilty that he had asked, guilty that he had forced me to take a still of that emotion and show it to him.

"Wherever we lay our hats, gentlemen," said Kevin, "wherever we lay our hats."

That night our hats got laid at the Out Bar. We didn't.

We arrived just after 11.30 p.m. and went straight to the bar.

"Whisky chasers?" Vikki asked.

We knew Vikki from our Friday visits. She usually worked the floor but was shift manager on gay night. She was the personification of a lesbian stereotype: fat, butch, clipped short hair, webs of tattoos pouring out of sleeveless vests, usually camouflage or some other military thing. Tonight was khaki.

"Dancing Queen" was blasting through the speakers and people were shifting to the dance floor, cramming onto the small space like overexcited sheep. It was the best time to be sitting at the bar.

"Fancy seeing you on a Wednesday," said Vikki.

"It was too early to go home," I said.

"You sure you're not on the turn?" Vikki enjoyed making guys uncomfortable, but I liked it. I was fascinated by the idea of quasi-intimacy with a lesbian; a connection, the lingering possibility of bending one's sexuality with someone, *for* someone; a man and a woman yearning for a wish to be intimate with each other, prohibited by instinct. Ruthless. SLAM! Forbidden intimacy. The ultimate frontier, an involuntary orgy of sexual numbness and cerebral desire.

Vikki was one of the most unattractive women I knew, and yet our flirting was real, we both enjoyed stepping out of our usual spaces and relished each other's reactions – toying like cats with a piece of string, not really wishing to catch what we played with.

Vikki handed us our pints. "The way you danced to Gloria Gaynor last time round has made some impact. People have been talking."

"That's what people do," said Kevin.

"It may be more to do with your double shots than with our music taste," I said.

"You know the rules: single shots only in mixers. Not my fault you drink straight liquor."

It wasn't a rule. She just liked to see us dancing to Gloria Gaynor. Or Abba. Or Queen. And she knew double shots would get us there faster, usually around midnight. Not that we put up much of a fight; ambiguity can be an attractive game, the natural step up from promiscuity.

Vikki walked over to our side of the bar to pick up a couple of empty glasses. As she walked past me, she brushed the side of her huge breasts against my arm, glancing at me sideways with a prankish look on her face: "If I ever turned, it would be for you."

"Oh, favouritism, uh. How about me?" said Kevin.

Vikki looked at Kevin with eyes like white hot metal. "Kevin," she said slowly, "it's because of men like *you* that I became a lesbian."

"What, aspiring engineers?"

They both laughed nervously. Kevin downed his whisky. I have no idea why Vikki was so angry with him, but that seemed harsh. He could be insensitive sometimes, all truth tellers are, but Vikki was no snowflake and I couldn't imagine her getting worked up by anything Kevin – or anyone else – might have said. Maybe he had tried it on with her. Maybe he had crossed a line. I never did find out, and Kevin swore he didn't have a clue.

41

THERE WAS a knock on my door. It was Terry.

He handed me a fat roll of twenty-pound notes. Must've been about £500 – what the Deptford locals called "a monkey".

"Hide this for me, will you?" He'd had a good night at the casino. His face looked ecstatic and terrified at the same time.

"Why don't you hide it yourself?" I said.

"If I keep it... it won't last long. Hide it, and only give me twenty quid at a time. And only when I'm sober."

"Ok. But count it first. I don't want any funny business."

He counted it. £20 shy of a monkey.

Terry handed me the roll and left. I shut the door and walked to the wardrobe. I grabbed one of the corners and shifted it a little to the left, then lifted a bit of carpet and stuffed the cash underneath. I pushed the wardrobe back into place, but one of the doors wouldn't close. As I was trying to stick a bit of cardboard under it to jam it shut, I heard the phone ring.

We didn't have a regular phone, just a payphone screwed to the wall at the end of the corridor. The coin slot was jammed, so it was only good for receiving calls. No one answered. I hopped downstairs and picked up the receiver.

"Good morning, sir, how are you today?" It was a woman's voice. Young. I knew she didn't give a toss how I was, but my brain couldn't help firing off a tiny spark on hearing those kind words from a female voice. Fake kindness is still kindness.

"I've just hidden a monkey under the wardrobe. You?"

"Oh, sir, where did you find a monkey?" She was phoning from some godforsaken call centre in the Philippines. Different currency over there. She thought I'd stuffed a small primate under my bedroom furniture.

"My housemate gave it to me. He won it at the casino."

"Sir, are you mocking me?"

"I wouldn't dare."

"In that case, allow me to introduce you to our new mobile phone offers. Do you have a mobile phone, sir?"

"I don't."

"Ok, ok..." I could hear her typing in confusion. "We are expanding our networks, and as a one-time only offer we're giving away fifty free mobile phones. Give me your name and address and I'll enter you into our prize draw."

"You should know my name and address, you called *me*."

"Well, if you could just confirm your name and address, I'll enter you into our prize draw."

Whatever possessed me to pick up that bloody phone?

Phones are a constant one-way window into the pits of Hell. You're sitting there minding your own business, musing about life, about things not being too bad when all is said and done and BANG! a hunchbacked demon with jaundiced eyes jumps in through the window and takes a shit on your breakfast.

"Sir, you're not interested?"

"I'm not interested."

"You're not interested in winning a mobile phone?" She talked as though she was offering me my very own fountain of eternal happiness.

"That's right."

"But, sir, why not? Why are you not interested in a brand-new mobile phone?"

"Mobile phones are evil."

"Evil? But, sir –"

"They give you brain cancer. I'd rather do without."

"Brain cancer? Where did you hear that?"

"I didn't hear it, I read it."

"Where did you read it?"

"A magazine."

"Ah…"

"Yep."

"But, sir, I assure you that *our* mobile phones do not give you brain cancer."

"You shouldn't make promises you can't keep."

"Have a good day." Click. She forgot the "sir".

Ten minutes later there was another knock on my door. Terry again.

"Alright, mate, can I have 40 quid? I need to fill up the car."

"You said I should only give you £20 at a time."

"No, no, I'm not gambling it, I need it for petrol, I've got a night shift."

"At the barber's?"

"No, man, I'm doing minicab work at the weekend for some extra cash."

I gave him the £40.

He was back half an hour later.

"Look, man, I need another £40, one of the rear tyres is giving up, I need to have it checked."

"At the bookies?"

"No, man, I've got a night shift, I need to get the tyre sorted."

He was back again an hour later.

"Look, man, I think the battery is shot, I need another forty quid."

"Here, take the lot." I gave him the roll of twenties.

"Thanks, man, thanks. You're a mate!"

The next day I looked at Terry's car tyres. Threadbare. It had been a good night for the bookies.

42

I STOOD BEHIND her as she stuffed a pair of tights into a brown handbag. Suddenly the whole night seemed like an unnecessarily contrived form of masturbation. Pleasantries, dinner, drinks. Feeble gateways to a few seconds of dopamine. The way to Hell is probably paved with pleasantries. And dopamine, definitely dopamine. I might as well have been a coke head. In fact, coke might even have been an improvement, but it was not an option, not on my salary. She shut the door and I felt sad and relieved at the same time.

Steph was a decent woman. I didn't want to break her heart, but I had no choice. Attraction leaves you no choice. Lack of attraction leaves you even less.

We'd been going out on and off for a few months now. One, long, one-night stand. Why did I hang around this long? I think I'd become addicted to her attraction for me.

Steph had ended up at my place less than two hours after we first met. She kept looking at her watch, worrying that she'd miss the last bus. Until we kissed, that is. Then she transformed.

Became inflamed. A wild beast that had been starved and caged for years and then suddenly set free in the middle of the savanna. I was dazzled by her intense desire. Her hands moved up and down my body in a craze, her tongue working away helter-skelter. I could see the struggle in her eyes, the primeval fuel running through her brain, the futility of her inner protestations as she wrestled with her own desires. But she couldn't stop herself. This uncontrollable attraction turned me on, injected an unknown energy in me – arousal inciting arousal. I'd always been suspicious of women who had rules about sex on the first night, especially if they stuck to them. That presence of mind, that following of rules over instinct, it's a sign of a woman who's not hungry for Man.

Steph was ravenous. She later told me she felt embarrassed at her behaviour on that first night. She even apologized. It wasn't an act, she really did worry about her inability to keep that explosive thirst for manhood under control. The irony was that her loss of control was probably the only thing I found attractive in her.

I was never crazy about Steph, but the sex was ok, conversation was mostly effortless, and her orgasms were generous. Everything is easier with a woman who comes freely; it takes the cloud away, then you can really focus on the fucking, like it was meant to be, like in the Serengeti. But even that wasn't enough now. I wanted a woman who made my soul spin, and Steph just wasn't that kind of woman. You could rely on her not to make your anything spin. Dear old Steph.

I always used a condom. I had a mission to fulfil and knew that screaming babies weren't likely to be welcome in Charing Cross Library. But condoms didn't have an easy life with Steph. She had this feisty, determined pussy that grabbed you, clung on like it was in free fall and my cock was the only anchor keeping it from plunging into the abyss. A combative, unforgiving space, air spurting out at every stroke, a sexual war of lust and physics, an unrelenting grip, a vice of vice. The condom never stood a chance.

It was a Saturday evening. I was on top of Steph stroking away and her pussy was holding on tight, gripping, working overtime. I was trying to build in some fluidity with my strokes, but the resistance was too great. I only managed jerky movements, as though my penis had the hiccups. Then Steph's breathing became faster. Her pussy started to pulsate, thumping at me every few seconds, getting stronger and stronger with every cycle. I tried to carry on like a horse ploughing through knee-deep mud but I eventually got out of sync. She must've felt me slow down, "Don't stop!" she cried. How do you not stop when you're struggling to stay in? Seconds later she came. Her muscles contracted so hard that she squeezed me right out like toothpaste from a tube. I glanced at the condom; it looked like a piece of cling film after three weeks in the fridge, all wrinkled up and with a gash on top.

I showed Steph her latest casualty. "Looks like we have a problem," I said.

Apparently it wasn't the first time. Steph became sad and I felt sorry for her. It was a real shame, being hampered by something that was so beautifully well engineered, so perfectly adept at its job. Afflicted with too much perfection.

Steph started crying, went on a rant of desperation about being cursed with razor blades in her pussy. She needn't have worried; the condom wasn't sliced – it was strangled.

I put on some clothes and went to the local pharmacy to buy the day-after pill. It was the same pharmacy where I'd bought the condoms the day before, and the same stubby guy in a white coat stood behind the counter. He gave me a casual grin. "Plan A didn't work then?"

"Plan A was doomed from the start. Unless you have merchandise that can survive a vacuum."

"I can't say that I do."

"Then we have no plan A."

He handed me the overpriced ball of hormones. I paid and walked out.

* * *

As luck would have it, Steph broke up with me two weeks later, some dumb idea about me wanting to fuck a brunette. She meant Gemma. Steph always pulled stuff like that at regular intervals. You could set your Swiss watch by her. The spiel went more or less like this: "If you want to fuck other women just tell me. You know, I'll understand if that's what you want, but tell me and let's be done with this, don't just go screwing around on me." Low self-esteem I suppose, but it was beginning to get old, so I didn't argue when she thought she had caught me sneaking around with Gemma.

But there was no sneaking around. Gemma had become quite close with Mrs Alaoui, and she started helping out in the shop at weekends. On Sunday afternoons Gemma and I would sit on the stairs for a chat while she took a break from the mop. She would light a cigarette, hand me a beer and we'd talk. Gemma was a simple woman, only worried about paycheques, rent, boyfriend. We never got into any deep discussion. There was a plain, direct honesty about her, the kind of honesty you might get from a loyal handmaid. Those mundane, superficial exchanges were like a hot bath for the brain; no need for mental focus, no pressure to sharpen the intellect, no juggling, no jostling to be head clown in the circus of charm and seduction, no fear of unfulfilled potential. Just words. Words for words' sake.

The irony is that sex with Gemma never crossed my mind. Worse still, in nearly a year of dinner dates and afternoon sex with Steph I was never involved with another woman. Absolute uncredited monogamy. And so it turned out that the scenario conjured up by Steph's fears was much worse, and more exciting, than reality had been. Not that the power of fear needed any proof (all the Greats had known of it), but here it was anyway.

I thought about Marlowe and I thought about Milton. I even thought a little about Judy thinking of Forster. Maybe it was time to make time. Then I thought about Lauren.

43

WHAT WAS IT about Lauren? I couldn't shake her off. There was that killer smile, of course. That supreme presence, gently unfurling. It began almost by stealth, spreading from nowhere, then suddenly flooding her cheeks, and with them anything and everything within a twenty-foot radius. It was the pinnacle of unfairness, the sort of thing that robs you of rationality.

And there was her walk. Sheer sex emerged from each tiny muscle and soaked every single move she made. A pure, distilled well of seduction.

But most bewitching of all was the way she placed her head on my chest after we'd made love. Gentle, effortless, yielding. You can tell a lot about a woman from the way her head lies on your chest. The erratic heads that weigh a ton on you and you can't wait to get out from under them, from under *her*. Or the restless heads, the heads that keep poking at your flesh and bones like a mad woodpecker, bruising your body a little and your spirit a whole lot. And then, once in a while, you find one that makes you wonder how such a large and rigid body part could possibly feel so soft and feather-like. This, I believed, was the sign of a truly kind woman. It was a belief that had served me well in the past, helped me to weed out bad ideas before it was too late. Even a woman who had kept her real self well hidden would eventually betray her nature and deliver unmistakable messages the moment her head touched my chest. The kindness, the malaise, the craziness or whatever else might've been carefully packed away deep in her core, would all come to the surface and be laid bare. Unambiguous. Magnified. Her innards spread on an operating table at the centre of a ruthless theatre. No escape, bright lights bearing down relentlessly.

But this was Lauren, and nothing was ever to be taken at face value with Lauren. Nothing was what it seemed, not even this innately primordial action. What if this too had been rehearsed? I wondered how much practice it took to make something so subtle feel so natural.

44

THAT SUNDAY Judy grilled me about Steph.

"You really *must* stop getting involved with these women you meet in bars," she said, then to Simon: "How does he do it?"

"I don't know, I presume he switches himself off."

"Yes, he must switch himself off, mustn't he…"

They were talking as if I weren't there.

Then Judy turned to me: "How do you find those women, how do you *choose* them?" She asked the question like a physician might ask details about embarrassing symptoms.

"I don't know," I said, "I look around, see who's there, strike up a conversation at the bar… or just put my arm around them, take them to the dance floor."

"My God, Si, it's worse than I thought!" There was alarm in her voice.

Simon agreed, naturally.

I didn't take it too seriously. "You know what they say," I told her, "when in Rome…"

"Well don't go to fucking Rome then!"

"What else do you suggest I do, put on my best frock and sit there waiting for a nice woman to chat me up? That's hardly going to happen. I have no choice but to *act*."

Judy turned to Simon again: "He's Miller, isn't he…?" she said in a flat voice.

"Trying to become what he doesn't want to be?" suggested Simon.

"No, not that Miller, dear – the other one." Judy's eyes were glazed over, transfixed, as though she was facing an invincible opponent, a tyrant. "He has the books and the dream, and now he is foraging for cunt."

Simon replied with a long, drawn out "Ye-es", his voice dropping a tone or two. My trial had begun. "You really must stop, Dak…"

The prying and probing went on for a while, then Judy

shouted, "Grub's up!" and everything else was put on hold as though we were actors in a play at the end of the first act. Simon went to fetch a bottle of wine. Judy came in from the kitchen carrying a big casserole dish with a large oven glove wrapped around it.

"Coq au vin," she announced. "My Neil's favourite."

She spooned a big helping onto my plate. "I used to make it for Neil in the summer, while he sat in the garden smoking his pipe and reading the Sunday papers. Afterwards we would drink tea and brandy and fuck by the fireplace as the sunlight came in through the French doors."

An unforgiving melancholy grabbed me tight; I too wanted the Sunday papers, a pipe, a wife who made me coq au vin. Even the French doors seemed irresistibly appealing.

Judy put down the casserole and sat at the table. My inner state must've been quite visible. "I know," Judy said in a motherly tone, "I know you want to fall in love, marry, maybe have a child – and maybe you will. In due course. But of course, in true Dak fashion, it has to be NOW!" She gave a roaring laugh. "You know what your problem is? You're obsessed with having a sex life," she tried to hold back her laughter this time – but couldn't. She was in a beautifully good mood, teasing me and Simon as if we were two old geezers and she an unruly young woman. "Look at Simon, he has no need for a sex life!" Simon made a face of pretend annoyance. "Maybe you should consider a sex life, Si, it might do you good, help you overcome your parental curse." She turned to me, whispering, as though trying to exclude Simon from the exchange: "Simon's parents had a sexless marriage, you see. He's been traumatized ever since." She laughed again, then faced Simon, continuing in a normal voice, "I mean, you have my love, of course, but you should do some fucking too. You know, seeing as we aren't fucking." She paused, then turned serious for a moment: "Si... why aren't we fucking?"

Simon thought for a while, then replied, "I don't know, dear. I suppose it's the age difference."

"Ah, yes," said Judy with conviction, turning back to me, "the age difference.

"At any rate, I'm actually glad you're not into fucking, Si – sex is in a bad state, it's all about the pornography nowadays. Better stay away from it." Then Judy gave one of those waves of her hand which indicated that the topic had been discussed to her satisfaction, signalling the end of the conversation. "Si, be a dear and put the kettle on, will you? And rinse the good teapot, I feel festive today."

Simon went to the kitchen and filled the kettle. He took a bottle of milk out of the fridge and poured some into a little jug – he too felt festive today. Then he looked for the good teapot. A solid walnut door that we knew to be beautiful and believed to be useful slipped from Simon's hand, sending a few teacups rattling. Judy called out over her shoulder, "Do be careful with that cabinet, darling. It's very dear to me – Neil used to fuck me over it after supper." Then she laughed. We all laughed. A twinkling laughter, the laughter that bursts out through your eyes at the sight of something profoundly timeless.

I was glad they'd got my trial over with at the beginning of the afternoon; now I could sit here in peace, enjoy the tea. Milk, no sugar. I could talk *with* them, be *with* them, soak up that feeling of being an intellectual adoptee in the house of life, love, and literature.

Simon came back with the good teapot and poured us all a cup. I sat proudly in what had been Neil's armchair. Judy talked about going to the National, about marvellous productions and ghastly productions and about Helen Mirren being variable.

45

I WAS USUALLY quite methodical in keeping my physical and intellectual endeavours separate, I knew how unforgiving the working classes can be. But sometimes you are in a hurry and a little tired and you get sloppy. This was one of those times.

I arrived at the garage just after 6 p.m., took off my rucksack and put it in one of the crates – we didn't have lockers, just wooden crates with time slots scrawled on them in automotive paint. You arrived between six and seven you put your stuff in the 6 p.m. crate. No need for padlocks, your stuff was safe there. The same cannot be said for your reputation though. Or your ribs.

I was doing some barbell rows when I felt a tap on the shoulder. It was Ray, holding up a copy of *1984*: "Are you some kind of poof?"

Ray was a welterweight contender – the Cannonball – Lewisham's new promise. Legendary for having knocked out a heavyweight during a sparring session, a big beefy guy thirty pounds heavier than him. Ray had such speed in his punches that he made up for the lack of weight behind them. That's why they called him the Cannonball. That's the thing with cannonballs, they are not as big or as heavy as a fridge or an oak tree, but they can do more damage. They come at you at speed.

So even though I could tell that Ray was *half* joking, I was still more than a little worried – I wasn't sure what the other half involved. I tried to explain I was on my way to bettering myself, but it didn't go down well.

"What, to become a better poof?" he smirked. Poor bastard. Ray thought all a man needed was a pair of gloves and a heavy bag. But no jockstrap can guard you against the monumental kicks in the balls that will come your way if you fail to read Orwell. Or Marx. He definitely needed Marx more than he needed those daily punches to the head. But his balls... his balls desperately needed Orwell.

Ray shouted over his shoulders, "Hey, Clint, we've got a contender!"

Clint was Ray's sparring partner. This did not look good. But I had no choice, I needed the garage. I needed a library for my body as much as I needed one for my mind, and I couldn't afford a gym membership. I stretched out my arms. They laced me up and I stepped into the ring.

Ray rang the bell and Clint began to dance around. His head bobbed left and right and he threw a few practice punches at the air. I tried to mirror his movements, looking like a ham-fisted shadow. I kept my gloves up and fended off a couple of jabs. Then another. Then the jabs started coming thick and fast. I squeezed my head between the gloves and backpedalled, retreating towards the ropes. Suddenly my flank was on fire. Left hook to the liver. It felt as though all my internal organs had shifted to one side, banging against each other like crazed bumper cars, squeezing lifeblood and bodily secretions out of each other. I flinched, desperately trying not to piss myself. I never imagined three minutes could last so bloody long.

I knew I had to get out of the ropes. I did a little shuffle with my feet that I'd learned playing football as a teenager; it worked. Clint moved to the left and I hopped over to the right. I was out – just. I figured I'd be better off centre ring, where I had more room to step around his punches. That seemed to work. I sidestepped a couple of straight punches and felt a second hook graze my side as I moved out of its way. Then Clint gave me an opening. I threw a right cross, really putting my hips into it. I caught him in the ribs, saw him slowing right down. He'd felt it.

Not for long. A few seconds later Clint was back charging at me. Jab, jab, one-two. I shifted my trunk round an uppercut and caught a glimpse of Clint's corner. Ray had a big grin on his face – the bookworm was gonna get it and he was gonna get it good. A short guy in a white t-shirt was shouting like a madman, spit drooling from his mouth like a rabid dog. I think it might have been Ray's brother, but I couldn't tell for sure, my vision was getting more blurry by the second. A small crowd had gathered on the top side of the ring and I saw two men in overalls walking in from the automotive garage. Some bald guy in a green jumper started taking bets: I was 9/1 to make it to the second round.

I didn't. My centre ring idea saved me from the body shots, but Clint was no mug. He'd been roughing up young contenders for the best part of ten years and knew how to hurt a man. I thought about Lauren; she knew how to hurt a man. Then Clint threw a couple of light jabs followed by a combination. I ducked and turned, then ducked again, lost composure, my cover-up came wide open. My teeth rattled and my neck stretched backwards like a rubber band, pulling my ribcage along with it. He'd caught me just under the left cheekbone. I went down like a sack of second-hand paperbacks.

The bus ride that night seemed endless. Every pothole was like another hook to the liver. It turned out Lewisham Borough Council also knew how to hurt a man. When the bus hopped over the hill at the Black Horse, I felt like I was going to puke my insides over the priority seats. C'mon, hang in there. Nearly home.

I hung in there for three more minutes. Then I staggered off the bus, took a few faltering steps on the pavement and hugged the bus-stop sign. Breathe.

My subscription to the body library was safe for a while, and I never again allowed my two worlds to come together. It wasn't easy, though. I felt like a bigamist.

46

MAYA WAS one of the office assistants. She had a timid smile and beautifully symmetrical breasts. From time to time the office manager would send her to the post room to pick up some leaflets. Maya would knock quietly, walk in and look at me with indecent green eyes that seemed out of place on her kind-looking, almost virginal face. Then she would lean on the counter, letting that cleavage hang. So unfair. That sort of stuff can cripple a man.

The guys at the front office drooled after her. There was this clerk who stood at the issue desk and looked at Maya with big pathetic puppy eyes as though she held the secret to eternal life and would she please, please consider giving him a peek. It was nauseating and heart-breaking at the same time.

I took the simple approach. I just talked to her and looked at her in the eye until she lowered her gaze, left her staring towards that hanging cleavage. I smiled genuine smiles, let her know I was dangerous enough to fuck her till she passed out but gentle enough to stay the night. It worked.

Except that Maya, well, Maya wasn't one for staying the night. It turned out she lived in a bedsit in Haringey with her boyfriend, Carl or Clive or something. I became her bit on the side and she had no intention of leaving Colin or whatever his name was. Maybe I'd overdone it with the dangerous vibes.

On Friday nights Maya and I would go back to my place after a few drinks at the Out Bar. She had this shyness about her, a veiled modesty of times past. Until the moment her dress came off – then she was a queen and a tiger, a sorceress and a wolf, a nymph, an empress. The transformation knocked me out every time, stupefied me, savagely blinding my mind's eye.

The sexual tension between us was otherworldly, as though we'd fucked in a previous life and were now desperately trying to relive the moment. We would go at each other's flesh like starved eagles, eventually collapsing on the bed, soaked in each other's sweat and barely able to draw a breath. Maya lay there, right arm resting on her forehead, left knee slightly bent, bathing in the intensity of my gaze. An intensity that came from deep inside my head with a force I could barely stand, a persistent thrust, an unstoppable urge, my brain cells wanting to gush out and lunge at Maya through my eye sockets. It was frightening.

Her skin was marble, and her labia had an ever so slight hint of pink. A cheeky tuft of blonde hair decorated her pubis with just the tiniest whisper of strawberry. I could've looked at her naked body for hours. Until 2 a.m., that is. That's when Maya smiled a forced smile and collected her clothes off the floor. I sheepishly walked down to Mr Alaoui's shop and called her a cab. Deptford to Haringey. Heavy words, beating down like sledgehammers on an autopsy table.

Every night I spent with Maya warped my soul a little, and Judy could sense it. One Sunday I went over to Judy's a handful of hours after Maya had methodically adhered to her curfew. Maya's punctuality was a punch in the gut; cold diligence nonchalantly trampling over her warm heart. Or what I believed to be a warm heart. Maybe her heart wasn't that warm after all. Or maybe she didn't have a heart. That, too, seemed possible.

"You need to stop this nonsense," Judy said. "That wretched woman cuckolding that poor man and fucking God knows who else. Really, Dak…" The disappointment in her eyes was a shard through my skull. "You're lonely. And you're still recovering from that heavy blow you received from Lauren."

"Yeah, ok," I conceded, "Lauren leaving shook me a little, but recovery sounds a bit much…"

"She *denied* herself to you! That's not something from which one may recover quickly. You may never recover at all. You've been hurt, don't you see that?"

I didn't really, not to the extent Judy had in mind.

"And so you keep stumbling into love affairs and commitment prematurely. With all sorts. With an immature little thing who indulges so blindly in her daddy issues. Don't you dare laugh! This is serious. Of course I can't say that *scientifically*," – she made a mocking gesture, and I briefly resented her for it – "but it's very, very likely. Just take a good look at how she treats you…"

"But –"

"What do you know about her? Nothing!"

"But I love her!"

"Oh do shut up. You love having your cock in her mouth, but that's hardly the same thing…"

I felt miserable. Judy made a subtle waving gesture with her left hand. Very subtle, as if my protestations weren't even worth dismissing. Then she sank back into her armchair and burst into laughter. But I knew she was angry at me. I should've walked out of there, turned around and walked out like a man, but I couldn't. That was the thing with Judy, I allowed myself to be seduced by the vigour inherent in her anger, the righteousness of outrage, and the allure of being accepted.

"You're committing to a woman you know nothing about," she continued, "and I mean facts, both psychological and ordinarily factual; schooling, parenting, siblings, friendships, previous lovers, likes and dislikes." she spoke calmly, but her fists were clenched tight by her hips. This mattered.

"Look, Dak, do I have to say it?" She turned to Simon: "Si, I have to say it don't I…"

Simon nodded.

"This thing with this wretched woman, it's intoxicating – of course – but it's also a dead-end. It hasn't the foundations to last. Pack it in, please."

I said nothing.

"You're an intelligent man, and your sex life is so very important; it deserves your contemplative attention. It isn't getting it now, you're all emotions. Emotions and illusion."

Suddenly, as if to prove Judy's point on emotions, I blew up. I screamed like a little boy, told her that she should trust my judgement.

"Oh stop being such a fucking wimp!" she shouted. Judy didn't just know how to build me up, she also knew how to disembowel me. Then, in a calmer voice: "Besides, if I trusted your judgement apropos of women, it would be extraordinarily silly of me, wouldn't it…?"

I couldn't argue with that, so I didn't.

47

I'D BEEN TO a public lecture on the philosophy of science where we learned the difference between the men of method like Newton and Feynman, and the quacks like Freud. Professor Cooper had a way with words and a faultless delivery that had me hooked from the first time I turned up to his lectures. He usually spoke at Senate House, less fashionable and more closely connected to the academic world, but this particular evening he was at the British Library. I made it my goal to attend every single one of his lectures. Well, what I really wanted was to *be* him, but failing that I would have to be content with being his disciple. I stepped off the pavement with a big smile on my face, Cooper's puns rolling around in my head, and a faint sense of achievement sitting in my gut. A cretin in a VW van nearly ran me over on the pedestrian crossing. God knows I love this city, but I swear it's going to be the death of me.

Fifteen minutes later I walked into the Rising Sun, alive. Kevin was in full flow: "Serious, deep conversation, and especially *introspective* conversation is the most intellectually rewarding experience a man can have. But with a woman you want to be intimate with…. Forget it. Deep introspection will kick you out of her bed quicker than fucking her best friend." He chuckled. "At least if you fuck her best friend there's always a possibility that she'd get curious and suggest a threesome. But deep introspection… never – *never*, forgives." He picked up his pint from the bar and took a sip. Hugh tried to do the same but splashed most of it on his shirt, then tried again, succeeded, and ventured an "uh uh…" in Kevin's direction.

Gus played devil's advocate: "Does that mean you've never had a serious conversation with a woman? Come on…"

"Of course it doesn't. I just had to forfeit physical intimacy. Just forget it." Kevin shrugged. It didn't even cross his mind that Gus's question might be a challenge. As far as Kevin was concerned, this was a simple exchange of factual information.

"And that's fine," Kevin continued, "sometimes you don't mind that, sometimes you even *want* that. All I'm saying is, you'd better know it." He took another sip. "And you can see it in her eyes too. They're wide eyes, wide with wonder, like a child's eyes. And that can be beautiful, but they're not wide with *desire*. The lust simply isn't there. Gone. That feminine fire, you know?" Gus and I nodded. "It's *vacant*. It's almost as if the part of a woman's brain that wets her knickers is the same that handles introspection – and it can only do one job at a time." Kevin's voice had a strange combination of sadness and detachment, as though the universe was both cruel and blameless at the same time. "It's like a curse, really," he concluded. Then he picked up his pint again, held it in his hand for a few seconds and took a big gulp. I couldn't help imagining that beer as a kind but futile nurse, tending to a pain that wouldn't be soothed.

My face must've noticeably changed in that moment because Gus gave me a puzzled look, then turned to Kevin and laughed. "Oh Kevin, you kill me sometimes. Come on, you must've had deep conversations with a woman you were intimate with!" Gus could hardly talk, his laughter interfering with his breathing, "What do you do, fuck and talk about the weather?" He gave a loud, self-confident laugh.

"Come along now," Kevin said, looking calm, benevolent, but also fired-up – like a kindly teacher moved by immense passion. He had a natural ability to remain dignified in the face of such brash criticisms. It was humbling. Well, *he* was. "Of course I have, of course you can. Come along now. You can talk deep about poverty, world peace, the Twin Towers or your grandma's childhood. Oh she's going to love *that*. She'll think you're so *sensitive*, so very considerate. But that's not the point." Kevin made a dismissive gesture with his free hand. "Going deep into yourself and digging deep into her *own* self, that's the killer. And it's not a neat killer, either. It's not a *clinical* killer." He waved his hand, emphasizing the finality of this point. Then he leaned in to us, as if wanting to make sure we didn't miss this part: "It's killing by hand grenade." Kevin's voice was so firm and his manner so grave that we stared at him in silence for a few seconds, like lost soldiers awaiting words of salvation from the oracle.

All of a sudden Kevin's face relaxed, like he'd just come out of a trance. He smiled, placed his pint on a stool and spoke again, but in a casual tone: "It brings out the one thing that women can't reconcile with taking their knickers off: insecurity. Yours *and* her own. Double whammy." He laughed, slapping his hand on the bar as if he'd just discovered the God particle. "She'll become coy and jittery, angry even. Anything but wet. It's not her fault, really. It's nobody's fault. It's *primal*, it's uncontrollable. But it's there."

Kevin spoke like a man who saw the truth but took no pleasure in having such privilege. Suddenly he looked tired, almost older, as though he'd just climbed a mountain. Maybe he had.

A little later Kevin raised his pint at us, then concluded, "Thrust deep into introspection or deep inside her, take your pick. It's a bloody shame if you ask me…"

We stood in silence for a while, then we drank up and walked to the bus stop, richer, and with a collective sense of mourning.

48

IT WAS A sunny Friday afternoon. The Rising Sun was packed and Liam had a hard time keeping people on the pavement. "Move over! If you end up under a bus they'll close me down for a week!"

Gus smirked at him. "But then we could have the wake here, with an open bar! That'd help people forget *and* it'd make up for lost revenue."

"Listen, I'll tell you one more time, move away from the fucking road! I have no intention of spending the night wiping your pea-size brains off the kerb." Then he turned to a couple who were standing at the corner with one foot off the pavement, "Oi, none of that! I don't want NONE of that!"

"Sorry, Liam," said the guy sheepishly.

"Oh you will be if you get run over."

Gus was pushing it now: "Hey, Liam, if we get run over I bet the Ol' Bill will make you pay for the funeral!"

Liam's eyebrows did a backward somersault. "I'll shove you in a bin liner and chuck you out with the empty bottles!"

"That's harsh…"

"Oh don't worry, I'll use an official liner, with a City of Westminster sticker on it an' all."

"Ah…"

"Yeah, that way I won't get fined by the council, innit."

Then Liam elbowed his way through the crowd and went back inside.

Kevin came out with a round: Pils and two lagers.

"No Maya tonight?" he said.

"Nope. She couldn't make it. Her boyfriend's having a party."

"Boyfriend?"

"Yeah…"

"Is he a bonus or a problem?"

"A problem."

"Ah. Does she know?"

"She knows."

"No change?"

"No change."

"I bet there were tears too, uh?"

"There were tears. She told me she wants to be with me but can't leave him, can't do that to him. And there were tears."

"She can't do that to him but she can fuck you behind his back? C'mon mate, she's playing with you. You've got to get out of there."

"She says she loves me."

"Do you believe her?"

"I don't know. She seems sincere."

"Oh, sincere," he said in a mocking voice. "That's a big word." Kevin and Gus laughed. That annoyed me. To be honest, I would've laughed too, but I was feeling defeated so I got annoyed instead.

"Do you want to be with her?" Kevin asked. "I mean, do you want her to leave him?"

"Yeah, but at the moment it's a game of cat and mouse."

"A *game*?" he said in disbelief. "It's only a game if you're the cat! You know what happens to the mouse, right?"

"I –"

"The mouse dies. The mouse always dies. So yeah, for the cat it's a game alright. For the mouse it's a matter of life and death. Which one are *you*?" He shoved his finger in my face. There was no need to answer, we all knew which one I was, and the odds weren't good.

I tried to make out I was cool about it. "Don't be such a stick in the mud," I told him. "Cat-and-mouse games can be fun."

"You're missing the point. No one in their right mind wants to be the mouse. No one. You've got to get out. If she was going to leave him she would've already. Cut your losses. Get out."

"It's easy for you to say, you have no passion!" I spoke in anger and regretted it immediately. My head was thumping. I'm such a prick.

Kevin looked at me with a faint smile. "Passion is all well and good when you need an explosion," he said, "but then what? Sure, sometimes in life you need to get aboard a rocket and launch yourself forward like some sort of haunted fireball. But it's not always about the launching, mate. Don't forget that sooner or later – if you want to survive – you'll need someone who can *land* the blasted thing."

I was humbled by his words, but that didn't help my restlessness. I needed something to take my mind off this whole mess, and lager wasn't enough. Whisky maybe… or a woman.

49

I ENDED UP going home with a skinny blonde who'd been scrounging drinks all evening. I don't remember her name. It may have been Sheila, or Linda – but I doubt it. At any rate, she turned out to be an old cat lady in the making, with not much making left to do.

The minicab dropped us off just after 1 a.m. We crossed the road and got in through the back. Mr Alaoui's house didn't have a front door, so I usually got in through the shop, but used the rear entrance after closing time. At the rear of the shop was a small backyard with a few clumps of grass and a whole lot of junk scattered across mossy concrete slabs: broken chairs, empty buckets, industrial waste bins, bits of old carpet soaked in rainwater and cat piss. Skinny blonde and I walked across to the door. I sidestepped a pile of broken crockery, stuck my hand in my pocket, pulled out the keys and began to sift through them. Mr Alaoui's cat leapt out of the rubbish bin, walked across a swamp-like piece of green tarpaulin and proceeded to stroke itself on skinny blonde's leg. It was a stinking old cat, a foul creature that Mr Alaoui kept as pest control. Skinny blonde picked it up. Hugged it.

"Do you like cats? I *love* cats!" She shoved that furry mess into my face. I gagged; it reeked of rotten meat and south London sewer rats. Cats, even clean ones, were never my kind of animal. And it's not just their obsession with rodents and dead birds. If I were to create an animal out of all the regrettable traits we find in humans, it would be a cat: arrogant, opportunistic, unjustifiably self-important and shamelessly ungrateful. I think it's fair to say that cats are the devil's deliberate attempt to incite misanthropy. Still, I would've rather hugged Beelzebub himself than Mr Alaoui's cat.

I found the key and unlocked the door. Skinny blonde made cooing noises and rubbed her nose on that four-legged ball of filth. Less than twelve hours ago its snout was buried in a pile of fly-infested guts that Mr Alaoui had been too lazy to clear out. Definitely not my kind of animal. I turned on the light. Skinny blonde put down that walking worm-incubator and we went up the stairs.

"I don't get it; how do you not love cats? They're *so* clever!"

"Not clever enough to have a bath once in a while..."

"Oh but they're very clean animals!" There was obviously something very wrong with this bird's nose.

Then she began to tell me that cats clean themselves with their tongue. The way she said it you would've thought it was some sort of superpower.

"I don't tend to see licking yourself as a form of hygiene..." I said, good will slowly draining out of me.

"Oh but they have a special tongue that –"

"Look, I hate cats, ok?"

"But why? I don't understand!"

There were probably loads of things she didn't understand. Entire libraries filled with stuff completely beyond skinny blonde's understanding.

"They shit everywhere," I said.

"Oh but that's just their nature! They mark their territory! It's actually a sign of their very perceptive nature."

It amazes me how understanding, how continually forgiving a woman can be of this "nature" when it comes to an animal that licks its own arsehole for a hobby. The same woman wouldn't think twice about chucking a man's possessions onto the street if he so much as dared to be himself for an hour.

Judy had warned me about this on a Saturday afternoon as we were leaving the National Gallery. We'd been to see some Hoppers that were temporarily on loan. Those colours blew my mind. All that blue, canvas after canvas awash with blue. And those greens, those opulent greens – sad greens, happy greens, peaceful greens, vengeful greens. I just had to keep looking at them, stare at them. I had to. I didn't know much about art, in fact I knew hardly anything at all, but those paintings kidnapped my mind – and when I got it back it felt cleaner, brighter, like the sun had been let in.

Judy took my arm as we crossed Trafalgar Square. "Yesterday I woke in the middle of the night and felt so well and happy," she said misty-eyed. "I lay there for some time thinking how very fortunate I am, to be having another life since Neil's death, and to be going to the National with two handsome young men of high intelligence and questioning natures."

We stopped at Nelson's Column. Judy turned to face me, slowly, a little unsteady on her feet. "I had such an exciting life with Neil, thirty years of seeking, investigating, disputing, and of course loving. A beautiful archaeological dig of the self. You and Simon are such pleasure to me." She paused, holding back the tears. "It pains me that I have to tell you this again, but I would be a fraud to you if I didn't: you've been hurt." She turned to look for Simon, saw him standing patiently a few yards behind us – he knew the drill – then turned back to me: "It's nothing unusual, it's how a lot of women are behaving, but there's no way you could know it." She shook her head and shifted her balance a little. "There are women who like men, but they're rare. Some, like me, prefer men to women, for personal reasons and utterly unfairly. But most women often bite men who are good to them. We're all sadists if given a chance, and women are no different." She shrugged, lightly, almost as if those words had been pushing down on her shoulders and she was glad to see them gone. "It takes a great act of consciousness to know you want to inflict pain and decide not to do it. It's even worse nowadays; there are so few good men who are prepared to do the work it takes to keep us in check. We're not easy." She steadied herself a little more, leaning against a bollard. The hint of a smile appeared in her eyes. "I'm grateful to my Neil for putting me right when I had that urge to be nasty. He knew how to do it, usually by making me feel deeply ashamed. I'm grateful to him for many other things, of course."

"He sounds like a great man," I said quietly, afraid that I might utter the wrong word and somehow end up soiling Neil's memory.

"He was, and he worked hard at it. He had three men as comrades in the first years of his life with me, all concerned with learning how to be with women. It's the journey of all good men."

Then Judy turned towards where Simon was standing. This time he walked over to join us, and we strolled around Trafalgar a while before taking the train home.

All this happened quite some time before skinny blonde ended up standing in my bedroom, so I should've known better. I shouldn't have been hurt by all that keenness to be loving and understanding of cats more than of men. After all, many women actually *like* cats.

But sometimes knowledge isn't enough. And so I went into a rant, berated skinny blonde for sticking her face in that bag of fleas, called her an idiot, accused her of reviving the plague.

I realized I was ranting. I knew it wouldn't bring about anything good, but I couldn't stop. The more she talked about that stupid cat the more I thought about Kevin, Maya, me being the damned mouse, and the more I hated the furry fucker. It was the sort of hate that wants to leave nothing good behind, the hate of scorched earth and blazing bridges.

The whole thing ripped the mood right out of me. I knew that feeling well. Failure was always only a few feet away, keeping an eye on me just in case I got too comfortable. Sometimes it was a noble teacher, sometimes it was bloody humiliating. Sometimes it was just bloody.

As luck would have it, skinny blonde wasn't planning to stay. "I rang my sister. She offered to come pick me up, so I'll probably leave around 2.30, you know, she's doing me a favour. I don't want to take the piss." How noble. She didn't mind taking the piss when it was her round in the pub. Twice. Some morals she had.

I went to the toilet, urinated, drank some water from the tap. Skinny blonde waited for me in the bedroom. When I walked back in I found her in my side of the bed, fully clothed. I lost it. "What the FUCK are you doing with your clothes on, you've been on the tube for Christ's sake!"

"I was cold, I wanted to get under the covers."

"Fine, but have the decency to take your filthy trousers off before getting under the covers!"

"I don't know you, I'm shy."

"Well, get over it then, or stay cold, you stupid cow!"

"Hey! Don't call me a stupid cow!"

"You know there's more harmful bacteria on a tube seat than in a public toilet? You just spread public toilet all over my bed, you... stupid cow!"

She froze, probably not because I'd won the argument, although I could've sworn I had (albeit the phrasing could've been more felicitous). At this point I only knew two things for sure: there was going to be no shagging tonight, and I was going to sleep on the other side.

50

IT WAS election month, and Westminster Council allocated funds for the updating of video and audio equipment. Some survey had shown there was a need to nudge the elderly to vote differently and push more students into the booths. Someone figured that libraries were the place to do it. Things got busy. The Head Librarian asked me to update the post room manual and told me that I'd need to train an Assistant Post Room Manager – a grandiose title for an overweight woman who helped out from late mornings three times a week. Then things got busier. First we had big pallets of brand new audiobooks coming in, and then Charing Cross received its very first VHS collection. I was put in charge of printing the barcodes and entering the new items into the library database. I'd managed to convince the Head Librarian to order a bunch of science and engineering documentaries: *The History of Flight*, *Longitude*, that sort of stuff. He agreed, reluctantly. He was big on WWII and he would've preferred to load the shelves with stories about

Stalingrad, but he was a reasonable man and he knew we needed variety. Besides, the arts councillor had specifically instructed him to split the selection in such a way that it would interest young and old alike, so he would've had a hard time motivating a full WWII collection. That's how I got hold of some good documentaries and the Westminster youth got to meet Quentin Tarantino.

I had a system. I would complete most of my photocopying and printing duties in the morning, forfeit lunch, work the franking machine till about 2 p.m., churn out new barcodes till about 3.30 p.m., and then sit in front of the VHS player for an hour with one of the science and engineering docs. This left me just enough time to get back to the post room at 4.35 p.m., pick up the sacks and carry them to the post office on The Strand before its shutters came down. I couldn't have done it otherwise. I tried watching a doc during the evening shift but it felt like cheating; evenings were for books. I remember how I made sure to watch each documentary before assigning it a barcode. It felt like some sort of privilege, like watching the premiere of a play or seeing a film before it's released. I was certain that's what being alive must've felt like during the Age of Reason.

The Head Librarian told me I had done a good job of cataloguing and arranging the tapes, and he decided to put me in charge of all the audio and video material. I would still work the franking machine and rush the sacks to The Strand, but some of the photocopying was now done by Nora, my new assistant manager, who hardly knew how to assist and didn't have a clue how to manage. She was meant to do all of the photocopying, but between her sandwiches, hot dogs, cream teas, cigarette breaks and whatnot she hardly ever made it to half, so most days I'd have to go in early in the morning to make the task more Nora-friendly. At least Nora never told me she didn't move like she was fat. In fact, some days she didn't move at all.

The supply teachers were ecstatic. They knew every single VHS tape by its library code and could tell just by glancing over the shelf whether the one they wanted was already out, way before the scanner had a chance to beep. One of the supply teachers was called Gary. I liked Gary. He was a bit of a ladies' man and he walked like he was in a constant hurry. Even when he wasn't walking he looked like he was late for an appointment, making sudden jerky movements with his arms as if trying to hurry the conversation along, constantly scanning the room with busy eyes, turning his head left and right as if the army were at the gates and he had to be ready to flee at a moment's notice.

Gary was really excited about our new video collection and he did all he could to build videos into his lessons.

"I'm supposed to teach the kids about civic responsibilities," he said once. "What do you reckon, shall I get them to watch *Terminator*? There's bound to be a lesson in there…"

Another time he crowbarred *Karate Kid* into a class on adolescence, and the week after that he played *Coming to America* as a lesson on the Royal Family. He was particularly proud of that one. Gary was a republican. "I'd rather be a citizen than a subject any day of the week." That was Gary.

Then we acquired a copy of a sex education tape, *A Comprehensive Study of Human Reproduction*. Gary thought it was hilarious.

"Hey, Dak, do you still have that tape, what's it called, *Debbie does Dallas*?"

"Yes, Gary, we still have that tape, and it's still called *A Comprehensive Study of Human Reproduction*."

"Cool, cool. Can I check it out please?" Then he'd hold up his hand in the shape of a phone receiver: "Yes sir, I'm putting the finishing touches on my lesson for today, sir. I just need to check out *Throbbing Hood*, sir."

People like Gary made me feel lucky. But I also felt like a swindler, like I had deceived the bosses into thinking they'd given me a job when in fact they were paying me to live an adventure. That worried me sometimes; I felt a duty to at least pretend I was suffering, reassure them they were getting their money's worth.

51

SATURDAY AFTERNOON the sun came out and I met Maya in Hyde Park. She brought ham sandwiches and I picked up a carton of Chardonnay on the way. We strolled along the Serpentine, Maya's blue summer dress floating in the air, occasionally revealing a white sliver of thigh as she walked. Then we found a spot under an oak tree and sat down on the grass. Nothing else existed; only the oak tree and the sandwiches and the cheap wine and a feeling that the world was alright.

Around 5 p.m. we flagged down the Number 36 and made our way to Deptford. We smiled at each other. We talked a while about Gary's lesson plans. Maya laughed a genuine laugh and I felt butterfly wings fluttering in my bones.

Half way along Peckham Road I noticed Maya shifting around on the seat, grinning. Then she sat still, looking in the driver's direction, still grinning. A few seconds later she shuffled around a little more, drew up her legs and plucked a pair of knickers off her ankles. They were the same blue as the dress and I was sure they smelled of wildflowers and joy. Pretending to hold my hand, Maya passed her crumpled blue trophy over to me, pulling the sweetest face of fake shock. We sat there like that for a few minutes – hand in hand in knickers in hand. Then we got up, rang the bell and got off the bus.

We went up to my room and Maya stood in front of the window in that flowy blue dress, casting an evening shadow like a piece of sassy topiary art. She had this shapely arse that was almost very nearly oversized but not quite. It had an unbelievable silhouette. Present, Fulfilling, Proud. A glorious sight. I felt grateful that it was mine for a little while.

I put my hand on Maya's knee, slowly caressing her leg as I moved up under the dress. I was still a good five inches away from her groin when I felt Maya's juices trickling down her thigh. I stood still for a second, savouring the moment, feeling

Maya's essence of excitement in my hand; then I grabbed her, kissed her, pinned her against the wall, still kissing, her tongue doing cartwheels in my mouth, she thrusted forward, she was slim and graceful but in that moment had the strength of a lioness, I stepped back to keep my balance, stumbled over one of my boots and fell on my back with Maya on top of me. Our tongues still pressed against each other like stubborn magnets. We broke off and she gave me an impish smile. Then she got up, stepped forward and stood with her legs parted across my head. I was a teenage boy, lying in a green field on a warm summer night, staring up at the Orion of her cunt. The trickle intensified. A stray strand of Maya's thick juices about three inches long spanned across from her inner lips and latched on to her thigh – a glistening bridge of desire. My brain was a flood of impulse. I shuffled back a little, grabbed Maya just below the knees and forced her to squat down on my cock. I was hard. I slid in with a grunt. She moaned, closed her eyes and sat still for a few seconds, her head thrown back as if my penis was a syringe draining her of all strength. Then she arched her back and went to town.

The next day Maya told her boyfriend she was going shopping and we met for a coffee in a new place just off Oxford Street.

"My friend Deena is coming along, I hope you don't mind," Maya said.

I kind of did. I'd rather have Maya's hands all over me than have Deena talk my head off, but it was just coffee, so I said, "Sure, no problem." The thing with Maya was, she fired the lust within me, even on days when I wasn't feeling amorous or even interested; she was an incendiary bomb of carnality. But she also knew how to make my chest burn with coldness, the coldness of pain and loss, that coldness that hit me every time I walked those stairs to ring the cab firm…

I arrived at the café and saw Deena gesticulating and shifting to and fro on her seat. Maya was sitting opposite, nodding politely. I pulled out a chair and sat down. Deena made a faint gesture of acknowledgement and carried on blathering, something about shoes or scarfs or whatnot. I sat there quietly, thinking of ways I could take Maya over the counter. Deena became background noise. Better.

Then the noise stopped, Maya pulled a face and I heard a thump under the table.

"What?" I said. "What's going on?"

"Nothing."

Something didn't feel right. There was a tension, and Deena wasn't talking. Something was definitely not right.

"What is going on?" I insisted.

"Nothing," Deena said, "I just asked Maya why she's not wearing her ring."

Maya looked away. I pried a little harder. What was the thump all about? It turned out it wasn't a ring. It was an engagement ring. Maya took it off every time I was around – cold, premeditated. The thump had been Maya's foot hitting the table leg, she was trying to kick Deena in the shin to shut her up. The thump of failure and deceit.

I was flabbergasted.

Deena went really quiet, scarily quiet, then picked up her shopping bags in a hurry and left.

I looked at Maya. There she was, the heavenly nymph with ice crystal in her veins. She couldn't bear my gaze, kept looking away, looking down, at her feet – approximately the same height to which my heart had dropped. My mind wandered back to when I was nine years old. My mother had caught me bringing bugs into the house and whacked me over the back of the head with a shoe. She was fond of using shoes as educators and I'd almost grown immune to their dull knock. But this time they were wooden wedge heels and she'd come up from behind and totally blindsided me. I froze. She stood there in guilty silence for what seemed like hours, staring at me with gritted teeth and murderous eyes. Suddenly she turned around and walked off. I could feel a bump growing on my head, pushing and pulsating as though my brain was trying to punch a hole through the skull. But the real pain was the lump in my throat and in my spirit. I didn't have my own room to run to – we lived in a tiny one-bedroom flat and I slept on a sofa-bed in the sitting room, which also doubled as dining room (the kitchen was minuscule) and sewing room – so I ran to the bathroom. I climbed into the bath, sat down and poured out the tears till there was nothing left to cry. I don't know how long I was in there, but I remember feeling cold, hungry and exhausted when I realized the lump in my throat had gone.

Sitting in that café now with Maya's knife in my ribs, I wished I could weep like I had done that afternoon in my parents' bath, let the tears flow in total hysterical abandon, like the virgin Mary at Christ's emaciated feet. And then some more, until there was nothing left to weep, until blood be forced to spill out through the eyes as replacement for the failing teardrops. Then the world would know. Then the world wouldn't be able to deny the smell of death in my heart.

No such luck. My tears dried up before the first drop had a chance to get going. I would have to find other ways of shifting those lumps.

I stood up and began to walk towards Warren Street station. Maya followed me. We got to the station and joined the queue at the ticket office. My face must've looked like a stone because for the first time I saw an expression in Maya's eyes that wasn't impertinence or seduction. But inside, I was a lump of molten lead.

This had to stop, I knew as much; but how do you stop a hurricane? I took Maya's hands in my hands, looked her in the eye and told her that this was it – him or me. Here. Now. Maya lowered her gaze once more, sobbed, and told me she was sorry. Sorry. That's all she kept saying – sorry. Then she walked out of the station, crossed Tottenham Court Road and was gone.

52

SIMON HAD TICKETS to see *Dr Faustus* at Greenwich Theatre.

I set off early. It was a mild October afternoon and Deptford looked mournful among the wet leaves. No doubt it had plenty to mourn. I walked along Creek Road, crossed the bridge and got to Greenwich just before one o'clock – a good two hours before curtain-up. Plenty of time to pop over to Hewlett's, where you could still get a slice of steak and ale pie with a big blob of mash potato and mushy peas. On Tuesdays they even served jellied eel and sometimes fresh cockles; a small taste of nineteenth century London. The woman behind the counter would pick up a ladle and carefully fish out the mash and peas from a large, bubbling pot, then slap two perfectly equal portions on your plate, with the slice centrepiece. It was wonderful. How it had survived Thatcher nobody knew, but a few years later it disappeared overnight and a Sainsbury Local turned up in its place. Tony had done a good job of finishing what The Handbag had started.

We took our seats in the gallery and Judy struck up a conversation with the young couple next to her. The man had one of those beards without a moustache, like that crazy Roman emperor. The woman had a handsome face, but her mouth was smeared with this heavy red lipstick that made her look like she'd been nicking cosmetics from a French brothel.

"I hear it's a good production," Judy said. "Marvellous play, can teach you a thing or two about life too."

"You've seen it before?" asked the beard.

"Oh yes, at the Old Vic. Exceptional production. And of course Simon reads me quotations, from the A text."

"Also known as the *correct* text," said Simon with a grin.

"He's very particular about the texts, you see…"

"You must know it very well then," said the French-brothel raider. Then she added, "It's our first time. We were planning to go see a musical, we always go to a musical on our anniversary – we've been married eight years! – but Arthur thought it may be good to do something new this year, something... more cultured." I suppose Arthur was the crazy-emperor-wannabe's name.

"Oh, it's an extraordinary story!" Judy said. "He was a scientist, a scholar, who longed for knowledge. A bit like you, Dak!" she turned to me briefly, letting out a loud chuckle, then lowered her voice to a more serious tone: "You ought to be careful with it, the power knowledge brings. It can cloud your judgement, make you lose sight of what's important." Then back to the couple: "Anyway, Faustus longs for knowledge, so he makes a pact with the devil: soul for knowledge. A bit like Feynman with Los Alamos." Simon and I smiled at the Feynman reference; the faces of Judy's captive audience looked entirely blank. Judy never so much as entertained the possibility that there could be someone on this planet who wasn't familiar with every detail of Feynman's life. She continued, "Then, over the next twenty-four years, he is steered away from redemption by threats and bribes from Mephistopheles."

"That's the same as the devil, right?" asked Arthur's wife.

"More like a kind of renaissance Alastair Campbell," replied Simon.

Judy laughed, then slapped Simon on the elbow and carried on. She looked truly happy. "So anyway, he goes through these twenty-four years of threats and bribes and then, eventually, he fucks a demon in the shape of Helen of Troy. And what a shape she was too!"

At this point Arthur & Co. had no idea whether Judy was a lunatic or a prankster, or whether she was actually serious. If she'd been a young woman they would've probably assumed foul play, but this was an old lady, how could she possibly... They weren't sure. Was there going to be a scene of the demon-fucking? At Greenwich Theatre? Surely not! You could see Arthur's face becoming increasingly contorted as he began to consider the possibility that Judy may have been relaying the truth. Shock slowly escaped through his eyes, and you knew he wished he'd never gone anywhere near those tickets.

"Anyway," Judy continued, "as you probably know, when you've fucked a demon you are now beyond redemption." She turned to me again: "That's something else you need to beware of, Dak. You never know what may be lurking in those bars…" Then she gave a roaring laughter just as the curtain began to rise.

When the play finished we took the stairs down to the mezzanine. Judy was buoyant. "What a *marvellous* production!" Then she told us how the whole evening reminded her of a time she and Neil had seen *King Lear* at the Young Vic. "We talked about it for days afterwards!" she said with brimming eyes. "Mostly about the fool, of course. That's the thing with a good Lear, everyone talks about the fool."

As we stepped onto the mezzanine we kept chatting about the play; Act 5, Scene 2. Judy made another remark about the marvellous production and I offered a few wisecracks about Mephistopheles; by now I knew how to sound intellectual, how to be intellectual. And I liked it. The working-class boy confabulating about hubris, the human condition, episteme and the *lex naturalis* – nonchalantly, matter-of-factly, as if he'd always known, as if those had always been his concerns, as if he'd never stood at a grimy lathe with a noose round his neck.

It was easy. The stuff just flew out of me like self-propelled confetti, making Simon smile with pleasure and Judy light up with pride. I was Cicero, I was Lord St. Alban, I was the eleventh Attic orator. I was Dakris Manell: Modern Intellectual.

It didn't last. An elegant looking woman in her fifties was listening in. "What a fine young man!" she said.

Judy turned on her usual sixpence: "Do be careful, he hates women."

"Oh I'm sure that's not true," said the woman.

"Well, he laughs at their love. And he absolutely hates Germaine Greer."

"And Greer hates me, so I suppose we're even," I said. "In fact, I don't hate her anywhere near as much as she hates me. So there, I'm still the better person." That's the thing with eloquence. Like science, like all good things, you can use it to cause more hurt more quickly and more pinpointedly. Sometimes against yourself.

"Ah, now you're a good person too? How did you figure *that*?" said Judy, looking at me through narrow eyes.

"At least I never told Greer she would most probably sexually abuse her own child."

"So you didn't."

"And you know why? Because I don't know her. Maybe she will, maybe she won't, I don't know, and I don't know because I don't know her. But not knowing me didn't stop *her*, did it…"

Judy turned to the elegant woman: "You see, he *hates* her!" Then she laughed, but it was a self-defeating laugh.

"Well, if she said those things about him I –"

"Oh don't you defend him now!" You could see Judy's jaw tightening, her composure buckling under the idea that some woman would take my reason over her conviction, over her hero's unrequited anger.

The elegant woman stood quietly, looking like a little girl who'd just been told off.

Judy looked at me, hard. "So you think she's stupid, do you?"

"No, it's much worse than that. She's intellectually lazy. And dishonest."

"Really, Dak, sometimes you're so rude!"

"Easy for you to say, you're not the one being accused of child rape."

Judy stared at Simon with her mouth hanging open. "Can you believe him?"

Simon shrugged. Judy let out a heavy sigh that ended in a grunt, then turned back to me: "What a stiff-necked obstinate bastard you can be! And how fortunate that you are so many other things as well – and that I love you."

It didn't seem like love. It seemed like the opposite of love. What if hate is not the opposite of love? What if the opposite of love is hurt? Hate is just one of the many roads that lead to hurt, and not even the most efficient one. But this…

Judy looked back at Simon, then stared at me for what felt like a very long time. She was motionless, didn't blink, just stared with her eyes gaping and her mouth ajar, like she'd just witnessed a terrible accident.

I felt sad at the thought of having disappointed Judy, and I was quite sure I'd disappointed her. But I had little choice, I was cornered, cornered by that cocktail of blind devotion to a papier-mâché hero and of wanton elevation beyond what is right, what is fair – and decent.

I offered Judy my arm to help her steady herself on the stairs to the exit. She pretended not to notice and grabbed hold of the banister instead. How could she expect me to simply take the nastiness? How could she not see the profound injustice?

Simon did nothing. Said nothing. He was the most emotionally courageous man I knew, but intellectually he was gutless. I felt sick. The chatter in the foyer was nails through my skull; the chandelier a catapult shooting thorns through my eyes. What of virtue? What of a virtuous man if we all carry the same unwashable criminal stain regardless? What of free will if we all have the sin of child rape already sewn upon us, if we are all beyond redemption by principle, by birth? Then we are all worse off than Faustus – doomed before any contract is even drafted, beyond redemption before we even begin to contemplate fucking the devil. This was unbearable, preposterous, and utterly corrupt. And yet Judy wouldn't hear of it. Simon stood by her, gutless, basking in her reflected self-righteousness and looking vaguely accomplished.

But the thing with the unbearable is that you can't bear it; so I had to tear away at it, rip it, crush it. Rudeness or no rudeness. I had to. And words were the only way I knew how, so I did, and I won the argument by logic, by common decency – and the elegant-looking woman by the stairs knew it, and rightly so. I had won and I had won justly.

And yet, among all the feelings thumping their way through my head, not a single one bore a shred of resemblance with being a winner.

53

IT WAS MY round. I walked through the Friday crowd and handed out the pints: Pilsner for Kevin and lager for everyone else. As we raised our glasses I fell into a rare moment of desolation. I knew I'd done the right thing with Maya, but I also knew that knowledge wasn't always a good nurse. I drained half of my pint in one swallow.

"I've climbed this thing, haven't I..." I said. "This thing that from the bottom looked so imposing, a big mountain, *majestic*. And now what?" A feeling of gloom advanced through my stomach. I'd listened to the warnings – Marx and Orwell. I'd tried to open my heart to the words of Yeats and Donne. I'd become devoted to Bacon and Feynman... Now what? Now that I stood on its peak, the once formidable mountain looked like a knoll among a thousand other knolls.

Kevin smiled at me, curling up only half of his mouth. "Ah, sweet melancholy," he said with a hint of cheek, "caresses you with one hand and stabs you with the other."

Gus laughed. "Bloody hell, guys, all guns blazing right from the off? I thought I was coming out for a drink!"

"It's a pilgrimage, mate," continued Kevin, "and each of those little hills is a beautifully sacred site. It's the hills that make up the pilgrimage. Reaching Mecca is not the point."

"Isn't it?"

"It's never been the point. If it were, you might as well go by bus and be done with it! But you know, there are no buses going to Mecca..."

"Really?" said Gus with a prankish look on his face. "How do the locals travel?" He knew only too well what Kevin meant, but Gus couldn't help it sometimes; he needed the laughter, he needed that reassurance, that crutch to help him wade the mud.

We sat, talked, and wondered. Wondered what it all meant, all the knowledge, the crafting the shaping the forging, all that drive and all that striving; what does it all mean? Will there be a time of redemption? Will he who strives eventually *be* striven?

"Does it have to mean anything?" Gus asked. "Does it?" But he quickly dismissed his own question, "Anyway, some say it all means nothing without the love of a good woman."

"Oh don't give me that Hollywood tat!" said Kevin. Kevin was a true Romantic, he couldn't stand how Hollywood had raped and pillaged the whole concept. "What makes you think that love would add any more meaning than – I don't know – sadness or amusement or terror, or any other emotion?"

"Well, love –"

"Love would add love, that's all."

"One more brick in the wall?"

"Exactly," said Kevin, staring both of us in the eye. "Love is a brick, love is *not* the wall."

"Or the mountain," said Gus, "or whatever the fuck your analogy has got to now!"

We laughed, the sort of laughter that reminds you of childhood. My desolation had melted; forgotten. This connection, this depth I had with Kevin always found a way of letting the light back in. It was the sort of connection that I craved with a woman but that had continually failed to materialize, elusive like the most ancient of Greek myths, an imaginary dance of drunken quicksilver, an insane ectoplasm of the soul. Whenever I tried to connect with a woman, I kept feeling that my words were too heavy, as in a dream of confusion. Words would leave my mouth, stagger through the air for a bit and then plunge to the ground, *slam!* – never make it to her eardrums. And I kept trying, god knows I kept trying, hoping, praying that my words might make the full journey, but they were just too bloody heavy. Then my tongue and my palate and my jaw would get weary and I couldn't say any more, I wouldn't try any more. Just too bloody heavy.

"Where did all this darkness come from anyway?" said Kevin. "It's not about Maya, is it?"

"Not specifically, but I guess she helped dim the lights a little, you know…"

"I know. So, what is it about her? If you even know, that is."

I smiled, unwillingly. "I wish I could tell you she was my Caryatid, holding up my temple, steadying me as I find my feet on this earth... but I have a strong suspicion it's all about looks. I don't like that, but that's how it is."

Kevin smiled, knowingly. "I know she's blonde and all that," he smiled again, this time wryly, "but you need to focus, mate. Don't be in a relationship with someone you wouldn't go to war with."

Gus emitted a loud snort, "Oh, we've moved on to war now, have we? That's a bit extreme!"

"So is life."

"Oh..."

"We're warriors. We need women we can march forward with in the knowledge that our flank is covered. And I mean *real* knowledge, the kind that you feel in your gut."

I nodded.

Gus took a sip of lager, placed the pint on a soggy coaster and wiped his mouth with the back of his hand.

"Of course," Kevin went on, "life has victories as well, and you'll have respite and repose and other such things describable by other such beautiful words. But you don't want to go in with a soldier who's only good for the rest days and the victory parades." He waved his pint in the air and spilled a few drops, bringing a shade of envy to Hugh's eyes. "That's the sort of soldier you pray and hope fills the ranks of your enemy's regiments. Then you'd have an easy life. But by your side?" He shook his head. "You don't want that by your side."

We all took a sip in silence.

"And anyway," Kevin said finally, "you chase the blondes, but you'll end up being tied down by a brunette. Mark my words."

I marked his words.

The conversation turned to London, as it often did with the four of us, especially on a night like this, especially when the meaning of life had been invoked. London was the adoptive mother we loved more than our birth mothers would ever know, the sister we never had, and the lover we couldn't forget.

"I guess," I said, "I guess sometimes I just wish I *could* get to Mecca by bus."

"But then it wouldn't be Mecca, would it…" said Kevin. "It would just be some city with a bunch of tourists."

Gus looked vaguely pensive. "Maybe the geezer is getting tired," he said. "You know, this city can bring you down sometimes; ask you more than you have left to give."

"Of course," said Kevin, "in London you can live on bitterness and regret, plenty of people do. But that's on you. London doesn't manufacture the bitterness, or the regret. London just opens herself to you, offers you her *cornucopia*," he enunciated the word slowly, rolling the "r" like an old-school Shakespearean actor, and made a gesture with his hands that resembled a flower opening up. "But it is you. You choose what to pick and mix."

Gus laughed. "Like a big sweetshop, innit!"

Kevin gave a faint smile, then carried on, "Choose wisely, my friend. She can be a tough mistress; gives it all but demands devotion. Fully. All great mistresses do – they wouldn't be great otherwise. That diligent equipoise, that's the source of their greatness."

All of a sudden Gus had a serious look on his face, firm, solid. "You'll be fine," he said matter-of-factly, as though he'd just been granted the power to know the unknowable. "We'll look after you, don't worry, we won't let you stray."

His words reassured me, which bothered me at first. I knew in my mind that neither Gus nor anybody could possibly know what was going to happen next, but it just felt good to have an older man tell me that things were going to be ok. My heart felt calmer, despite my mind.

That night I went to the late-opening newsagent on Oxford Street and bought a first class stamp. Then I walked to Charing Cross, let myself in to the library and picked up a university application form. I grabbed a pen. My hands were shaking. I saw a headmaster in a mortarboard shouting at me in a squeaky voice: "You have no qualifications, you fool!" His stooges gathered around him in a circle and laughed at me, baring their long yellow fangs, repeating the headmaster's verdict in chorus: "You fool! You utter, utter fool!" I thought of Gus's words again, of the feeling they had brought me in that precise moment he'd delivered them, the moment they'd entered my brain forever. My hand steadied. I felt my spine straightening up. Under "subject" I wrote "Cognitive Science". My hand was clammy with sweat. I filled in the application, shoved it in an A4 envelope, sealed it, put on the stamp, walked out, dropped the envelope in one of Her Majesty's finest pillar boxes. I stared at the red pillar for a while, then I turned around and walked to Trafalgar Square to catch the night bus. Now we wait…

54

KEVIN HAD BEEN going out with Patsy for nearly a year now. She was a wonderful soul. A professional volleyball player who travelled up and down the country every weekend and was in the gym five days a week. They didn't see each other very often, but when they did it was Calliope and Oeagrus, infinite orchards and splendid songs.

That Patsy was beautiful anyone could see – symmetry had really done a number on her. But it was her gaze that really stayed with you, the way she looked at you with inquisitive green eyes that always seemed to be less than a second away from a smile. Her cheekbones rode high, and her spiky black hair almost seemed to signal the high voltage that ran through her body. Ah, her body; the body I imagined the Amazon goddess of war would've had, a Minerva of the Amazons, if the Amazons had had a Minerva and if Minerva had had the gentle heart of a dove.

Phoneys are always talking about "energy" as if plastering a scientific term over a vague idea would somehow magically make it plausible. But with Patsy I could swear there really was an energy surrounding her, a force field that made you want to spend time with her, made you want to be within her orbit. And orbit is the right word, for Patsy was a whole planet: she had warmth and storms and volcanoes and green fields and deep blue oceans filled with sharks and corals and sea turtles. Maybe a few shipwrecks too, but I knew nothing about that.

I could never have her, of course. I couldn't even think about not having her, because that involved the thought of having her, which I could not. She was Kevin's woman, and that was that. So I flirted with her sister. That's as close as I was ever going to get.

Bethan, that was the sister's name, was ordinary looking, but turned out to be funny and charming, so the more we talked the more good-looking she became. She was a good friend of Vikki's, so at first I thought she might be a lesbian, but she turned out to be bisexual, which suited me fine.

One Saturday night Kevin and I stayed in the Out Bar after closing time. Patsy's team had just won a big tournament and were determined to carry on celebrating into the small hours. Bethan was doing a lot of giggling. We downed a few vodka shots and things started to get lively. A couple of Patsy's teammates were dancing on the bar, pretending they were Formula 1 drivers on a podium and spraying soda water on each other. The team physio pulled out a brick of hash and proceeded to slice it with a flick knife, while the coach was bent over in a corner coughing like a maniac after trying to drink lager straight from the tap. Kevin took Patsy upstairs. Vikki pulled the shutters down, then called me over.

"You can use my sofa if you want," she said. "Just be sensible, don't jizz on my cushions."

I took Bethan upstairs and looked for the sofa.

It was a nice flat, sparsely furnished but clean and tidy, not at all what I imagined a butch lesbian's bachelor pad would be. There was a little table in the corner with a large hookah on it, and on the wall there was a print of Hopper's *Nighthawks*. Vikki had good taste.

The sofa was in the middle of the flat. Small but comfortable. I unbuttoned Bethan's shirt and slid my hand under her bra strap.

"It's a Wonderbra," she said nervously. "Don't be disappointed when it comes off."

I smiled, trying to look reassuring, then kissed her again.

There was nothing disappointing about Bethan's breasts. They were smaller than the bra had advertised, but they were perfectly shaped, almost deliberately engineered to fit in my hands, and with beautifully rosy nipples that stood to attention as soon as I freed them.

After a little more kissing and fondling Bethan unzipped my trousers, undid my belt, sat me on the sofa and took me in her mouth. She was terrible at it. It felt like she was blowing on my penis the way you blow on a candle. Maybe she thought that a blowjob had to involve actual blowing? I suppose we've all been guilty of taking things too literally at some point or other, but this seemed like a whole new level.

The stair lights were on and I could see my penis in Bethan's mouth – clear as day – and it certainly looked like Bethan was sucking on it, but I felt nothing of the sort. My mind started to wander as I looked at Bethan's head; the human head is rather large, this is a human head, it's rather large, a rather large head. Not surprising really... after all, it's the head of a large mammal. Isn't it odd that we insist on thinking of female humans as gracious creatures? Look at that skull! It's definitely a large skull... the skull of a large animal, an animal that could easily, *easily* bite the head off a bird. Then I thought about my grandmother, how she could wring a hen's neck in a matter of seconds. She'd put on this long black apron, walk out into the yard, open the chicken shed and pick up one of the hens. The hen would go into a frenzy, flap its wings like mad, as if desperation could finally allow it to overcome its evolutionary shackles and let it fly off into the sunset. But the commotion wouldn't last long. Grandmother would put the hen under her left armpit, holding it close with her forearm and stroking its head with her free hand – a dark, leathery hand whose skin had been baked by the sun and pickled in the rice fields. She would keep doing this for a few minutes, until the hen calmed down and became almost motionless, hypnotized. That's when grandma would take the bird's neck between her two thumbs and *snap!* deliver instant death. All this she did matter-of-factly, with no more thought or consideration than when she was stirring soup or sweeping the floor. I saw grown men sheepishly knocking on my grandmother's door with a hen under their arm, their head bowed, their heart too soft to snap the life out of a defenceless creature. Men who'd fought in the Second World War, who'd pushed a bayonet through another man's chest, but didn't have the heart to kill that oversized feathery thing that had laid their breakfast for the best part of a year. So they'd turn up at Mrs Manell's door, bow their head, and hand over the hen, together with a half dozen fresh eggs – for that was the fee, a full dozen if they wanted the bird plucked as well. Then they'd wait quietly outside the door for their family's dinner. Grandma would take the hen, turn around and immediately start stroking its head. Death has no time to waste.

Meanwhile Bethan was still trying to put out my candle. I took another look; that's definitely the skull of an animal that could wring a bird's neck. Definitely. Never mind birds, this is the skull of an animal that could easily tear your face off! Why don't we see more of that? Why are we so hell bent on seeing gracefulness in a woman? We should see less of the gracefulness and more of the face-tearing. The face-tearing is real, the gracefulness I'm not so sure.

All of a sudden I felt sorry for Bethan. She seemed to be working hard at it, or at least trying anyway, putting real effort in. I made some noises, about thirty seconds' worth, caressed the back of her neck – the neck of a large mammal, not the kind you could snap with your thumbs – and gently pulled her away from my crotch. Then I stood up, turned Bethan on her back and mounted her. She made little movements with her head and breathed heavily, like she couldn't handle the excitement. That turned me on immensely. I started pumping with purpose. Bethan's eyes opened wide, giving her face a comical look between surprised and terrified. I held back a chuckle. Then Bethan grabbed my forearms and dug her nails in before throwing her head back and squeezing my hips between her thighs. She was shivering. I slowed down, slid out and rolled off. She kept shivering.

"Are you ok?"

"Yes… yes," she said, punting, her teeth chattering as she breathed in, "It's just too much…"

"Too much?"

"Too sensitive. I can feel the air between my legs…"

I got up, found a blanket and put it over her. The shivering was beginning to freak me out. Then Bethan took a deep breath, wrapped herself tight in the blanket and sat up.

"I've never come before with – you know… a man inside."

That explains it, I thought. I felt stupid for having almost freaked out at something like that, something to celebrate.

"Glad to be of service," I said.

She laughed, stood up and gave me a kiss on the cheek. I could see the same sharp sweetness I had seen in Patsy. I wondered whether Patsy too shivered as she came. Then I went to the bathroom, stuck my head under the cold water tap and put that thought out of my head. Well, I tried anyway… so full marks for effort.

A week later Kevin and I were back at the One Bar, this time on a Wednesday, when Vikki was shift manager. We brought a few other guys over from the Rising Sun and two girls we'd met at a bus stop on the way. Shift managers got a cut of the night's takings and I wanted Vikki to have a good night. We didn't tell Gus it was going to be gay night. He wasn't impressed, but I convinced him to stay for a drink.

Vikki saw us and made a sign to the DJ. A minute later Gloria Gaynor was blasting through the speakers.

"So," Vikki said," how was my sofa?"

"Comfy. We had a good time," I said.

"I hear Bethan had a *great* time; *memorable* one might say. I always suspected you had hidden talents." Then she smiled and pretended to flick me in the crotch.

Word got around. I was in demand after that, had a good few months. All thanks to Vikki.

Vikki and I never did end up in bed, of course. But our flirting continued like some illicit underground activity, a quasi-incestuous fantasy. The whole thing seemed paradoxical. This big, brutish-looking butch with graveyards and scissors and middle-fingers tattooed on her arms liked me more than any woman I had slept with. And I don't mean "like" in the way schoolchildren like custard or puppy dogs. She *liked* me. She liked *me*. She asked after me, asked me about my life, my obsessions, the daydreams and the night terrors. Truth be told I think Vikki liked men, she just couldn't fuck them, that's all. And she definitely saw something in me, whatever that was. Maybe she even loved me a little. She sure sent a lot of loving my way that spring. Short-term love, phoney love; but still, it kept me busy at night.

55

SPRING TURNED INTO summer and summer into autumn, and failures with women continued to shape my life more than the successes.

Flora worked at a coffee bar on Whitehall. She was a slim twenty-two-year-old with a round face and a silver tongue. We would chat a couple of times a week as I picked up a coffee on my way to the bus stop.

One Wednesday evening the coffee bar was very quiet. Flora was wiping the counter with an old sponge.

I threw some sarcasm her way: "Are you using that to spread germs around?"

She looked at me with piercing eyes. Her demeanour excited me.

"White coffee, no sugar?" There was a hint of coyness in her voice. I imagined taking her over the counter.

We chatted for a few minutes, then I glanced at the clock on the wall behind her, "I need to get going," I said, "but I'll be back." I looked at her straight in the eye.

"If you're back at eleven you might catch me at the end of my shift," she said.

I was back at eleven.

Flora had finished her shift, true to her words. She asked me to wait a few minutes, then went to a staff room; came out two minutes later with her hair loose and a hint of makeup. She had this slim, athletic, almost boyish body and beautifully olive skin. She intrigued me.

We went for a walk around Leicester Square, chatting and people-watching. Flora liked to make fun of tourists. "Look at those two, zig-zagging around. They haven't yet worked out that the quickest way from point A to point B is a straight line."

"Maybe they don't want to get there quick," I said, somewhat absent-mindedly.

"I reckon they don't understand straight lines."

I liked her sense of humour, but sometimes it seemed to rely too much on putting others down.

A couple of hours later we went to her place, somewhere in Willesden. She poured two glasses of wine and handed me one.

"Would this be a good time to kiss you, then?" I said. I was feeling presumptuous.

"I don't know, you're gonna have to find out for yourself."

I took her free hand and pulled her towards me. She pushed a strand of hair behind her ear and looked down shyly. It was a genuine shyness, at odds with her usual brazen demeanour. Many a woman has turned into a little girl in the presence of a confident man. I wasn't a confident man, but I had learned how to put it on, and that was almost as good, though it didn't *feel* that way.

I put my forefinger under her chin, raised her head up a little and kissed her. She was motionless at first, but then returned the kiss with some passion. We kept at it for a while, stroking each other's back and neck. There was no bra strap across her back.

Flora was a decent kisser, darting her tongue around energetically. I lowered my hand onto her hip and felt my dick getting harder. She put both her hands on my lower back and pulled me closer. She had small, firm breasts and I could feel her nipples piercing through the yellow blouse. I slowly began to slide my hand into her knickers. She grabbed it and pushed it away. "I'm low," she said in a monotone.

I wasn't sure what that meant, but it looked and sounded like the opposite of excitement.

Back to kissing and stroking above the waist.

This happened a few times, maybe four. I started to feel I was losing my erection. I bet she decides she's no longer "low" the very moment I go soft, I thought. I'll be damned if I get caught with a limp dick after a good fifteen minutes of throbbing! I wasn't going to take the fall for her failure to be ready.

I stopped kissing her, stepped back and said, "Let's just leave it, then."

Suddenly she looked angry; dark circles sprouted under her eyes: "WHAT?"

"Let's leave it. Where's your bathroom?" I turned around as if she had motioned that the bathroom was behind me. She hadn't.

"Oh, great," she said, sarcasm all over it. "Now you're not gonna *fuck* me?"

I didn't answer. I kept walking as if I knew where the bathroom was.

She caught up with me, grabbed my arm and shoved my hand down the front of her jeans. I think she was wearing lace knickers. "Come on!" she said, "let's GO!" She was angry.

"Look," I told her, "let's just have another drink and go to sleep."

"Great. THIS IS JUST GREAT! Now you can't even *fuck* me? Screw you then!"

"Ok, whatever."

I went to the bathroom, had a piss, threw some water on my face, then came back and sat on the sofa. Flora was in the kitchen banging dishes. It was 2 a.m. and the last tube had long gone. I lay on the sofa and tried to get some sleep.

56

YOU MAY NOT be surprised to learn that very few people checked out *A Comprehensive Study of Human Reproduction*. Apart from Gary, of course. But this one Thursday was going to be an exception. A woman in her early forties came in as I was tidying some shelves and started browsing the catalogue. She looked very distressed, like she'd been crying and was now trying to hold back the next flood of tears. I asked her if she was ok. She started sobbing. I fetched her a drink of water from the cooler.

It turned out she was looking for a sex education tape to show her fifteen-year-old daughter. I explained that *A Comprehensive Study of Human Reproduction* was the closest thing we had, and I tried to explain there was nothing in it that a fifteen-year-old didn't already know. But she was desperate she said; she'd take anything we have. As I took the catalogue from her hand the Head Librarian came over and asked her if everything was ok. He must've thought I was molesting her or something. She became hysterical; launched herself at the Head Librarian, grabbing onto his tweed waistcoat and weeping uncontrollably.

She relayed the story between sobs. She hadn't slept in days, worried sick that her fifteen-year-old daughter was having sex. How did she know? She'd found a condom in her daughter's purse, that's how. A condom! Smart kid was my first thought. You should've seen the terror on the woman's face, you would've thought her daughter had fallen into the lion's enclosure or something and had been maimed for life. It's not like she'd got syphilis – that could've been nearly as bad as the lions, granted – but the girl had *condoms* for god's sake, all she was getting was a bit of dick. Freud was way off the mark as usual with that drivel about women having penis envy, but some women definitely have penis *phobia*. Of course, no one is going to touch that hot potato, not even Freudians. Cowards. Yeah, it's better kept hidden away, deep down in society's dungeon, with all the other tricky terrors.

I put the catalogue back on the shelf and walked towards the post room. As I turned around to shut the door I saw the Head Librarian trying to pull the woman up from the floor and off his waistcoat.

That evening I had dinner with Simon and Judy at a small trattoria in Bloomsbury. I hadn't seen them for some time after that business about Germaine Greer, and it took a while for the ice to thaw. But eventually we got talking.

Judy went first: "It doesn't matter who's right and who's wrong. You must know that my love for you is beyond whatever disagreements we have."

That felt good. Surreal, and heavy, utterly unmatchable – but good. Nobody had ever told me anything like that.

Then I told them about *A Comprehensive Study of Human Reproduction*, about Gary, about the mysterious condom and all that commotion for a bit of dick. "You'd think the girl was playing with assault rifles or something."

"That's what happens when mothers think they can do a father's job," said Judy.

"Do you think it's the mother's fault?" asked Simon.

"You know, Si, I don't, but I just about had it with women this week. I probably think *everything* is their fault!" She threw her head back in laughter like she so often did when she caught herself being unfair. She had an astounding ability for self-reflection, enough to know she had blind spots, and found them incredibly amusing.

"Bloody women, eh!" said Simon with a mock-macho look.

"Yes!" Judy agreed between bursts of laughter, "Bloody women indeed!" Then, in a more serious voice: "It's Cynthia."

I had no idea who this Cynthia was, but judging by the sudden change of expression on Simon's face it was not the first time Judy had been upset by her. Later Simon told me that Cynthia was suffering from depression and Judy phoned her regularly to get her talking, to help her get out of the rut, as Judy put it. But Simon was now worried about the effect Cynthia was having on Judy's own wellbeing. He had tried to stop Judy from contacting her, but to no avail. Judy knew it wasn't good for her own health, it upset her gut she said, but she felt a duty towards Cynthia like she did towards all women.

"The things she does to that poor Howard," Judy said, "it's shameful really. I think she may be a sadist." While she said this her head was tilted to the side, as though she was trying to gather her memories. Then she turned to face me and Simon, and added, "We're all sadists of course, as you know, but some of us struggle to keep it in check."

"When was this?" I said.

Judy ignored my question and carried on; it was obviously not pertinent to her story. "She threw one of her tantrums. In the post office. It was chock-a-block. She said she was aggrieved!" Judy laughed a dismissive laugh. "But I know it was a tantrum. Howard told her to stop it at once – she was being silly, of course – and he was looking out for her, guarding her dignity. But Cynthia being Cynthia… she didn't." Judy made a gesture with her finger as if to underline the obvious silliness. "You know what she said after telling me all this? She said, 'Who does he think he is?' Can you believe it? Who does he think he is! How ghastly! How very ghastly! Trying to cripple his manhood like that." Judy rested her head on the palm of her hand, as if the whole story was weighing her down. She sat in that fashion for a few seconds, then added, "I mean, the man is a frightful bore, but 'Who does he think he is'? Awful. Absolutely awful." Judy's hands dropped down onto the armrests as if the bones in her arms had suddenly turned to dust. Then she looked at Simon, a gloomy curtain unfurling across her eyes and face, and in a slow, beaten-up voice she said, "Really, Si, some of these women are beyond saving. Sometimes I think I'm going to give up on them. I won't, of course – I can't. But the things they say sometimes…"

"I bet the Greeks had a solution for women like that!" said Simon with a grin. He was trying to get Judy's thoughts away from this Cynthia person. It worked. Judy laughed, then made a deliberately bored face and said to him, "Of course. Go on, Si, *tell* us about the Greeks."

"Well, they did have a convincing way of dealing with parents."

"Ah, yes, parents," Judy said, "another lot that need to watch out for sadist tendencies. It's so easy to give in when you have a little defenceless creature in your arms. We all have it."

"Oh, but the Greeks had a solution!"

"I'm sure they did, hahaha…"

"I know you're a fan of Socrates, but: Aristophanes disliked the modern ideas of Socrates – these modern folks all immersed in their ideas – and so what does Aristophanes do? He has a pupil of Socrates persuading his father that it is right for a son to beat his own father."

"Jolly good!" Judy said.

"Well, so this pupil, after giving his dad a good thrashing, he says, 'I know what will cheer you up, father – I shall go and beat my mother!'"

Judy laughed. "That will teach her!"

"Now," concluded Simon in a serious-sounding baritone, "if that's not the cradle of civilisation, I don't know what is."

At this point Judy had tears of laughter streaming down her face. She pulled out a white handkerchief, dabbed her cheeks gently, and said, "The cradle of civilisation indeed!" then turned to me, pretending to whisper as if not to be heard by Simon, "Last month he was into Heraclitus. He read me bits that he says are witty. Apparently Heraclitus was a good laugh!"

After lunch we walked through Russell Square. Simon told us some more stories about Aristophanes, then tried to bring up Heraclitus again, but Judy wouldn't let him – she'd had enough Greece for the day. We walked by Gordon Square, looked at the plaques: Virginia Woolf, The Stracheys, T.S. Eliot. "Thank God for the minds of dead people," said Simon. "They keep us all sane."

57

ONE MONDAY EVENING I got home just after eight o'clock and went in through the restaurant to pay my rent. Mr Alaoui greeted me with a big grin. "Come back down in half an hour," he whispered, "I'm shutting early tonight."

"What's the occasion?"

"I got testicles," he announced proudly. He covered his mouth as he spoke and looked around furtively as though he'd just offered me the dodgiest deal of the century.

A stream of loud, angry-sounding Moroccan vernacular came through from the kitchen. Mrs Alaoui clearly disapproved of the idea. I presume she was worried about their licence, but it was strangely reassuring to imagine that a woman was so distressed at the loss of an adolescent calf's masculinity. Mr Alaoui replied with a monosyllable and shrugged the way a man shrugs when he's run out of explanations. I gave him a faint smile, trying to communicate I was on his side but also taking care not to seem disrespectful to his wife. A fine balance. I must've pulled it off because he patted me on the shoulder and sent me on my way. I handed him the £50, went upstairs, had a quick shower and walked back down. Mr Alaoui was pulling down the shutters, looking around with an unnecessarily shifty demeanour. Judging by his behaviour you would've thought he was planning to push heroin outside a nursery.

Several minutes later a big boyish grin appeared on his face as Mrs Alaoui drove off in their family car. He walked back towards the door as gingerly as his chubby legs allowed and turned over the CLOSED sign.

"Salim is waiting in the basement," he told me. "Go get Terry, I promised him a taste."

I turned around and opened the back door. I could hear Terry cursing from the bottom of the stairs. I went up. He was waving his hands excitedly at Mickey, a tall guy in an ill-fitting BT uniform. When Terry saw me his eyes lit up: "Wait till you see what we've got planned for YOU!" he pointed his finger at me in a half-menacing manner. I don't think that was his intention, the menace, not on this occasion anyway, but he couldn't help it; that's the only pointing his finger was used to doing.

Eventually I gathered that Mickey made a bit of cash on the side installing dodgy phones in friends' houses. He would run a line from some adjacent building and hook it up to a temporary socket attached to a rotary phone. The rotary had belonged to some old lady who Mickey duped into believing that modern lines only worked with keypad phones. And that's how he got 10% commission for selling keypad phones to the elderly and cash in hand for passing on the rotaries. It's also how we ended up with a phone in each room working off the line that ran to New Cross fire station. The only problem was that when one phone was in use the others wouldn't work, as all the phones ran off a single line, so you'd get a busy tone whenever one of the receivers was off the hook. Typical Terry's bodge, but we all felt positively aristocratic at the illusion of a private phone. It didn't last long. Mickey's job must've messed with the fire brigade's line, and a few months later a BT van turned up outside New Cross station and all our phones went dead.

I left Terry and Mickey haggling over the price and went back to Mr Alaoui.

Terry's loudness followed me down the stairs as I walked to the basement: "A pony? You're having a laugh!" I closed the door behind me.

In the basement, Salim was splashing some kind of marinade over a linen bag full of what looked like pinkish prunes. Mr Alaoui was standing behind him in expectation, occasionally pointing and giving instructions.

"Nearly there," he announced. "Let's go fire up the grill."

And that was it for the night; by which I mean I don't remember what happened next, except that Terry came in with an ounce of skunk and two unmarked bottles of gin.

58

IT WAS 7 P.M. The reading rooms were nearly deserted and I was on my last batch of leaflets for the day. The Head Librarian had rushed home to sort out a plumbing emergency, or a bored housewife, I forget which, so I had to stay behind till 9 p.m. That would've been fine if only we hadn't scheduled a public lecture on something like "The Cultural Imperative" or "The Social Imperative" or some other boastful title like that, to be given by a sociocultural anthropologist no less.

Social anthropologists were almost as intellectually stale as literary critics, but their arrogance and self-righteousness tended to intertwine with larger doses of sanctimony and a slice of phoney do-goodery. It was at times like this that I thought about Upendo, wondering whether he'd outsmarted us all, took the easier way out; at least he could shoot his enemies dead and move on, wash away the injustice with spates of blood. Not so easy for us – not yet anyway, the shooting of anthropologists was still considered illegal.

This particular specimen featured the usual regulation corduroy suit and compulsory neck beard accompanied by foul breath. He introduced himself as Jonathan P. Irwing, pausing halfway through as though that P mattered somehow. Jonathan P. Irwing liked his name to be pronounced in full. When Nora made the mistake of referring to him as "John" you would've thought she'd just tried to piss on his shoe. Not that his shoes couldn't have been improved by a little piss. His breath *definitely* could. I imagined that Jonathan P. Irwing's breath started off in his lungs as fresh mountain air and then turned foul on contact with the rot that floated around his ersatz mind.

Nevertheless, I honoured Judy's teachings and did my best to be a good host. I made pots of tea and coffee and placed a bottle of water and a plastic cup on Jonathan P. Irwing's desk. He thanked me, then put his hands in his pockets and proceeded to tell me every detail of his three-hour train journey, dwelling in particular on how successful he had been in changing train at Derby – all the while breathing out like a moose who'd been chewing on fresh turds.

I tried to move away, subtly at first, but the old sod was half deaf and kept leaning in. I thought about grabbing a seat, but decided against it, knowing I'd be trapped if he followed me along. So I kept standing, backing away slowly at every opportunity. This social anthropology palaver was hard work. Finally a dishevelled old hippy with a chipped tooth and a squeaky voice approached us and asked him to sign her copy of his book. I took my chance and sidled up to an empty seat.

At 8 p.m. I asked Nora to call Jonathan P. Irwing to the podium, let her deal with the stench of social anthropology for a change. And so it began. It turned out that Jonathan P. Irwing had been to Australia, and that he said "quote unquote" a lot, especially when he talked about industrialized societies and the developing world. He clearly thought that was witty. No one laughed, but that didn't deter Jonathan P. Irwing one little bit, as he also turned out to be one of those who laugh at their own jokes, heartily, and with the occasional bout of smokers' cough. And so he carried on. He talked about this Aboriginal tribe where women were encouraged to be promiscuous. You could see the sense of high virtue in his eyes. He delivered the information in a monotone, as if to deliberately underscore the point that he, Jonathan P. Irwing, was entirely at ease with this cultural expression – while also secretly hoping that others wouldn't be, so that his virtue could be unique as well as high. His phoniness stank almost as much as his breath. Possibly more.

This preference for female promiscuity, he told us, was

rooted in the cultural belief that sperm from different men would mix in the woman's womb, bringing with it all the best traits from each man the woman had intercourse with. So the more diverse the sperm a woman gathers, the better the children she is going to bear: they will have the height and strength of one sexual partner, the intelligence and compassion of another, and the wisdom and social skills of yet another. A sort of positivity-driven genetic cocktail. It was a great story, and it did make me think about the lengths to which a culture will go to manufacture virtue. But Jonathan P. Irwing relayed it as though it was more than a belief, as though it was somehow *true*. I raised my hand, asked him how come they don't realize that the children take after a single father, that in actual fact only one set of traits gets through. Surely they can see that each newborn looks an awful lot like one particular guy from the village?

Jonathan P. Irwing did not like that question. He tensed up inside the corduroy suit, scratched his neck beard and went on a long disquisition of how the aboriginals' beliefs are "True to them, and therefore it is their truth. It is an aboriginal truth." That's what he said: *their* truth. "Truth is cultural belief," he said. And he said it with a straight face. That's how Jonathan P. Irwing used his intelligence; he used this large brain evolution had gifted him, this freakishly capable product of nature, he used it to intellectualize self-aggrandizing crap. Crap that deep down he didn't believe himself of course – and it showed. Because when push came to shove, when the time came to travel to the Sociocultural Anthropology Society and meet up with other self-aggrandizing conmen, then you would see Jonathan P. Irwing queue up in earnest to get on an aeroplane. An aeroplane built by engineers relying on science relying on objective truths. Not once did Jonathan P. Irwing turn up at an anthropology meeting on a flying broomstick, or a magic carpet.

Between the pseudo-intellectualism and the stench of Jonathan P. Irwing's breath assaulting my senses I felt a churn in my stomach. I was angry. Mostly angry at myself for being angry at that educated halfwit. People like him took my own good will, my own commitment to keeping an open mind, and turned it against me; attacking rationality, my rationality, on a whim – while they themselves had no intention of acknowledging the bridges and the rockets and the skyscrapers that rationality built. A cheap trick. When you confronted them, they would tell you that rockets and skyscrapers pollute the world, conveniently forgetting that the same rationality also built aqueducts and defibrillators and sewage plants. But I suspect Jonathan P. Irwing didn't like to talk about sewage plants, they reminded him of his breath.

And yet, there was a part of me that felt compelled to hear Jonathan P. Irwing's intellectual acrobatics, a part that considered listening to his nihilistic drivel, that part of me that whispered: "Just in case..." I felt defeated, wished I could've had that part of me surgically removed. But open mindedness can't be selected, you can't pick and choose when to have it. If you lose it, you lose it all, not just the bit that can be hijacked by educated halfwits. So I decided to give the surgery a miss. I stood up, walked out and made for the bus stop. The cool evening air felt good in my nostrils.

59

SOME WOMEN only give head when they absolutely have to, as a duty, a chore – or worse, a favour. But not Hannah.

Hannah had the passion of a trumpet player and the rhythm of an orchestra. Oral sex is like theatre: timing is everything. Hannah had impeccable timing. Her performance was a glorious ceremony of lust and vigour, a celebration of unbridled womanhood. Bowing to your cock and reigning over it at the same time. She didn't just swallow your come, she swallowed the whole of you.

Hannah was in her mid-thirties and you could see wrinkles beginning to form around her eyes, as though her smiles and squints had outstayed their welcome. She picked up some shifts at the Out Bar, but this particular Friday she had the night off and was sitting at a table with another woman, drinking and grimacing. Sometimes the grimaces made it into smiles and occasionally into a laugh. Hannah had a wholesome laugh. She also had very straight teeth, very evenly distributed and perfectly aligned, like she'd picked them out of a catalogue. She occasionally looked our way. I told Kevin we should go over.

"Nah, you go if you want."

"There's two of them," I said. I knew it would work better with support. "I need a wingman. C'mon."

"You go first, I'll join you in a bit."

"There's two of them, it works better with a wingman."

"Yeah, the wingman comes later."

Kevin didn't quite know what a wingman was.

I walked over. "Hey, I was telling my friend he should come over and talk to you, but he wouldn't, so you'll have to make do with me. I'm Dak."

Hannah looked at me as though she'd known this would happen, and she probably had. Her friend smiled and fiddled with her cocktail, stabbing pieces of fruit with a giant toothpick.

Two hours later I was throwing Hannah's shirt on the floor with one hand and unhooking her bra with the other. I played with her breasts for a while, but she didn't seem very interested; I had the impression there was something else she wanted to get on with and this breast-fondling business was holding her up. Then Hannah unzipped my trousers, threw a pillow on the floor and knelt opposite me. She looked at me for a second, then bowed down and took me in her mouth. I closed my eyes and let her skill envelop me. I could feel my dick throbbing as she worked away, her head dancing between my legs.

She broke off. "You have a beautiful cock," she whispered, "very... what's the word, proportionate?" Ah, I thought, the lure of symmetry – and this time I'm on the right side of it. I lay back and allowed myself to experience Hannah's deluge, a hurricane let loose on my cock.

For a good half hour afterwards I couldn't get my breathing

back to normal. I kept feeling that my two lungs were fighting with each other, each insisting on its own rhythm and throwing the other off beat.

"So, when was the last time you had sex?" she said.

"That's quite the personal question!"

"We're in bed together, naked."

"Fair point." I was beginning to like her. "Few weeks ago. You?"

"Since August."

"Ex-boyfriend?"

"Summer fling. Didn't last."

"Why not?"

"He was boring."

"Ah, one of those who get too comfortable?"

"Not even that, he was boring from the start. But he was good-looking and I was going through a bit of a dry spell, so…"

I was definitely beginning to like her. I think most women don't get this, but there's something very attractive about a woman who's unashamed of her sexuality. Most women I met were either blatantly vulgar about it or kept it buried away in some old bulletproof coffer they opened only when the lights were off. *All* the lights. The tight coffers thought themselves virtuous, while the other lot thought that blatant was the same as unashamed or free or emancipated; but the truth is that sex is like food, and neither anorexia nor obesity are good signs. Hannah was a gourmet. Her coffer was wide open in full daylight, and yet she didn't molest you with the contents; she laid them out suggestively and invited you to hold out your hand, but never flung them at passers-by or poured them on your head. She was comfortably erotic.

"As I get older," she said, "I understand my body more, my needs. I now know that sex is for my pleasure too, and that most men actually *want* to please me."

"You know too much," I said with a grin.

"You'd better get used to it, honey."

I slept well that night. And I think Hannah did too.

60

HANNAH DIDN'T LIKE fucking very much. Her mind always seemed to be preoccupied with other things, like she was rearranging the furniture in her head or something. She seemed impatient, too, like she was waiting for the *real* fun to begin.

One Sunday afternoon we made a big fry-up: eggs, bacon, Lincolnshire sausages, tomatoes – the tomatoes were from a tin, I never had any fresh veggies in the house, they didn't last an hour; Terry was like a wild goat who'd swallowed a giant tapeworm – beans, fried bread and mushrooms. Heavenly. Then we made about a gallon of tea by boiling water in a saucepan (Terry had taken the plug off the kettle to fix the TV in his room).

No one else was home and we had the whole house to ourselves. I lounged around in my bathrobe and Hannah spent most of the morning in her blue underwear. She kept walking back and forth by the curtainless window, trying to catch the eye of a passer-by – it excited her.

After lunch I went down the shop to buy some orange juice. When I got back the dishes had been washed but there was no one in the kitchen. I put the juice in the fridge and went upstairs. As I walked into my room I saw Hannah on the bed, naked. I jumped in and we burnt off some of those heavenly calories.

After a few minutes of missionary work I turned Hannah around and took her from behind. Hannah was a tall woman, so I needed a little help. She complied. I hung on to her hips and thrusted myself into her. Long, deep strokes.

We'd been going a while and I was running out of breath. I slowed down a little. The phone rang. Hannah raised her head. Without a thought I slipped out of her, walked across the room and picked up. My cock stood proud in the air, sweat running down my neck and chest.

"Hey stranger!" It was Lauren. My heart skipped a beat and my cock twitched.

I winked at Hannah. She was still on the bed. Still on all fours. She gave me a faint smile, turned on her side and sat up with her feet on the floor. I think she didn't mind, she wasn't crazy about fucking anyway.

"What's up?" I tried to sound uninterested. It wasn't easy – my erection belonged to Lauren now.

"Guess what, I'm being transferred to London! Can you *believe* it?"

"Uh-uh."

"I'll be landing at Heathrow Wednesday morning, 11.25 a.m. See you there?"

"Cool, I'll see what I can do." I hung up.

Hannah was sitting on the bed, wiping sweat from under her breasts with a towel. She looked puzzled but said nothing about the phone call. That's just as well, because I had no idea what possessed me to pick up that phone. I liked Hannah a little more after that.

I walked back across the room and towards the bed, my dick still pointing upwards, twitching a little for Lauren and a lot for what was about to happen. I placed a hand on Hannah's buttocks and motioned her to get back on all fours. She threw the towel on the floor and turned around, presenting me with that magnificently firm, plump arse.

"Where were we?" I said with a grin. Her pussy was still moist.

"Somewhere about here," she said, wiggling that arse.

I put my hands on her hips and entered her again from behind, picking up where we'd left off. I only lasted a handful of strokes. Heathrow here I come.

61

LAUREN'S FLIGHT LANDED twelve minutes ahead of schedule. We arrived at her place just after one o'clock, a flat in Islington with a concierge and large windows overlooking the Grand Union canal. I felt like I was in a different London, a parallel universe that shared only its name with the city I called home.

As we walked through the door Lauren kicked off her shoes. Then she unbuttoned her dress and let it fall to the floor. There she stood, like the fountain of sex that she was.

"I need a wash," she said.

I took off my clothes and followed her into the shower.

Lauren washed with such grace that I had an erection as soon as she laid on the soap. I watched her, mesmerized, my dick upright like a flagpole waiting for a flag. She was my delirium.

"I guess that needs washing too," she said, her customary cheek flashing across her lips.

She began to soap me up. I poured some soap on my hands and lathered up her shoulders, moving slowly down her back and to her buttocks. Solid as a rock. A smooth, maddening rock.

All of a sudden Lauren rinsed herself off and got out of the shower. She wriggled her behind at me, picked up a fresh towel and wrapped it around her head like a turban; she looked like the incarnation of a mystical Babylonian heiress, her naked flesh glistening with tiny water droplets. Then she turned slightly and looked at me over her shoulder, mischief pouring from her eyes. She curled her finger at me and motioned me to follow her. I stepped closer. Lauren grabbed my penis and led me to the bed. I felt like a teenage boy discovering sex for the first time. How did she do it?

We made love through the afternoon, starting and stopping every time one of us got out of breath. Lauren let out little gasps, then called out my name, then took the Lord's name in vain, then called my name again. I was in good company.

"You've got some long game mister!" Her chest was moving in and out fast between each word.

"I like touring," I said.

"Touring?"

"Yeah, you know, a bit of this and a bit of that, then change position for a bit of the other, then stop for a chat, a smile, maybe a sip of wine, and back on the saddle. It's all about the journey, baby!" I chuckled.

"You're an odd duck."

"You love it…!"

"Don't count on that."

And just like that, Lauren sponged up all the affection and sincerity I cast in her direction, giving nothing in return. Not a thing. I grabbed her hand and put it on my cock. It rose. I turned her around and entered her from behind.

A few positions later she popped a big one, then fell on the bed with her forearm across her face. I lay next to her.

"I am numb," she said, almost absent-mindedly. "I think I'm broken."

"Come here, love." I palmed her head and brought her closer, motioning her towards my chest. "Get into your favourite nest."

"That nest is *dangerous*."

"Only if you fight it," I said, longing for that symbolic kindness, that primordial lightness. "Just nestle up, let go…"

She did. And it was every bit as magical as I remembered – fresh lavender buds gently cascading onto my body and soul.

Suddenly Lauren looked sad. A true, honest sadness. Her face showed me lines I had never seen before. She turned her head slightly, adjusting it on my chest.

"Lying here on you like this… I know I should feel," she whispered. "But I can't."

Her voice was velvet, her words thundering blades of fire. The hurt was sudden. I did my best not to let on. "Maybe you just don't like me," I said with as much cool as I could muster. "It happens."

"But some things seem so easy with you, so *natural*. Except for those times when I want to kill you." She laughed, her lines back to her usual poker face.

"Whatch'ya gonna do," I ventured in a mock New York accent, trying to conceal my own sadness ramming at the gates.

"Maybe I'm just empty. I don't know. I really don't know." Those honest lines appeared again for a second, then they were gone. Lauren put her hand on my crotch. My dick unfurled slightly. She smiled. This she did know. Was it ever going to be enough?

Lauren closed her eyes. Her breathing got heavier. We napped in each other's arms for the rest of the afternoon.

62

LAUREN AND I sat at the flat all day, talking, laughing and taking Polaroids. Dozens of them. They were mostly pictures of each other, kissing, smiling, staring, Lauren pretending to pull up her stockings, striking Betty Boop poses. I was deep in a new fantastical Bohemia.

I tried taking pictures of Lauren when she wasn't looking, when she was standing around naturally, relaxed, unaware. It wasn't easy. Every time I went quiet she became suspicious, she'd turn suddenly in my direction and stare at me with venom in her eyes: "What are you doing!? Stop doing that!"

She made me feel like a thief. I probably was. I was trying to steal a glance at the woman behind the game, to catch another glimpse of those honest lines she had inadvertently exposed the day before. No such luck. Lauren only liked having her photos taken when she was in control of the pose, the angle, the clothes, the hair – no pictures near an open window on a breezy day – the mood. Her highest goal was to pose so impeccably as to leave no trace of the posing. A perfect hustle.

I got out of bed, poured myself a glass of water and popped to the offie for some beer. When I came back Lauren was standing at the sink, filling up the kettle and fiddling with her jumper.

"I scratched my neck," she said. "Will you kiss it better?"

There was a line of raw flesh across her neck. "Blimey, that looks nasty! What are you like…"

"I know, it burns like hell now."

"Why don't you just leave it alone? But then again, I love kissing your neck…" I felt a little corny, the delivery maybe, but the message was true – Lauren's neck was more than a neck, it was the essence of sex. It seemed wrong that her breasts or her pubic bone were so carefully covered by clothing while her neck could just be out in the open like that, as though it didn't hold any secrets, as though it wasn't part of anything. Culture is such a bizarre form of mental illness.

"You do?" Lauren said, her mischievous smile splashing across her face. "That's good, 'cos I like having my neck kissed. Of course I despise it too because sometimes I lose control when you do it. But that makes me like it even more."

She stretched the collar down past her shoulder to reveal the full length of her neck, down to the clavicle. I felt a buzz deep in my groin. A woman's clavicle can form the most attractive contours when the light falls on it just right – and the light seemed to fall just right quite a lot when it came to Lauren's clavicle. I gave in to the urge and kissed her three times, softly and deliberately, taking time between each kiss. Lauren's skin quivered, her shoulder twisted up in a quick twitch, shivers moving rapidly down her body.

"I like kissing you," I told her, "but I like it even more when *that* happens."

Her eyelashes fluttered, like a siren call luring me to my demise.

All day long we cooked, ate and made love. Flowing, plentiful, bliss. It was the Serengeti all over again, it was the wilderness, but without the wild cats trying to disembowel you. It was freedom and it felt like happiness.

* * *

I woke up an hour later. Lauren was at the window with a pad in her hand. She'd been making a drawing of a photo we'd taken earlier, the two of us kissing. She showed it to me. It looked amazing. In a strange, inexplicable way that drawing looked more real than the photograph, as though Lauren had captured some essence that wasn't visible in the cold lines with which photography so faithfully reported reality. I couldn't draw a stickman to save my life, so perhaps that's why drawings always fascinated me. They seemed like things of magic, and the person doing them a magician, a sorcerer of dust and colours. All of a sudden it hit me that I had no idea Lauren was one of these magic-making sorceresses. I knew she was a sorceress alright, but not of this type. I wondered what else I didn't know about her, what other skills she'd kept from me; what dreams, hungers, regrets, sparks, fears. I felt an urge to know it all. I wanted to enter her body and look inside her, I wanted to melt my brain into her brain, fuse her mind with mine and mine with hers.

Just when I thought my desire for her couldn't grow any stronger, Lauren put the pad down, walked to the kitchenette and began talking to herself while making a coffee, giving stern orders to the cafetière.

"You're funny sometimes," I told her.

"Oh, I'm hilarious."

"Yeah, just not always on purpose."

"Hey!" Her eyes lit up and her mouth curled up a little on one side. She looked irresistible. I wanted her more than anything, more than humanity would allow, more than penetration could offer. I wondered whether I was going mad. I couldn't afford to go mad, I hadn't even finished *Thus Spoke Zarathustra*. Can you get hold of Nietzsche in a madhouse?

63

THE NEXT EVENING I booked a table at The Cellar, a hybrid between café and restaurant just off the Edgware Road. In The Cellar there was no wine or beer in sight. A hospitality paradox. Kevin had told me that the owners had lost the alcohol licence a few years back but couldn't afford the fees to change the name of the place, so now customers had to bring their own bottle of wine and be charged fifty pence for uncorking. The food was decent. You could order smoked salmon, crackers, gammon and cheese on toast for less than a fiver. The seats looked like church benches and the walls were covered in flowery wallpaper and old-fashioned paintings of chubby men in bowler hats. It was very popular with young crowds that had big dreams and small wallets.

We got off the bus at Oxford Circus. Lauren was a few feet behind me. I stood on the pavement waiting for her to catch up, then put my arm around her waist and led her towards the pedestrian crossing. I took her by the hand, pulled her gently across Regent Street, making sure to time our steps in between the bicycle attacks. Lauren was quiet for a while, then burst out in an incredulous voice: "Did you just try to hold my hand? You pervert!"

I smiled, but only on the outside. She'd sooner grab my cock in the middle of the Oxford Street traffic than conceive of holding my hand. Her coldness burned like white embers through my gut. I imagined us in a dimly lit slum, rubbing against each other like meat robots, dead eyes wide open, staring blankly, thrusting mechanically at each other. Why does it have to be all about the fucking?

Lauren slowed down and turned to face me. Then, as though she'd read my mind, she said, "I'm a little twisted. Addiction to a sense of control, I think... Having the upper hand. Self-preservation I suppose."

I'd suspected all that game-playing would've taken its toll on her soul. Now she was confirming it to me in a rare moment of humanity. I felt a sudden kinship with her. I said, "Do you miss the game playing? Do you think you can get out?"

"Not sure I actually liked playing, but I'd get a quick high – you know – enough to keep me going back."

I was certain she had no idea how those words hit close to home.

We kept walking along Oxford Street in silence. When we arrived at The Cellar Lauren was transfixed. Even her facial features looked different; something intangible ran through her and it showed. She kept saying how great the food was and how much she loved the place, but the food had nothing to do with it – she was just working hard to keep her emotions stowed away, stuffed in that dark closet she had hidden deep inside her bosom. If I were a betting man I'd say she was deeply touched, dazzled by the whole thing, by the possibility of doing things together, being out together, *being* together.

The waitress arrived with a corkscrew. I pulled a bottle of Bordeaux out of a carrier bag. Suddenly I thought of Elly, the dormer window, Kensington Palace, the dry humping, those huge wobbly breasts. I thought about Elly sitting on me sat on that chair.

Lauren was playing with her wine glass, stroking the rim with her middle finger in a circling motion. I knew she had sex on her mind.

"I haven't been with a man since I last saw you," she said.

"That's good to know," I said, feeling a little buoyant at the news.

"Oh don't flatter yourself. I've just been busy with other things, that's all."

A little heartless, I thought. And yet I couldn't help loving the wit. That's how she always got me. And so the dance continued. A hazardous, debilitating dance. Was I the mouse? *Again*? I sucked at the Bordeaux and hoped I wasn't the mouse.

64

I HAD A series of repeated encounters with sleep deprivation. The Head Librarian was at the London Book Fair for the week and I had to put in extra hours to cover. I was doing overtime in Lauren's bed and spent nearly three hours a day on various bus routes between Islington, Deptford and Charing Cross. I was losing track. I dutifully continued to put in my hours at the reading table, but soon realized that not much was getting in – I was just going through the motions. Most reading sessions turned into mindless page-staring diversions, meaningless words blending into each other like streams of black soup. I needed something to refocus my mind.

I got on the 188 at 6.45 a.m. and put in some extra work at the photocopier. By 11 a.m. I'd cleared out my in-tray, which meant I could take a full hour for lunch. I walked over to Trafalgar and into the National Gallery. I went straight to Turner's suns. They hung there in that chapel-like dome as if they were holy icons imbued with divine powers. And maybe they were. I stared at the explosions of rust, my mind getting lost in the accurate vagueness of their contours. They say Turner was the very first impressionist. He'd definitely left an impression on me. Turner the first. How do you become a first? I wondered. What force, what vision needs to possess you to be a first? A true first *must* be possessed, of that I was sure. He must be taken over – that's the only way he would be able to produce something that couldn't possibly have been learned. Turner the executioner, putting behaviourists to shame a hundred years before their first whimper. Plato would've been proud. Turner the pupil and Turner the master, knowing without learning and seeing without having seen. Fuelled by that elusive knowledge that does not come from experience – and yet there it sat, right inside him. That it couldn't be learned knowledge was obvious: it wasn't there until he himself made it be. That's what being a first is. It wasn't there yet, and yet it flowed inside of him. Knowledge that was simultaneously there and not there, at once of this world and not of this world, non-existent and yet in existence. Turner the first, Turner the magician. I checked my watch – ten minutes to one. I walked along the corridor, rushed through the portico and made my way back to Charing Cross Library.

65

I CARRIED ON with my 6.45 a.m. plan, sorting out my in-tray by 11 a.m. and going back to the National for almost a full hour every day, immersing myself in Turner's magic.

One evening Judy phoned me and went on a rant about how I didn't love her. I hadn't spoken to her in nearly three weeks. I felt guilty. I hung up the phone, bought some flowers from the off-licence and walked to New Cross. I knocked on Judy's door. The door opened. Her face lit up and she threw her arms around me. Flower petals darted in all directions. Then she took the flowers to the kitchen, filled a vase with water and put them in.

"Beautiful," she said, "and I do like yellow."

Simon walked in.

"Si, have you been in the loo all this time?" Judy seemed very upbeat, nothing like the mood of the phone call we'd had less than half an hour ago.

"Yes, dear," replied Simon.

Judy turned to me: "I've been nagging him about the roses, they need pruning." Then she turned her head and called over her shoulder, "Haven't I, dear?"

No answer.

"I've been nagging him, but he won't admit that. I don't even know why I do it, I hate those bloody roses." She gave a quick laugh, then added, "But that's women for you. Sometimes we just have to feel that we matter." She laughed again; it was a fuller laugh this time, like one would laugh at an incredible absurdity. "I don't know how he puts up with me sometimes…"

Then she called out again, "Si, you're such a dear, how do you put up with me?"

Simon walked over to where Judy was standing and gently placed his hands on her shoulders. "Well," he said, "I just find that I end up taking longer and longer shits."

Judy doubled over with laughter, struggling to hold on to the cookbook in her hand. "Oh, Si," she said finally, gasping for breath, "you bring such joy to my life."

Simon smiled, his eyes tearing up. Then he picked up a butter dish and walked to the fridge.

We sat down and I told them about my struggle to refocus, my trips to the National.

"You're so selfish!" said Judy in excitement.

"Oh, am I?" I apologized, but that's not what she had in mind.

"Oh no, don't be sorry, it's great to see!"

"Selfishness?"

"Yes! Honest, unadulterated selfishness is a great thing! And you have it. Usually only children have it, but occasionally you see it in an adult and it's so uplifting."

"I don't know how to take that," I said.

"Oh don't be a fool," she dismissed my misgivings with a wave of her hand. Then she turned to Simon: "Isn't he wonderful, Si?"

"Yes," he said in a baritone, as if making a statement of grave consequence.

The flattery worked. I kept going to the National every day for a month. My reading became more focused, the words on each page slowly disentangled themselves and reclaimed their meanings.

"Sometimes you just have to shock yourself out of idleness," said Judy. "Simon had to do it too, you know, that time when he rebuilt himself."

"It sounds like Dak needed someone to feed his inspiration," said Simon. "Terribly clever of him to choose Turner."

Judy's face lit up. "Yes! He is a clever bugger isn't he..." she paused for a few seconds, staring at me, then continued, "It's like when Feynman saved my life. It happened soon after my Neil died, I'd been –"

"Ah, yeah," I said, "you already told me that story."

"So?"

It was obvious, right? She had already told me the story. I knew the story.

"I know the story," I said. I also knew I'd made the wrong move. I knew it instantly.

"Well, maybe I want to tell it again!" Judy said crossly. "It's called 'sharing'."

Simon chipped in: "Really, Dak, sometimes you haven't a clue how love works. People don't just tell each other stories to deliver *information*."

"Yes!" said Judy. She had anger scattered all over her face. "Will you stop focusing on information? FUCK INFORMATION!"

Simon allowed a second of silence after Judy's outburst, then added, "It's much more than that."

"Of course it's much more than that," Judy said, "I'm sharing my state of mind with you." Then she looked at Simon and spoke in a lower voice, like she was delivering sad news: "He doesn't understand."

Judy turned to me again, her face a battlefield of emotions, "It's sharing, it's *living*." Anger was the Chief Marshall on this battlefield. "Don't you EVER tell me you already know a story again! Just LISTEN! – stop being so fucking rude and listen!"

Simon chipped in again, as he always did when numbers were on his side. He had the courage of a coward. "Yes, Dak, show Judy respect, she has lived these stories, they *are* her." That was a good point. The coward had made a good point.

66

A COUPLE OF days later Lauren and I arranged to meet up in the West End. We spent a whole afternoon talking, laughing, occasionally fondling each other by the kerbside.

When we got back to the flat we tore each other's clothes off and jumped into bed. I began to play with her naked body. She responded. I climbed on her and pushed in. Her excitement intensified, her voice deepened, and an image of pleasure appeared on her face. I must be doing something right, I thought.

Sex with Lauren was often a haze, a dreamy state that possessed me from the moment we kissed, dragging me through a foggy ecstasy till the moment we fell back on the bed in exhaustion. But this time my mind was unusually clear, there was an unfamiliar sobriety running through me. I caught a glimpse of Lauren looking at herself in the mirror. I focused, surprised that I could do that at all. I saw her flirting with the mirror, looking, staring, glued to her own image like a junkie to a needle. She tilted her head, chasing a better look, a more complete look at her own body. An expression of intense lust was now forming on her face. She'd never looked at me like that. That's a bad sign… I wondered whether she had any interest in me, my presence, my body – a man's even. She seemed to have no such interest. My body, my extremities, were merely flesh props in her own porn fantasy. That's a very bad sign…

I felt a sudden burst of excitement. I bent forward and gently bit Lauren on the thigh. She groaned, then laughed her beautiful laugh. I wanted to fuck her hard – throw her up against the wall and take her, but also hold her in my arms and stroke her hair, all at once. She was my innocent Madonna and my filthiest Whore. My heart felt light as a feather and Freud was still a fraud. I slid my right hand under Lauren's back and turned her over. She sprung onto her knees; her pussy puffed up, her arsehole puckered, and I exploded inside her.

Lauren had the hots for me, even if she was never going to admit it.

An hour later I noticed Lauren staring at the desk in the far corner. I looked at her, wondering how much distance the mirror had put between us. She seemed miles away. Then she shook her head, smiled and turned to me: "We've never had sex on a desk, have we?"

"We kind of did."

"What does that mean?"

"Over the countertop, remember?"

"It's not the same."

"It's the same height."

"It's not the same."

"It's the same position."

"Ah."

"Sometimes I remember things," I said, "things we did, but in places we didn't do them in."

"So it's made up, then."

"Oh no, it's not made up. They *happened*, just not in those places. They didn't *quite* happen, but they happened."

"Oh, like, creative memories?"

"Yeah, like that."

I felt a strange happiness, gratifying – a bowel movement of the heart. Sometimes she gets me, I thought. Squarely and precisely, like a laser missile.

67

THE PHONE RANG. It was Kevin. He sounded buoyant. "Hey geez, I'm getting married!"

I didn't take him seriously – he didn't even have a girlfriend. Patsy had been out of the picture a while, left for Tokyo a few months back. Apparently Japan was one of the few places where you could make good money playing volleyball.

But Kevin insisted, "I'm having a whisky on the way to church!"

"Church? What church? Where are you?"

"I'm in Germany. I'm getting married to a German, man!"

"Are you serious?"

"Like a liver shot."

It turned out that two months ago he had rekindled with Bettie, an old girlfriend he'd met at university nearly ten years before. They used to sit in her dorm room after class, talk for hours about life and philosophy and the spontaneous flow of raw emotions. After graduation Bettie moved back to Germany to work in her father's company, while Kevin went back to the Isle of Wight before deciding to move to London. They wrote to each other for a while, but life got in the way and they lost touch. And now he was five minutes away from marrying her. Bettie had got back in touch after her fiancé stole the wedding rings and disappeared. Gambling problems. Kevin flew to Berlin and proposed to her the same day, near Checkpoint Charlie, by the ruins of the Wall.

Kevin and I had a complicated relationship with romanticism. As a way of life it was appealing, alluring even, especially if you allowed yourself to romanticize the romanticism. But it was also a distraction. It watered down our ambition, weakened our determination. I had my share of struggles with it, but Kevin might've had it harder than me on this one.

I was lost for words. All I could muster was a crass "Good luck, mate."

Kevin hung up.

I put down the phone. I felt drunk. The kind of drunk you feel just before the hangover kicks in. What just happened? It seemed like a heart-warming story, but this was Kevin's life, an actual man's life, not some kitsch romance novel that you could sell to a second-hand bookshop after a skim-read. Was this really happening? I hope he's going to be ok, I thought. I hope he knows what he's doing.

68

KEVIN'S NEWS rattled me. Was it the end of an era? I called Lauren. She thought it was wonderful news. I wasn't so sure.

"I don't have a good feeling about this," I told her. I realized I was speaking in a beaten-up voice.

"Oh get over it, you're just being needy."

Her words flew at me like steel pellets. "That may be true," I said, defeated by my unwillingness to fight back, "but it doesn't help to point it out."

"What, you want to be coddled?"

"I just want some kindness."

"When have I been nasty to you?"

"Absence of nastiness isn't the same as kindness."

Lauren scrunched up her nose, as if my words had released a terrible smell. "I don't like you today," she said, "you're not amusing me."

"Sometimes life is not amusing." My voice was almost a whisper now.

"So what's your problem then?"

"Some of your words stick, you know..."

"Which ones? What have I said that stuck?"

I wasn't going to get into that back and forth business; no good would come out of that. "Look," I said, "all I'm saying is that a little sympathy wouldn't go amiss, that's all."

"Good luck getting that from me."

More steel pellets. This time coated in ice, driving bruises deep into my spirit. Kevin's wisdom echoed in my head. Would you want her by your side in a war? Not if your goal is to stay alive. She rode my strength when I had it, fed my weakness whenever it dared to surface, gave it a stir, nursed it into certain misery. That's how you cripple a good soldier. Sarcasm is fun, but sometimes a man needs a little humanity.

I put on some clothes and walked to the garage. Ray was at the heavy bag. He smirked and nodded in my direction. Clint was mopping the ring, picking up the fluids he'd punched out of some poor rookie a few hours earlier. I walked to the benches and took some of my frustration out on the oil cans. It felt good. Necessary.

I got back to Deptford just before 9 p.m., took a shower and sat on the bed. An articulated lorry shot over the hill by the Black Horse and the whole house shook like in an earthquake. It felt strangely soothing. I turned on the radio, lay down and closed my eyes.

The phone rang. I ignored it, but they wouldn't give up. Dickhead. If I was going to answer I would have by now.

The caller must've sensed my mood because the phone went quiet – but only for a few seconds. It rang again. An adamant dickhead. I picked up the receiver. It was Lauren. I hadn't expected that. "Look," she said in an almost kind voice, "maybe I was selfish. My life's been a mess, I nearly died several times for Crissake!"

We all nearly died several times. But I didn't say that. I didn't say anything; she was giving me something and I wanted it all.

"Talking to you makes me feel better, you always have such *clarity*. It grounds me." She paused, as if needing to catch her breath. This was physical. "I didn't think about what that means to you, what it might do. I'm not always sharp that way. I told you, I'm broken. You still there?"

Her honesty moved me. I tried to speak but words resisted me. A sliver of love tore through my body. She had me. Again.

69

I WAS AWAKENED by a punch in the face. Or at least that's what it felt like. I'd been thrashing around in bed and ended up dislodging one of the bricks that moonlighted as a leg. The bed tilted over, sloping sideways like a crooked roof. I rolled down the makeshift hill and slammed my face on the skirting. I was soaked in sweat. Then I remembered. I had been dreaming that

I was chained to a stake. Mephistopheles himself stood opposite, shouting incomprehensible orders at me, hurling spit in my face with every syllable. A crowd of ugly medieval peasants with rotten teeth squealed like damned souls in Hell and brandished their pitchforks at me. Suddenly Mephistopheles's eyes turned white. The noise subsided, his voice became soft and feminine. An old witch with an aquiline nose and a huge hairy mole on her chin passed him a black cape and a hangman's hood. He put them on. Then, in a delicate, sensuous tone he whispered in my ear: "You know my determination… my fledging career… my growing ambitions… my future… you know all that time and sweat and tears I've invested in my personal growth? You know all that hard graft? You can have it. HAVE it! It's yours. All of it. Just give me a smile in return." That's when the bed gave out and I tumbled awake.

I took a fresh towel out of the wardrobe and dried the sweat off my face and chest. That's fucked up. That's not my worth. That needs to stop.

I went downstairs and washed my face with cold water. I felt like I'd just cheated death. I saw my reflection in the mirror: pale as an albino corpse. My heart was drumming inside my chest, knocking violently against the ribcage. The walls were closing in. I walked out the door and marched into the street. I strode along the pavement, crossed the road and kept going, staring ahead, hands in my pockets and shoulders hunched forward like a hunted man.

An hour later I ended up at Judy's.

"She's relentless," I told her. "Chipping away at me, at my humanity. *Our* humanity." As I uttered those words I imagined Lauren placing her hand on my heart, covering its nose and mouth and pressing down, firmly, until it struggled to draw air; then release it a little, snigger, and press down again.

"Do you think she's a sadist? You have to be careful of sadists," Judy said.

"It's possible, I guess…" It seemed very possible. The female equivalent of the wife beater; one day she looked at me starry eyed, enrolling the sexiest of voices to tell me how much I meant to her, how my presence centred her – and the next day she screamed at me like I was some stray dog who'd just shat all over her geraniums.

But unlike a wife beater she didn't bother with black eyes, cracked ribs or any of that superficial hurt that heals inside of two weeks. No, she went straight for a liver shot to the soul.

"Maybe she's just mad," I suggested.

"That could be too, there's a lot of madness among women nowadays. They've all lost touch with their instincts. You only have to look at Cynthia – mad as a hatter!"

"The madness wouldn't bother me if she wasn't so bloody hurtful."

"Ye-es," said Judy pensively. Then added, "Women need to learn to be gentler with men. That's a mother's job really, to teach little girls the importance of being gentle. But women are so bloody wretched nowadays, they don't do it. And so little girls grow up without realizing. Their genitals are all safe and tucked in, you see…" she made an inward, wrapping motion with both her hands, "that's why they don't realize, that's why they need to be told. It never crosses their little mind that boys don't have that privilege, that your genitals are all out in the open – vulnerable."

Simon and I listened intently. He was sitting motionless, as if he were under a beautiful spell that could be broken by the tiniest movement and he was doing everything in his power to avoid spoiling it. We were in the presence of something wonderful, and we knew it.

"It was ok when we were monkeys, you know, on all fours," Judy continued. "We had our back as armour to protect the genitals," now she made a bowing motion, mimicking a pronograde posture, "but as soon as we became upright, then everything changed – and it became a woman's job…" she hesitated, "a *mother's* job, you know, to make little girls aware of that, so they don't be reckless with little boys and don't grow up to be reckless with men – with men's feelings. But nowadays women are too busy trying to *be* like men, so they forget. We're doomed, really…" She sighed. "Simon, be a dear and get me a glass of water, will you?"

Simon looked like he'd just been awakened from a dream, his eyes almost vacant and his face muscles set like fresh concrete. It took him several seconds to switch back on and get up.

"Yes," he said in a trembling voice. He walked to the kitchen.

After that Simon and I were silent for some time, fearful that our voices might disturb Judy's words still hanging in the air.

Finally I ventured a thought, "Not being reckless with men's feelings," I said, slowly, replaying Judy's words in my mind. "Women nowadays complain that we men don't *show* our feelings."

"Really?" Judy laughed, throwing her head back. "Oh God, it's worse than I thought!"

I thought she was joking, surely everyone had heard of this. But Judy was not everyone.

"How do you mean, worse?" I said.

"The last piece of dignity a man has is to keep his own bloody feelings to himself! And these wretched women are *complaining* about it? Shocking." She looked truly contemptuous. "Besides, have you ever slapped a dog on the nose when he drinks from a puddle?"

I laughed. Simon didn't.

"Well, if you've done that, you'll know that he's not going to try again. And that's what happens with men's feelings. Women are reckless with them, slap them on the nose. Clever men catch on quickly, and learn to never do it again." Judy waved her hand dismissively. "It's the mothers, I told you."

I nodded.

"There's no excuse for it, the recklessness I mean." She spoke with a hint of anger, as though reprimanding all womankind. Then, in a loving voice: "Yeats tried to tell us all those years ago, of course: 'Tread softly because you tread on my dreams.' But many of us do not listen.

"So please, Dak, listen to me, be careful with women. Don't be fooled by the bright smiles. You're likely to be bitten by them; certainly not appreciated or loved."

Her wisdom was hard to swallow. I took a swig of sherry to help it down. I felt the blood rushing through my cheekbones.

Judy sat up straight in her armchair, placing her hands flat on the armrests. She looked regal in her posture. Then she said, "It is a pleasure to know you and watch you as you 'fill out', so to speak, become more of a man every day. All that reading you've been doing, it's awfully good."

I smiled. The honesty of her good words was almost too much to take. My ears weren't used to it. My body, my mind, my gut and my soul weren't used to it.

"You're becoming almost daily more male and mature, and you were clever to start with, so it will have to be a very ok woman who can take good care of you."

The flattery sweetened the pill a little, but not for long.

"Manhood is not easy. Most men nowadays choose to escape it, which leaves those of you who don't overburdened. And I know how trying it is. I hoped Lauren was an easy woman to have around, someone you could just hang loose with, you know... take a rest from doing anything except what you want on the spur of the moment. Now it doesn't look that way." She sighed. Her eyes looked sad, of a raw sadness that emerged from deep within. "Be careful, Dak, opium comes in many forms."

70

LAUREN WAS in a great mood.

"I want to dance tonight," she said twirling round, her skirt fanning out to reveal those ivory thighs and a glimpse of that sweet spot just beneath the undercurve of her buttocks.

"There's a new place in Shaftesbury Avenue with live music," I said, "we could go check it out."

"Great. I'll wear my leather skirt. It's *very* short."

"We may need to queue, you'll be cold."

"Oh, I won't be doing that! I'll tell you what. If there's a line we'll find a dark alley to explore." She flicked a pair of knickers back into the wardrobe. "I'll go pantiless, just in case you need quick access." Then she smiled, and I followed suit. Lauren's flirting was infectious, she could turn the most mundane conversation into pure excitement.

"Hold your horses, young lady! I won't take my trousers off in an alley, it'll be freezing!"

"That's perfect, the cold will shrink your huge balls down to average size."

"I don't like the sound of that…"

"Why not? I love your huge balls, they're mesmerizing, like the ocean or people-watching."

"Ok, when you put it like that… it sounds both poetic and disturbing."

"Just like you, then," she whispered. Then she pointed her finger at me in mock condemnation and shot me a big grin.

All week Lauren had lashed out at me over all sorts of inconsequential crap, looking at me with raving bitterness in her eyes. I felt drained and bruised. And yet she could still make my insides smile. With a curl of her lip, the twitch of an eyebrow, a sweep of her eyes – she could soothe me like honey, like a cool flannel over a feverish brain.

I turned on the radio. Lauren stood by the bedroom mirror and began trying on different skirts. I walked up behind her, put my hands on her hips and kissed her on the neck, just below the ear. She tilted her head and smiled. Her knees buckled. She turned her head to me: "I want to ride you and then I want to wake up with you." We kissed. I unbuttoned her skirt and slid it over her knees and down along her legs till it hit the floor, forming a loose ring of blueness on the beige carpet. Lauren stepped out of the ring with the tiniest of movements. She moved with the rhythm of a ballerina and the dexterity of a leopard. If leopards could do ballet they would move exactly as she did in that moment – of that I was quite sure. I picked her up and put her on the bed. We kissed again, a long, hungry kiss. Then we made love, grabbing at each other like drowning beasts. I thrusted into her like it was my very first and last ever fuck. Lauren moaned her deep intense moans, giving out sudden whimpers as if on the brink of hysteria. It was wonderful.

We lay in bed panting through vague smiles. My mind started racing, replaying every moment Lauren and I had spent together. Life with Lauren was *hard*. Her behaviour was erratic, her moods explosive, her brain like a spinning wheel on crack. Starting a conversation with Lauren was a game of Russian roulette. Nah, conversation isn't the right word for it. Her method of communication was the conversational equivalent of carpet bombing. She was a tinderbox on legs. Great legs, which made the problem a thousand times worse.

A heavy fog descended on my brain. I wished I could just slash my chest open and show Lauren my insides, my heart, the lot – then she would know. Then she would have no doubts about me, my nature. Then she could stare my innards right in the eye and know exactly what I know, feel exactly what I am.

But the thing with slashing your chest open is that it kills you. Bloodily. The result? She'd likely throw up all over your futility – or worse, turn away. So I grabbed a pillow and put my arms around it, my chest unscathed.

All through this Lauren was asleep, her chest rising and falling at short intervals. Suddenly she opened her eyes, "You're all kinds of man," she said, looking at me suspiciously.

"Yeah, I am a lot of things to a lot of people."

"Oh don't be smug now, you make me want to take it back."

"Do you want to take it back?"

"No." She smirked.

We lay there breathing quietly. Lauren caressed my arm and I ran my fingers along her thigh. Then she rested her head on my chest, like only she knew how, just like it was meant to be.

71

I WOKE UP feeling like I had been asleep for a century. Lauren was standing at the window in her skimpy blue gown, gazing toward the canal. She looked exquisite. All five feet one inch of her stretched up, chest pushed out like a soldier and right leg slightly bent like a schoolgirl. I could just make out the line of her thigh muscle tensing as she leaned on one leg. A distilled sex potion; could drive a man to insanity with her mere presence. I was transfixed. I could've watched her for hours.

Then she noticed me. "What are you doing?" she snapped. She'd caught my stare with the corner of her eye.

"Looking at you," I said.

"Well, stop that!"

"Why would I?"

"I look hideous."

"You're pretty far from hideous if you ask me..."

"Weirdo."

I could feel the anger seeping through her now croaky voice.

"You look gorgeous," I ventured, thinking it might appease her. Also, it was true.

"Oh don't give me *that*!" She tensed up, straightening her leg. Now she looked like a wild cat ready to pounce.

Lauren was so effortlessly sexy, but she could turn on a sixpence, go from honeydew to cluster bomb in a matter of seconds. Having her around was like living in a labyrinth littered with mouse traps of a million different sizes. And I was the mouse, and a blind one to boot.

She turned away from the window and walked off with a grand gesture, like a dame who'd just been irreverently addressed by an impudent servant.

I sat up in bed, wrestling with my self-respect. I thought about Hannah. She was as far from Lauren as you could get. Different species. Thoughtfulness and tact flowed from Hannah like honey off a hot spoon. I knew she was the woman a man needs by his side, a woman you can strive by. But I couldn't control who I was attracted to. Just another straitjacket I had to live with. Some call it "thinking with your dick," but thinking has nothing to do with it. When her naked body is stretched out on the bed and she looks at you, pleadingly, lusting for your sex, your attention, your manhood, and you feel like a piece of cold dead rock at the bottom of a river, what good is your thinking then?

I noticed I'd slipped back down into the bed. The sheets were all corkscrewed around one of the blankets. A pillow had fallen on the floor. I stared at it. It looked desolate and lonely. Lauren shouted lumps of bloody hurt through the bathroom door, then went quiet. Eerily. I began to feel like an innocent man on death row.

Nothing will send you to Hell faster than a fair face with a heart of stone.

Half an hour had passed. I walked to the bathroom door and called out to Lauren: "What are you doing in there?"
"I wanna kill you right now!"
"Oh, come on, baby, come out of there."
"Fuck you! You sit there watching me when I'm all skanky!"
"Maybe I like you skanky."
"Stop RIGHT NOW or I'll throw this bottle at your face!"
She was serious. Talking wasn't an option. Explaining myself definitely wasn't an option. I had a hunch that a kiss might've worked but I didn't fancy the odds. I'd have to sit there until the shrapnel fire died down.

And so I did. I sat there and waited. And with every minute, with every glance, every syllable, Lauren was dismantling my good will, mashing up my self-esteem and throwing the whole sorry mess on a scrap pile. I stared at my reflection in the window. My eyes looked hollow. I thought about Judy, about the opium of the fools, about vampire stories and gullible men, men with chalky white faces, the life drained out of them, their head falling to one side, their limbs giving out. I stood up and went to the kitchen. I poured a glass of whisky, drank it down.

Why couldn't it all be as easy as the fucking? Merging, blending into each other, working together, cooperating? Why did the everyday have to be so tediously exhausting? An immense sadness assaulted me. I felt numb, as if my whole body and soul were turning into sand. An autumn breeze came in through the window and caressed my face. I stood there, like a man who had nothing to give.

72

AN HOUR LATER Lauren came out of the bathroom, walked over to the bedroom and flung her gown on a chair. She stretched her arms in the air, stark naked, her breasts perking up as the pec muscles pulled upwards. She pretended not to be looking in the mirror, then tilted her head up and smirked, thoroughly in love with herself. I called her out on it, thinking she might turn in my direction and shoot me a lusty look to prove me wrong. She didn't. Instead she mumbled something about the importance of self-love and looked through me like I was invisible. A mannequin. A cheap see-through mannequin. Heavy loads of desperation fell on my chest. I was desperate for Lauren to see me, desperate to see her eyes widening with excitement as she took in the contours of my body. But she just couldn't do it, it was as though something inside of her didn't connect. Maybe she too needed to read Forster. Lauren reading Forster? I smiled, thinking about what Judy would make of all this. She'd probably tell me how women's anxiety cripples them, makes them unable to empathize with men, especially the men who tend to their wounds – "Just remember the White Feather Brigade!" Then she'd probably tell me about women's career lust and status lust. How about self lust? I didn't know. What seemed obvious was that Lauren only had eyes for herself. All else was hopeless. And desperation without hope is the antechamber of Hell. No idea why Hell even needs an antechamber, but here it was. I saw myself sat on a charcoal bench engulfed in red flames and orange flames and yellow flames, waiting to be called in as Cerberus launched into frenzied growls, yanking at his chains with blazing eyes, frothing at the mouths. I was close. Really close.

In that moment I realized all the raw sex that Lauren so prolifically exuded had to come at a price. I knew I couldn't keep on paying it. Not indefinitely. And Hell was one hell of a price.

I willed myself out of my reverie. "Do you want to go out for a drink?" I said, adamant to make it work, but unsure what "it" was.

"You still want to go out with me? You must be *mad*!"

"Mad about you, baby!"

"Nah, you're a glutton for punishment."

I wasn't. I hated it. But I just couldn't get her sweet smile out of my head. The smell of her skin, her small, tight body, the elegant sexiness of her moves. It really was hopeless.

My mind floated to Judy once more. I remembered the time she had told me that the way you carry yourself defines you. We were sitting in her garden sipping tea and Judy was leaning back into her chair, arms stretched out along the armrests. She liked to soak up the early summer sun.

"If you let someone treat you like an idiot, you will eventually start to behave like an idiot," she professed. "That's why you need to choose your friends wisely. Shame you can't do that with your family." She laughed a hearty laugh.

I hardly had a chance to laugh along with her when Judy interrupted me, her face turning serious all of a sudden. "It's not funny," she intimated. "The world desperately needs good, strong, decent men, men who are prepared to work on themselves. Of course the world also needs good women, but I have no patience for women at the moment." She waved her hand in dismissal: "We're not talking about women now." She sighed, realizing she'd side-tracked, then carried on, "Being a good man takes work, you're like fertile ground, you can bloom, but only if you take the trouble to do the weeding. Fertility can fuck off just like that." She made a tiny flicking motion with her wrist. "Surround yourself with people who are keen to join in with the weeding. Look at Simon, he's come such a long way since he left that wretched woman."

Simon smiled for a second, but quickly went back to a serious, attentive expression. When Judy spoke, you listened – and he knew that.

And so it happened. After allowing Lauren to treat me like a worthless idiot for three days straight, I brushed my teeth, put on my coat, tied my shoes and went to the bus stop. The 188 approached and I went through my pockets searching for the bus pass. As the doors closed behind me I realized it was the first of the month. Too late. The bus pulled off and I held on to the handrail with no money in my wallet and an expired bus pass in my hand. I sat down in slow motion, feeling like a little boy who'd just dropped his ice-cream on the tarmac. Judy's prediction had come full circle, and I was the idiot. I slouched back into the seat and waited for my stop.

As we approached the Bricklayer's Arms the driver slid his side window open. The bus slowed down and lurched to a stop. Doors opened then closed, and the words "Tickets please!" smacked me around the head like a headmaster's cane.

I was charged £10 I didn't have and escorted off the bus. The driver shot me a pitying smile. An old woman turned her head slowly to look at me in disgust; I was obviously everything that was wrong with this country.

I pulled up my collar, shoved my hands in my pockets and walked to Charing Cross. I got to work thirty-five minutes late and was docked an hour.

73

I'D BEEN PRINTING leaflets all morning and the sooty smell of toner was beginning to get to me. I made a cup of tea and was about to sit down outside the reading room when Judy walked in.

"Hello, dear," she said, beaming. Simon had dropped her off on their way back from the National.

"We've just been to the Titian exhibition. All that ultramarine..." she brought her right hand to her face, gesturing a flash, "awakens your eyes. Anyhow, mustn't waffle. Tonight we're going to the Lyric in Hammersmith to see *Mourning Becomes Electra*, will you join us? A friend of Simon's got us circle tickets. It's supposed to be very good."

I said yes, then made Judy a cup of tea as we waited for Simon to pick her up. She told me he'd gone to UCL Hospital to enquire about her slow recovery after a hip operation.

"He's been engaged in conflict with the bloody complaint department for weeks now, over the balls-up by that damn woman, Da Silva." Da Silva was the surgeon who'd carried out Judy's hip replacement. "He's doing it very well, bless him. Can you believe they had the nerve to say how sorry they are that I've been upset? Not sorry about my hip, about my upset! Which of course is not what Simon is complaining about." She shook her head. "Really, I could go crazy if I had to do it myself." She took a sip of tea, then looked up and smiled one of her sincerest smiles, "It's such a pleasure to have a good man taking it up." The smile turned into a quick laugh, then she added, "I'd very much like to go into the complaint department and have hysterics! Hahaha. I wonder... could one find the complaint department do you think? It's probably in a bunker."

At 11 a.m. Simon walked in all flustered, looking like he was being chased by a pack of wolves. "I'm double parked, let's go! Oh, hi, Dak!"

Judy looked at me with a raised eyebrow, mildly amused by this minor commotion. "Oh well," she said cheerfully, "must dash, no rest for the wicked and all that. See you at seven, Dak, lots of love, cheerio!" Then she took Simon's arm and left.

The rest of the day went on as usual: leaflets, booklets, a sandwich, barcodes, quick nip to the National, half an hour in the life of Ivan Denisovich, more leaflets. At 5 p.m. there was a public talk by a Raquel Roderick-Proudfoot, an intellectually barren spinster who got off on calling herself a sociocultural musicologist. I timed my shift so that it would end at 5 p.m. sharp, sparing myself Raquel Roderick-Proudfoot's attempt at smuggling Marxism into Charing Cross by disguising it as a talk on "The Myth of Beethoven's Curse". You can always tell when you're dealing with a member of the socio-cult, they throw around the word "myth" the way an illusionist does with abracadabra.

But it was ten past five and Nora hadn't turned up, so I had to wait around a while. I locked myself in the post room to make sure I wouldn't be caught in the Head Librarian's last-minute trawl for attendees. I heard him rounding up issue desk staff: "That's the spirit! We want our guests to feel welcome don't we? Come on, Claire, you'll like this, it's about music!" It definitely wasn't about music.

Oh Shit. That's the distinct sound of the Head Librarian's brogues travelling in my direction; I stood quietly behind the door, holding my breath. Come on... Phew, just about. The Head Librarian must've thought I'd left and didn't knock.

The relief was short-lived. Raquel Roderick-Proudfoot's posturing could be heard through the post room's plywood door: "Beethoven has been used," she began. "Used to normalize hearing and construct deafness as its pathological opposite."

For the love of Jesus.... Where's Nora?

"But deafness itself is merely a social category. A construct."

Fucking plywood.

"Modern society views deafness as a pathological defect, a deviation from the *normal*." You could hear the disgust in her voice while she uttered this word, "normal," as though each consonant brought with it a spoonful of castor oil. "In my recent book, I show how the notion of deafness has been culturally constructed as the absence of hearing." Did one really need a book for that? It seemed to me that a two-line dictionary definition would have sufficed. Then I realized, not without a mild sense of defeat, that I hadn't dodged this evening's sermon after all. I might as well have a look at how this woman keeps a straight face through all of this. I cracked the door open. "This hegemonic consensus is toxically enshrined in our worldviews, and new frameworks are needed to overcome it. Frameworks that view deafness as a different way of life rather than a shared disability, and the deaf community as an alternative culture." A haughty grin temporarily interrupted Raquel Roderick-Proudfoot's vacuous look of self-importance every time she uttered the word "culture," as though she was the only person in the universe with the physical ability to pronounce it.

She carried on. Still no sign of Nora. "Deaf culture is perceived as threatening by many hearing people – indeed, in my book I liken deaf culture to a kind of 'immigrant' culture – it is therefore apparent" (how was it apparent?) "that deaf culture is the victim of cultural shaming. Just like Jews were forced to wear yellow badges in order to make their Jewishness visible and mark themselves as 'other'," here Raquel Roderick-Proudfoot flinched, gulping down a few more spoonfuls of castor oil, "so deafness is made to be visually identified via the wearing of hearing aids and the presence of cochlear implants. And thus hearing people mark deaf culture as 'other', forcing deafness to be identified as deviant, deviating from the category they construct as 'normal'." More castor oil. I turned to pick up a ream of A4, 300 gsm. I opened the photocopier's bottom drawer, then froze as I realized that Raquel Roderick-Proudfoot was not-so-subtly likening ground-breaking, life-changing technology to Nazi propaganda. At this point I half expected her to advocate the abandonment of research into hearing loss treatment, perhaps bringing in vivisection as a comparison. I was spared. Not entirely though. A few minutes later she began a just-so-story about Beethoven, how Beethoven's deafness had been shamelessly constructed as disability although – Raquel Roderick-Proudfoot was quite sure – it had actually been a socially-conferred identity. Raquel Roderick-Proudfoot spoke with such conviction and self-assurance that if your sense of time had been a little shaky you would've been forgiven for thinking that she was a close friend of Beethoven's. His personal confidante, the only person to whom the composer had relayed the whole truth about his new cultural choices, secretly revealing to her over a cup of tea how he picked deafness as a lifestyle in the same manner he had picked Vienna for a place to live.

A few minutes later Raquel Roderick-Proudfoot paused, stretching her neck upwards as though readying herself to look down on the rest of the world, then flashed a fake smile and wrapped up the forty minutes of insanity that she had so skilfully dressed up as knowledge. The Head Librarian opened up the floor for questions, which inevitably began with the usual mini-lecture disguised as a question. A guy with a nasal voice draped in a mixture of self-pride and disappointment declared that Raquel Roderick-Proudfoot's talk should've been about something else entirely. Something to do with the construction of irony in the historiography of Beethoven's life. Apparently the really important thing was not deafness, but the irony that a great composer had gone deaf. And oh, wasn't it a cruel irony? Ah, the injustice of the universe! The fickle wrath of the gods! Oh, didn't the cosmos punish the poor man! Why hadn't Raquel Roderick-Proudfoot brought in the role of the cosmos?

Nora walked in, soaked to the skin and apologetic. She nodded toward the podium. "Any good?" she said.

"Beethoven."

"Uh?"

"The poor bastard contracted syphilis. You get eighteenth century syphilis, you go deaf. That's the deal."

Nora shot me a look of suspicion. "Is that it? Sounds simple."

"Well spotted." She was learning.

"What?"

"Raquel Roderick-Proudfoot is too simple for simplicity."

"Ah."

"The copier is stocked," I told her, "I'll see you tomorrow."

It was pouring outside. I picked up an umbrella from the lost property cabinet and walked to the bus stop.

I arrived at the Lyric just in time. Simon and Judy were waiting in the foyer. Simon handed me a ticket. I am very lucky, I thought. The bell rang; we walked in and took our circle seats.

Very good seats, smack in the middle and not too far from the stage, but also not too close that you had to sit with your neck all crooked.

The curtain went up. There was singing. A few exchanges about some army general. Bickering between husband and wife. Then, somewhere in the middle of Act I, Helen Mirren walked out of the portico, playing *a tall striking-looking woman. She has a fine, voluptuous figure and she moves with a flowing animal grace.* She didn't look like she had to do much playing. She seemed effortlessly elegant. Though she was nearly twice my age, an "old" woman by all accounts, I had this absurd feeling that I could love her – and I mean *love* her, erotic love. But then again, I felt I *could* love most women – maybe that was my trouble. Jim Morrison's voice flashed through my head: "Hello, I love you..." That's a man's curse; loving a pretty face before he even knows her name, let alone her character. Helen Mirren wasn't just a pretty face, though. She spoke in a strong and confident but sensual voice; an unlikely, almost otherworldly combination. And she moved. She embodied that flowing animal grace with all her being, as though those words had been written for her and she forged for them. Some women have it, I thought. It doesn't matter how far their tits have sagged, some women just have it.

74

LAUREN AND I had another argument. Or, more precisely, Lauren brewed up an argument and catapulted it in my direction. The whole thing was about something so trivial that I was sure it must've been about something else. I don't remember what started it but I remember Lauren's jaw tightening as she screamed, hurling insults at me with an infernal energy, her eyes hollow with fury, a fury that did not belong to me – it couldn't. It was so absurdly disproportionate that it made the use of a sledgehammer to crack a peanut look like a perfectly sensible hardware choice. Where did all that fury come from? By what mad alchemical process was it being concocted? And with whose first matter? The image of a conveyor belt loaded with swearwords and bile popped into my mind. I stifled a giggle. Halfway along the conveyor belt was a giant hammer attached to a hydraulic piston hanging from the ceiling. The hammer moved up very, very slowly and then *slam*! it crashed down on top of each piece of bitterness, magically moulding the swearwords into the shape of a thunderbolt. A trapdoor at the end of the conveyor clunked open to reveal a dark void. The belt dumped the foul-smelling bolts down the void and into a large stainless-steel container, steam billowing out of the darkness. A hellish sound of muffled screams escaped briefly as the trapdoor slammed shut. I smiled. Lauren stood by the bed like a block of ice; her expression stone dead, her eyes stone crazy, her heart stone cold.

I went for a walk to clear my head. I wandered around aimlessly for a while and ended up in Camden. In a misguided spurt of adulterated romanticism I bought a wooden carnation from one of the market stalls. Handmade. I desperately wanted things to be alright.

I took a bus back to Islington, walked into the flat and put the wooden carnation on a chair. Lauren didn't notice it. I took off my boots and hung my jacket by the door. Part of me was glad she didn't notice the flower, spared me having to face my feeble attempt at fighting assault rifles with carnations.

For the first time in a long time I felt utterly powerless. She had me. And the irony was, she could've had so much more if only she'd allowed herself to take a leap once in a while, if she had not burned every single bridge before I had a chance to lay the first plank. A plank… Maybe that's why I'd been drawn to that stall of wooden flowers, I was looking for planks, planks to lay under Lauren's feet so that she may tread carelessly upon them. I felt sick. I wondered what it would take to make a wooden flower wilt.

Suddenly, as if wanting to put my mind at rest, Lauren glanced at me: "I was thinking about us kissing. They're a good fit, our kisses, aren't they."

A second wave of romanticism swept over me. I stepped toward her, still eager for things to be alright. It didn't last long. Lauren proceeded to dissect the whole thing as though our kisses were some vapid piece of literature and she a female Adam Norther. The only saving grace was that she used shorter and less pompous words than Adam Norther ever considered doing. But the result was much the same. She took our kisses apart, gutted them, called them "weird", and by the time she was done I'd forgotten all about the beautiful thought she had begun with. The romanticism escaped my body in a sudden gush, like sewage from a burst pipe. I saw Kevin's smile. "When they call you a hopeless romantic," he had told me once, "you can't help but romanticize the occurrence, think how wonderfully *uber*-romantic you must be to elicit such emphatic remark. Your own romanticism fools you into believing that the focus of the remark is on the romantic. It isn't. The focus is on the hopeless. Take heed, for that's the informative part." I could feel my face going pale. I went quiet. Really quiet.

I woke about twenty minutes later, exhausted. My insides felt as though they were slowly melting, hanging loose over my bones like Dali's clocks on the parched tree branches.

"Are you staying tonight?" Lauren said. "I wanna wake up with you in my bed."

"You sound lonely. Maybe you should learn to treat men better."

"Oh stop whining!"

"There it is."

"What?"

"The attack. They're constant."

"Well, maybe you should take them like a man, stop being a little bitch!"

"A man?"

"Yeah."

I wondered what gave her such a warped idea of men. The words "You don't know" escaped through my lips before I could stop them.

"What don't I know?" she said, bitterness firm in her voice.

"Never mind."

"Don't fucking do that! What is it? WHAT? I WANT TO KNOW!"

A dry coldness flooded through my body. "We don't always get what we want, do we…"

"You're pissing me off right now!"

"It seems that happens a lot."

"Just fucking tell me! WHAT IS IT?"

"A man?" I said despite myself. "A man who puts up with this sort of stuff has two options: he is either the kind who throws you across the room and then comes back for more, maybe an apology, or he is a weasel who doesn't fuck you, or fucks you up, or worse, fucks you *over*. I'm not that kind of man."

Lauren's stare bore down on me; blankness soaked in anger, sizzling.

"But if that's the kind of man you want," I told her, "I'll ask around, see if I can introduce you to one."

Silence. She always went quiet when she knew she'd been had. Self-preservation, I guess.

A few minutes later Lauren put her arms around my waist, and in a low, silky voice she said, "You should fight for me a little, you know... My brother once drove all the way across the country for a woman."

"Did it work?"

"Well, no, but – argh! I HATE you!"

I said nothing.

"You should still fight for me!"

I probably won't stay, I thought. Or maybe I will. It's going to be a long night either way.

75

THREE DAYS LATER we were sitting on a bus on our way to Paddington station. Lauren had to fly to New York to train a fresh batch of interns. I didn't say much. Lauren wore shades throughout the dull, cloudy morning. Dali's clocks persisted, and they were more than a memory.

The bus took a left and merged into the traffic on Edgware Road. A few more minutes and we would catch a glimpse of the Victorian train shed. I felt relieved the Russian roulette was coming to an end. No more sinking, no more churning, no more loitering in Purgatory. All tears under the bridge now. And yet I still wanted her – her smell, her skin, her tongue.

We stepped off the bus and walked down the ramp into the station. Lauren shot straight for the ticket office. I followed her. The queue was short. Lauren put the ticket in her jacket pocket, then took off her shades and stuffed them in a handbag. We kissed. A long, fierce kiss. Her sweet scent rose up and shook my nostrils, then my brain. Her tongue weaved and waved onto mine like a painter's brush flirting with the canvas. Soft, determined, firm in its grace. I never knew you could miss something even before it was gone.

And then she was gone.

76

ONE THING WAS clear: she hated me.

I never figured out whether Bettie had ever been in love with Kevin, but they were proud of one another and had a deep admiration for each other's minds. I would take that over fairy-tale love any day. The problem was that Kevin and I also admired each other's minds, and Bettie couldn't stand that.

The first time I met Bettie was late on a Saturday evening when she was in London for the weekend, a few months after the wedding. Kevin and I had been working late and needed food. He phoned Bettie and asked her to join us. We went to a Greek restaurant near Russell Square, sat down by the window and ordered a bottle of retsina. Fifteen minutes later we saw Bettie walking along the pavement. She had a brisk walk and oozed confidence. She walked in.

"Good evening, boys." She smiled.

"It's nice to finally meet you," I said, feeling strangely timid.

It was her confidence; it unsettled me. I'd been around confident women before, and I was usually well grounded in their presence, even feeding off their vibes, but this was different. Bettie had a force field around her that made me uncomfortable. This surprised me and bothered me at the same time.

She stared straight at me: "I have a bone to pick with you!"

I scouted her face for the slightest hint of a smile. No luck. She was dead serious.

"You keep your intuitions off my Kevin, you hear me?"

She spoke calmly, in a soft voice, but her words felt loud.

"You're safe," I said. "I'm not into guys."

Her eyes narrowed. "Oh I'm not worried about sex. Sex is cheap. I know he has women after him, he is an accomplished man, why wouldn't he. But no frock can tune into his wavelength the way you do."

"He does that to me too. We can't help it."

"Never mind that. That's not what I'm talking about."

"Ok…" I said, my tongue mired in hesitation.

"I've never been jealous of a woman, *ever*. But I'm jealous of YOU!" Bettie's voice had risen for a split second, then immediately returned to a calm tone. This change happened so swiftly that I wondered whether I'd imagined it. Then I noticed her index finger pointing at me with gritted teeth. I definitely hadn't imagined it.

I sat in silence, barely managing a dopey smile. Bettie was right. The bond between Kevin and me was visceral. I had never experienced that with a woman, and I couldn't imagine it happening. Maybe the same was true of Kevin and she knew it. It was more than mere jealousy, but it must've hurt all the same. Bettie was right. And there wasn't a thing any of us could do about it.

Kevin knew it too. He smiled at Bettie and then looked at me with a resigned expression on his face. "Come on, enough of this. What are you drinking?" he asked her.

"Vodka and tonic."

"Come on, Dak, go get the lady a drink."

Kevin knew how to diffuse a situation. But Bettie's words lingered like the smell of gunpowder after a mass shooting. I stood up and went to the bar. I felt a daze coming on, as though half of my brain had passed out and the other half was watching over it.

77

IT WAS DEFINITELY a Tuesday. Someone knocked on the post room door just before 10 a.m. It was Nora.

"There's a letter for you," she said. "Needs to be signed for. The postman's waiting upstairs."

It was a large brown envelope, heavy, with "London University" printed in big letters across the top left corner. I stared at it for a while. It's too heavy to be bad news, I thought. Surely they wouldn't put all this weight into a rejection? Nah, it's probably a prospectus, advertising material, nothing to do with my application. Some intern in the university mailroom got hold of my details and sent off a bunch of glossy papers — I knew the drill, we used to do the same thing at Charing Cross before our funds got slashed. I grabbed the envelope and tore it open, disappointed at the anti-climax I'd just manufactured in my head. Inside was a hardback with a light blue cover and, in the centre, a drawing of a human head. Under the drawing was a title in black font: *Cognition and Human Nature*. A university book! I couldn't believe it. A University Book. It was like any other book, of course, but that brown envelope and those words in the top left corner gave it a magic aura. I held it in my hands, trembling. Then I picked up a pencil from the issue desk and sat at the reading table, transfixed, fully intent in memorizing every word. There was a white slip of paper sticking out. I pulled it out, it said:

Dear Mr Manell,

Please find enclosed an introductory text in preparation for your interview.

Best regards,

Prof. V. M. Slater
Professor of Cognitive Science
London University

I put the slip in my pocket and started reading, skipping the introduction and any page marked with Roman numerals — this was too important. I must've been three or four pages in when I realized that I'd been copying down every single word. I tossed the pencil across the table and kept on reading. I was done in less than an hour. I closed the book, went to the loo, urinated, washed my face, walked downstairs to the kitchenette, poured a pint of water and gulped it down. Then I walked back to the reading table and started again. I did that three more times, then I put the book in my bag and walked out.

78

THE INTERVIEW was in less than a week and I needed a suit. Most interviews I'd had were for catering jobs, so I'd usually turn up in a shirt and jeans. For the library interview I'd worn black trousers with a white shirt and no tie, on Upendo's advice. I asked Terry if he knew anyone selling suits on the cheap. He didn't. He gave me a long diatribe about the restructuring of the docks and how they were driving small entrepreneurs out of business – by which he meant they were making life difficult for the artful dodgers – then moved on to a speech on how to select a good second-hand suit from a charity shop. I listened.

"First," he said with a strange look of excitement, "check that he's been a good boy, you know, that he wore underwear. You do that by looking for yellow marks around the inside of the fly. Give it a sniff if you're unsure." Say what you will about the nutter, but he did have a system. Rudimentary perhaps, and more than a little revolting, but a system nonetheless. I decided I was going to rely on visual inspection only, and wear two pairs of boxers just in case.

"Then you want to check the jacket, particularly the armpits. You don't want to stink with some other fucker's sweat!" I certainly didn't. "Look at the lining around the armpits, make sure it's nice and white."

"Ok," I said.

"Check the elbows too, feel them between your finger and thumb, make sure they've got some thread left in them. Ah, that reminds me, do the same with the back of the trousers. If it's thin, thanks but no thanks. They'll split the first time you squat."

I wondered whether I'd have to sit down for the interview. Maybe I could go through it standing, just to make double sure?

"And that's it," Terry declared. "That's how you get suited up for a fiver."

79

THE FOLLOWING MONDAY I turned up at London University with my light-grey Oxfam suit – £4.75. The black tie was a loan, courtesy of Charing Cross Head Librarian.

I arrived twenty minutes early and nearly ended up being late. The Head Librarian had told me that it was bad practice to arrive early, you should arrive on time, that's what the time is for. When they give you a time, you arrive at that time; not before and certainly not after. So I walked along a row of university buildings looking for number twelve, that's where the Department of Cognitive Science was, and made sure I knew where I needed to be. Then I strolled around campus killing time for the remaining sixteen minutes. I didn't want to make a bad impression by arriving too early.

When I walked back to the Department I had two minutes to spare, ready to knock on the door at 11 a.m. sharp. Panic set in when I spotted a sticker near the door handle. Crap. How did I miss it? This was bad. Wasn't it there sixteen minutes ago? How the fuck did I miss it? Well, it certainly was there now, nonchalantly staring at me in its laminated ruthlessness. It said: "Exit Only. Please use rear door for enquiries." My chest was thumping. I ran around the building and knocked on the rear door, panting. A bemused secretary ushered me in with less than ten seconds to spare. It turned out there was a whole room full of interviewees waiting to be called in. I could've arrived an hour early and it wouldn't have made one bit of difference.

The secretary pointed me to the end of the corridor. A large wooden door with a gold-plated knob stood before me, the kind of door that seemed to have been manufactured with the specific intent of making me feel small and insignificant. There was a white sign on it at about waist height: "Prof. V. M. Slater."

I knocked.

"Come in."

I went in.

"Mr...?"

"Manell."

"Ah, yes." Slater stared at my face inquisitively, as if I belonged to a newly discovered species. He didn't even so much as glance at my suit. All that trouble for nothing. It was clear that Prof. Slater was after much more than a decent dress code, a realization that both relieved me and terrified me – what if my potential is bogus? Standing still is all I have to do to keep the suit from splitting, but what if it's me who comes apart at the seams? At least the suit won't crack under pressure. I wasn't so sure I could say the same about me.

"Pleased to meet you," Prof. Slater said, shuffling through a pile of papers on his desk and placing a little booklet on top. It was my application. "This is usually a formality," he told me. "We just make a conditional offer pending A level results; in and out in less than ten minutes. But you have no formal qualifications. Close the door please. This is going to take a while."

I closed the door.

"As I was saying, you have no formal qualifications." I was beginning to wonder whether he was trying to test my resolve, see if I'd collapse to the floor under the weight of those three words: No. Formal. Qualifications. Then he added, "But you do have glowing references from the Head Librarian at Charing Cross." He looked up: "Did you read the book we sent you?"

"Yes." I stifled an insistent "sir." It didn't seem like the right thing to say.

"Ah. Then you will be aware of the concepts of spreading activation, matching, and inheritance." He stood up and walked to the whiteboard that hung on the wall behind his desk. He began to draw a diagram. I'd never seen it before. Shit. My books let me down. How could they! Did they? Was it me? Did I read the wrong books? Or maybe I forgot everything I know, shit, no, no, I would know if I lost my memory. Would I? Would I know? How would I know…? If you lose your memory you won't know what you used to know and you can't know what you no longer know. Fuck. Ok, ok, calm down. Breathe.

I breathed.

As I tuned back in I realized that Prof. Slater had filled the whiteboard with ovals and letters and arrows and arcs and upside-down triangles, and that he'd been talking all the way through: "Let a directed graph be populated by nodes 1 to node N, each having an activation value A which is a real number in the range 0.0 to 1.0. Further, let a link L in the range i, j connect to a source node s with the target node j with each edge having an associated weight W, itself a real number in the range 0.0 to 1.0. Now, if activation originates from node N minus 1, what variation of the algorithm permits marker passing to distinguish the paths by which activation is spread over the network?"

Ok, I thought. I get it. This is where he's going to explain to me why I'm not cut out for university. He's laying this thing out in front of me as proof of how inadequately insufficient my knowledge is, how infinitely far below university level my mind is loitering. What was I thinking…, of course, university is not for the likes of me, what a fool, he did tell me after all, didn't he… he was honest from the get go, he did say "you have no qualifications" …Twice. Yeah.

I wanted to get out of there as quickly as possible. Go home and forget all about it. Drink. Sleep. Just forget about it. But why is he dragging this out? Why not dismiss me straightaway? Is he a sadist? Maybe he is a sadist. Sweat was running down the back of my shirt, my parents' demands of mediocrity thumping loud in my head, bouncing from one end of my skull to the other.

Prof. Slater turned away from the whiteboard and looked at me blankly. I nodded, wanting him to know that I understood, he didn't need to feel bad about rejecting me, the diagram made it clear I wasn't up to the mark, there was no need to feel bad. I didn't want him to feel bad. But then the same thought bubbled up in my mind again: why didn't he just dismiss me straightaway? Why did he ask me to come here? He must know this stuff wasn't in the book he sent me. Why didn't he just send me a letter of rejection? I took courage: "I've never seen a diagram like this before. I don't know what the answer is."

"I know you don't. But I want to see you try to work it out."

"Ah."

He handed me a green marker pen.

I walked to the whiteboard and stared at Slater's creation.

"Oh," he said, "and you probably won't be able to work it out either, it's second year material. But I'm interested in how you go about *trying*."

I uncapped the marker pen and tried a few possibilities, drawing lines between source nodes in the diagram.

"Isn't the value of W necessary to the solution?" I said. "I don't think it can be solved without knowing W."

"Uh-huh. What are you going to do about it, then?"

My mind was a riot of doubts. Then I remembered Thomas Kuhn: "Truth emerges more readily from error than from confusion." I wrote a random number next to W. Eleven I think it was. At least I'd have something to work with.

"Uh-huh," Slater said.

I carried on drawing lines, making more assumptions about the different values of several other variables. Slater uh-huh'ed and mm-hmm'ed at every step, occasionally flagging potential issues by asking a question: "Wouldn't that miss the target node? Won't the edges supersede the source node?" and so forth. Far from putting me off, his commentary encouraged me to carry on, to keep driving those Popperian piles deeper into the swamp, looking for firmer and firmer ground. I had no certainty about any of the steps I was taking, and yet all doubt had fled my mind. I felt as though I was living in a vacuum outside the known universe which contained only Slater's knowledge, my own mind, and a green marker.

Nearly an hour had passed when Prof. Slater motioned me to sit. I did.

His face looked much more relaxed than it had done throughout our exchange. He smiled as he told me what the actual answer was.

"You were rooting around in the right direction," he said

with a kindness in his eyes, "though you didn't quite get there."

I smiled. I was so elated from the intellectual high I'd just experienced that I forgot I was under scrutiny.

"I can't offer you a place on the Cognitive Science with AI course, you don't have a programming background, you see. But I'm offering you place on the BSc Cog Sci. Congratulations." He held his hand out. I wiped my hand dry on the Oxfam suit and we shook. Suddenly I felt knackered.

I walked out into the thick London air and stood next to a pedestrian crossing. Dry pollen tickled my nostrils. I've only gone and done it.

80

I COULDN'T SLEEP. I lay in bed staring at the ceiling all night and into the early morning, then finally fell asleep at 6 a.m. and woke up an hour later in a panic. I felt like I'd been torn out of sleep by a terrible realization, the realization that I'd robbed a bank and my mugshot was all over the news. Have I been deluding myself? I'm nearly thirty years old. I've been living on a shoestring for years and I'll be past thirty by the time I graduate, competing with twenty-three-year olds who'll have the same qualifications and half the bruises. Forget about it. Time to stop daydreaming, find a proper job. Or stick with the library, maybe I can make Head Librarian one day, or go back to the café and make manager; Hasan is bound to screw up bad at some point, then they'll have to let him go and offer the job to me, I'm the only guy they ever employed who has some shred of dependability. I could make a decent living and get my own place, my own fridge even, keep my beers safe, have my own cupboard for my own peanuts.

I was wallowing. I knew it. But that's the thing with self-pity, sometimes all you can do is let it burn on out.

The shift at the library felt endless. I went through it like a zombie on Valium. At 5 p.m. I walked to the Rising Sun for some time to mull over a drink. Scotch – straight.

The place was nearly empty. I sat by a stained-glass window depicting a man carrying a large plank on his shoulder. The kinship was immediate. Here's to you, Plank Man! I drained the scotch and ordered another. An hour passed. At five past six Kevin walked in. He instantly knew the self-pity was strong.

I told him the whole story.

"You know what's going to happen, right?"

I had no idea.

"The years are going to go by anyway, with the only difference that you won't have been to university. So you might as well do what you've been wanting to do all along, at least in three years' time you'll be where you are wishing you were today – and that ain't half bad."

"Yeah, but fresh out of university at thirty-one?"

"Oh you'll still have to deal with being thirty-one, don't you worry about that. But if you don't go, then on top of it you'll also have to deal with the fact that you didn't follow your passion – you'll have to deal with being a sell-out.

"Don't do like Gus. For the last twenty years he's been regretting that he didn't read philosophy. Too idealistic, he thought. He bought into the story that a sensible lad would study law, or business; wouldn't muck about with *ideas*. And look at him now. No matter how much philosophy he gobbles down, he just can't forgive himself for doing a business administration degree."

I knew Kevin was right, but the devil had to push his advocate. "It's not that bad," I said with no heart, "Gus has the best of both. Business administration earns him a good salary, and then he reads all the philosophy he wants in his own time. Seems like a good deal to me."

Kevin looked at me with impatience. He could smell the rot of a devil's advocate a mile away. "It's fucked up, that's what it is. Doing business administration and *then* reading philosophy? Do you have any idea what that does to a man? There's no way you can administer a business after you've read Kant."

I smiled.

Kevin stood up and motioned me to do the same. We embraced. Kevin patted me on the back, grinned and walked to the bar.

It turned out I did have everything that mattered. But one thing had now come into focus. Between the faint light peering through the stained glass, the dense clouds of vision-crippling smoke pushing up against the low ceiling, between the doubts whirling, the head pumping, the chest thumping, the itchy feet, the gritted teeth and the long haze of a drawn-out zombie day, between all that, one thing stood out as clear as Liam's last orders bell: Potential doesn't last forever.

It was time to deliver the goods.

www.ingramcontent.com/pod-product-compliance
Lightning Source LLC
LaVergne TN
LVHW031604060526
838200LV00055B/4480